I would like to say, "thanks mate," to Brenda Murr for her transcription work in my dark ages, when a computer was the size of a sofa and I found using the latter much easier than operating the former.

Mythistrone

by
Eddie Woods

Michael Terence
Publishing

First published in paperback by
Michael Terence Publishing in 2019
www.mtp.agency

Copyright © 2019 Eddie Woods

Eddie Woods has asserted the right to be identified
as the author of this work in accordance with the
Copyright, Designs and Patents Act 1988

ISBN 9781800940321

All rights reserved. No part of this publication may be reproduced,
stored in a retrieval system, or transmitted,
in any form or by any means, electronic, mechanical,
photocopying, recording or otherwise,
without the prior permission of the publisher

Cover images
Copyright © Ikonstudio, Teguh Mujiono, Martin Malchev, Verzh

Cover design
Copyright © 2019 Michael Terence Publishing

I

JUST MARRIED

Newlyweds Paris and Helen were relatively new to the area. He spent most of his time looking cool and statuesque when he wasn't down the pub with the boys being rat-arsed, the second of which wasn't surprising considering his home life.

Helen just wasn't your average homemaker; in fact, if she had applied for the position of spouse to the fishmonger, which was advertised recently in the local branch of the Odysseus Date-a-Mate and Employment Agency, she would probably have been rejected on the grounds of overqualification.

Did she give the poor guy earache or what? It was all the fault of that cocky tart Venus, in a marketplace in Sparta. He was quietly minding his own business doing a duty-free booze run when a golden delicious apple rolled across his path and he picked it up, then the interfering fairy stories started. Why did he pick that apple up he often wondered.

The face that launched a thousand ships indeed. Paris had another view which could only be developed with hindsight. After personally bringing about the economic downfall of the richest nation on earth, through the misuse of credit facilities in various millinery, haberdashery and chintz outlets, the face that sank a thousand ships - along with three quarters of the younger generations of two great nations and a goodly amount of plundered rich stuff - would perhaps be a closer description.

All the time she wanted more - change the leather sofa, why? It's the wrong colour that's why, which would inevitably lead to the curtains being too long, too wide, too kitschy and the carpet being the wrong shade of wrong, followed by changing the up-lighter shade for a downlighter one and the whole thing would progenerate from the washing machine in the back place to the shell-shaped soap dish with the purple rose on it in the shag pile carpeted en-suite bathroom.

Money, all money, all the time more bloody money. Would the bitch ever be happy? Priam, his father, being a bit longer in the tooth, had seen it coming the day she showed up in Troy with the duty-free load. He just knew she was going to be high maintenance. He'd given it a few months for the novelty to wear off, it didn't and eventually he'd settled a few bob on her and dispatched her to Egypt as a foreign envoy.

Paris for his part suddenly had a lot of Egyptian international relations meetings, or holidays as they should have been called, to attend. Then the war started and the accountants had taken over. Helen became another statistic on a debit tablet that just kept getting paid. She'd cleared out all of Priam's available collateral right down to his personal current account and run up so much credit that the poor chap had to declare himself bankrupt and watch the whole war effort fall apart, along with any semblance of family life.

What was he, Paris, supposed to have done? She was after all the most beautiful woman in the world and he was the most handsome man that ever got horny and, love conquers all. She couldn't stay away any more than he could and after nine years of long-distance passion, Helen returned to Troy – for good!

They'd left town rather sharpish after that one - Paris glancing over his shoulder once or twice and firing off his remaining arrows in a haphazard fashion, one of which he noticed ricocheted off the bell tower only to be deflected by a bloody wooden horses ear, which had been left indiscriminately standing around, to end up embedded in some big guy's ankle - with the intention of starting all over again somewhere else.

Helen had continued with the 'spend and save ethic' - as it was expounded in many a company advert under the guise of, 'buy one of these and look how much you can save!' – that she had always been so good at. She did lots of the former and none of the latter and told Paris to get up off his arse and get a job.

Paris, still to some extent trying rather unsuccessfully to reason with his testosterone, looked her up and down and thought, man, what a woman, looks great, smells good, tastes divine and the sex is absolutely amazing. So, after once more servicing his lover for life, Paris set off down the hill to Odysseus's place to seek gainful employment. He hadn't gone more than forty yards along the newly laid cobble path when he felt the squelch, the squelch that one invariably dreads but knows so well, the squelch that instantly tells one that looking down for confirmation is not necessary for that particular purpose but more for the damage and spread assessment. Paris looked down and there all over his brand-new Gucci Jesus sandals and oozing playfully up between his toes, was the biggest, softest imaginable form of the canine aftermath and it was still warm. He scanned the immediate area and instantly spotted the culprit.

"Oy, you, yeah you!"

"Me? Are you addressing me? I have a name you know."

"Yeah, an' you also gotta dog."

"Oh, are you a dog lover then?"

Paris shook his leg rather in the way that a cat with diarrhoea would shake its rear one shortly after having coated it with said diarrhoea.

"No, I certainly am not a bloody dog lover."

The stranger with the dog took Paris's hand in a vice-like grip that could have left Einstein second in the atom-splitting stakes. "The name's Hercules, performer of labours to the rich and famous."

"Oh, so that's who you are. I guess you won the court case then, they let you keep the dog?"

"Yeah, it was a hell of a fight but he's such a lovely dog, well worth it. Sorry, what did you say your name was?"

"I didn't, it's Paris," replied Paris, trying in an un-obvious fashion that was totally obvious to re-align the fractured bones of his right hand. "That's the trouble with mythical creatures, they tell you about the three heads but, legend being what it is, the smaller details are left out, they don't tell you that each one has an exit hole too, just look at my Guccis!"

Cerberus gormlessly licked Paris's injured hand with one head while sniggering a lot with the other two.

"I'm sorry about that," said Hercules, "he got hold of the leftovers from last night's takeaway curry, it's not his fault."

"Yeah well, from now on sod off down the park with him for a shit!" Paris turned on his turd be-sodden heel and looked for a piece turf or a crooked cobble to scrape it on. Not finding anything suitable in the immediate area, he squelched his way towards the river just off to the left of town.

As he washed the fetid crap off his foot an old fellow, of beggar like appearance, came over and extended a rather skeletal hand. Paris looked up at the shape outlined by the mid-day sun and shaded his eyes, as well as smearing shit across his forehead, to get a better look. "Oh no, piss off Charon, you I just don't need, not today." Charon remained with extended hand. "Look," said Paris. "Bugger off and pay for your own boat repairs, it's your own fault, using that bloody sickle thing as an oar."

Charon did not move but he did do something most unusual, for him at any rate, he spoke. "Look, pal, they had a bit of a get together up the side of Olympus and they all got pissed up and decided to privatise a few assets. What you are looking at is the river Styx P. L. C. I'm in charge here and if you want to chuck shit in my river you can sodding well pay for the privilege, so either cough up or remove it."

More money, thought Paris. "You're just another parasite who's after my cash, you're all the same. Do you know a woman called Helen by any chance?"

Charon thought for a moment. "Yeah, real good-looking doll, knows how to dress, long hair, cute ankles, knows how to have a good time, that Helen?"

"That's the one," grunted Paris.

"No, mate, never met her but they all come by here eventually. Now cut the pleasantries and pay the sewage toll before I go and get Geryon out."

Having encountered a three arse-holed-shit-in-unison dog already that day, Paris was in no mood to meet the three-headed, winged, aerial version, which could probably crap from a great height with surprising accuracy, so he paid up and attempted to resume his original errand.

Large bold capitals over the shop door proclaimed –

THE ODYSSEUS DATE-A-MATE AND EMPLOYMENT AGENCY

Arrows strategically shot through the woodwork indicated the range of departments:

1. Redeployment and re-training, extreme left
2. Youth experience and general exploitation, not so extreme left
3. Male and female dating, straight up (well, what else?)
4. Blue and white-collar potential servants to the gods, not so extreme right
5. Kings, queens and various assorted royals, extreme right

Paris, having had the benefit of a private education and therefore being fully capable of understanding the signs, took the extreme right, only after mistakenly having had a dose of straight up. He entered the door marked Employment Clerk and was invited to take a seat. Now times were hard granted but he had thrown better seats than these in the royal skip on many an occasion and declining the offer decided to sit on it instead.

"Name?" said the clerk.

"Paris," said Paris.

The clerk raised one eyebrow closely followed by half a face to inquire. "What about it?"

"What?"

"Paris, what about it?"

"What do you mean what about it?"

"What about Paris?" asked the clerk, "that's in the newly acquired territories, we haven't even officially named it yet. How do you know about Paris?"

"No, you dopey excuse for a donkey's distended gut, my name is Paris."

"Aaaha, would that be Paris as in Paris, France?"

"No! That would be Paris as in crown prince, son of Priam and heir to the Kingship of Troy, Paris."

"Don't take that tone of voice with me, sonny boy. Crown prince and thronal heir are ex-job descriptions so far as Troy is concerned. You ex-royals get right on my tits you know? You come in here full of bloody heirs and graces, arrogant to the point of ignorant and try to lord it over the lowly clerk who is just doing his lowly job. Well let me tell you, sonny, you are redundant, sacked, disinherited and well and truly arse kicked, do you understand? You need me, I can get you another job if I feel so inclined, so don't come in here with your heavy-handed, high minded, obnoxious strutting about and take the piss out of me, okay?"

Paris looked at the half-face that had just risen to animation and spoken to him. "I take it," he said calmly, "that career fulfilment and job satisfaction are not at a premium in your present position?"

At this point, the clerk, who was one camel's extra straw and a Prozac short of a straight jacket crumpled down on to his desk and blubbered incessantly. "You don't understand. You don't know what it's like. I run all these departments from extreme left to extreme right whilst that tosspot owner Odysseus goes jaunting off about the world, chatting up Sirens and shafting Cybeles and Shape-changers. I get no help around the place at all. So I complain and he says get the wife to give you a hand. What a laugh, I mean, she's

Mythistrone

totally useless, she just sits in the back room pissing about with a bloody shuttle and a loom and along with bewailing her fate says, "yeah okay, when I've finished this tapestry." Then the old cow rips it all back and starts again. I mean, stone the crows, she's got suitors in and out of here at all hours of the day and I'm the twat that has to give them a shit load of excuses and get shot of them, as well as deal with you shower that thinks the world owes them a living. I can't take it, I just can't take it anymore. I'm a god-fearing kind of bloke, I live a decent and honest life and when I ask god, why me? What do I find? I'll tell you what I find, I find that a jumped-up bunch of reprobates and spoiled kids like you have had a fucking war and changed all the bloody gods again - and then I have to start all over again. It's so disheartening and soul-destroying and you lot, you don't give a bugger, coming in here whinging and whining about wanting a job, so just sod off will you? Come back later, there's a worldwide recession going on in the royalty ranks. We can't find positions for the good ones, you amorous, don't give a toss about anything but your dick bunch, have got no chance, so do us all a favour and bugger off will you?"

Paris stood up and, deciding that the original offer was probably about as good as the day was going to get, left with the chair.

His duty discharged for the day Paris decided that he just had time for a swift pint down at Andromache's Bar and Bistro, which he knew, rapidly following that first swift pint, would quickly turn into a right skinful.

Two-thirds of a skinful later, Andromache leaned over the bar, imitating the yet to be invented product of a double jelly mould with a cleavage, and said, "Aint yer 'ad enuf yet Par?"

"Watcher Andro, how's tricks?"

"That's my business but between you and me it's been a damn sight easier since your dumb brover 'ectar got 'is 'ead kicked in."

Paris, by now, had passed the point where decency and coherence exerted any kind of binding social conduct on his behaviour.

"I've alwaysh fanchied you, you know Andro an', an', if it wasn't for Hecktar I'd 'ave married you, you know, 'cos I fink you're, really good lookin' bird you know."

"Shut up Paris, you only say that when you're pissed."

"Thatch 'cos of you runnin' a pub, sho I only shee you frough a bar haze but you're alwaysh good luckin' when 'am pissed."

Thud!

Splash!

Andromache had removed the tankard that was propping up Paris' chin and incorporated its contents with his hair.

"Time you went 'ome to your long sufferin' wife Paris," said Andromache, as she deftly whipped round the bar and equally deftly, kicked the stool out from underneath him while grabbing him by the scruff of his collar and impelling towards the door all in one neat, easy, well-practised manoeuvre.

"Waih a minit," slurred Paris, as he reached out and picked up his chair, with which he zigzagged down the cobbled pavement in a direction opposite to that of his morning journey. He turned the chair up on his shoulder and began to play the, yet to be invented, bagpipes while bouncing off the occasional garden wall, lamp post or public waste bin. Suddenly, right out of the blue, Paris sort of heard but more sort of felt a very familiar, '*squelch!*'

"Oh bollocks, 'son the ovver bleedin' foot naah."

He wiped his foot, while balancing his bag pipes very professionally in his ear, on the doorstep of the Odysseus Date-a-Mate and Employment Agency. "'Sa crap plachase anyhow," he sniggered, leaving a number of upturned horse-shoe-shape gouts of dog poop decoratively spaced along the step and continued on his wayward stumble in a vaguely homeward direction.

He paused at the front door and fumbled a great deal with the latch, until he realised that it was the letterbox. The door eventually swung inwards and Paris upended his bagpipes into their former incarnation and placed a chair on the floor. He stopped, looked around and instinctively ducked, as only one who instinctively knows that he is instinctively in deep do-do instinctively would.

Dunck!

Too late, he realised as his eyes began to re-focus on the love of his life, who seemed suddenly very tall and who was still menacingly wielding a telescopic rolling pin.

"What bloody time do you call this?" she screeched at him.

"Iken exchsplain…" he tried.

Kdunck!

Should have been ready for that one he thought, eventually making it to an upright stance just prior to falling over a chair that some prat had left in the doorway.

"You drunken sod Paris, mother was right, you'll never amount to anything."

Kerduhnk!

"And don't you dare tramp that dog shit in all over my nice clean carpet."

"But - it's been a hell of a day, love, you wouldn't believe what happened on the way to the job shop…"

Dunck!
Kadisch!
"Ouch."

The Trojan Bunch

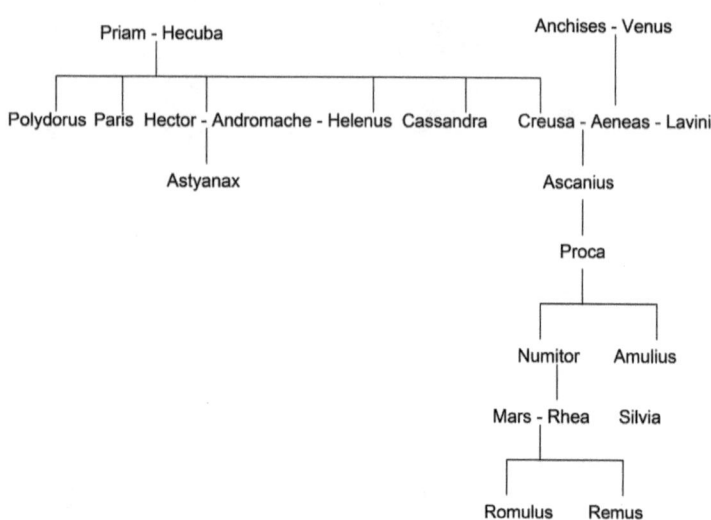

II

PEOPLE IN GLASS HOUSES

Theseus stood in the back garden of his three up, two and a half down semi, admiring how well the tomatoes were doing this year, the rake gave a tell-tale creak as he leaned on it. Theseus, recognising an omen when he saw one or in this case heard one, wisely straightened his gait and shifted his weight sideways.

Thwakiesszzz, tshinkle! Theseus watched in horror as two panes of glass crazed with large radiant, spider-web reminiscent holes in them following their reaction to the interaction of two feet of knicker elastic, a forked stick and a chunk of rock. Rapidly after that, the horror increased as the panes collapsed and sliced his tomatoes to ribbons.

Theseus turned, glowing at the ear lobes with rage as he realised - for Theseus may have been many things but slow on the uptake wasn't one of them - that if the rake had not creaked ominously the rock in the greenhouse would now be wedged somewhat painfully right between his buttocks.

"Hoy, Astyanax, you little snot rag," he bellowed at the recalcitrant child, who was perched on a ten-foot-high wall displaying the upstanding middle finger of his right hand and most of his tongue, "when I get my hands on that catapult you're going to have an embarrassing time explaining to the physician how it got stuck in that sunless place, wide end first!"

The boy laughed and jumped down on the far side of the wall as Theseus bolted for the gate and ran straight through it in hot pursuit. Suddenly the air rang with the sound of a matronly voice. "Astyanax, Astyanax you little shit, you get back 'ere this instant," screeched Andromache as she ran across the bistro cart park, stopping only to trip over her elastic-less knickers, in pursuit of the brat. Astyanax saw the dangers of this two-pronged pursuit and took an immediate vector alteration.

Andromache picked up her skirts, and her elastic-less knickers, and decided to circle round ahead while Theseus brought up the rear.

Astyanax now ran - as though all the slayers of all the monsters, in all the hells, were after him and breathing hotly on his tail, which was not too far from the truth really - looking over his shoulder now and then to see only Theseus still in the game.

Theseus, as ever, not slow on the uptake, slowed down. Andromache was missing which was, if he knew anything about harbingers, a devious, dangerous one. This, he decided, was going to be fun to watch.

Astyanax took a last look over his shoulder, before the next turn, at the apparently flagging Theseus and was gone.

Thwaumph!

Astyanax suddenly re-appeared from his last turn performing a double, full-twisting open back somersault, followed very closely by the hand that had just transformed him into the erratic gymnast.

"Ow, ya bitch," wailed Astyanax as the owner of the hand entered the scene and, while using the other one to keep her knickers aloft, let rip with a stream of invective in the way that only a pub landlady can, whilst all the time employing the gymnastically inclined hand in pursuit of the boy's ears.

Andromache was an awe-inspiring sight on full throttle, Theseus watched in rapt admiration - from a safe distance.

"You miserable little wretch…" *Thrash!* "…It's tough enough bein' a single parent…" *Slap!* "…Without you continually acting the prat…" *Smash!* "…Now let that be a lesson to ya."

A sound resembling, *tewanng*, was followed by a nifty manoeuvre, which replaced the knicker elastic in its rightful place and that was followed by what was now becoming a familiar sound.

Thump!

"An' don't get upsettin' the neighbours no more either, got that? The poor bloke next door 'as been through two wars an' a bloody minotaur so the likes of you can 'ave a good life, show some respect you little git." With that final admonishment the boy was hauled to his feet by one rather enlarged and throbbing ear and towed home.

Theseus cracked up laughing - making a mental note that the forked stick of the catapult was still out in the sunshine but then too much excitement in one day wasn't good for one - and returned to his garden to find his wife, Hippolyte, standing in the gateway, arms folded and wearing her grim and irate face. "Where the hell have you been sloping off to? It's always the same, anything rather than mow the lawn. I swear Theseus, since we moved here you do absolutely nothing to help me about the house, when you're not down the pub with that good for nothing Paris, you're out pratting about with the neighbourhood kids, you're a complete waste of space and, your ex-wife, you know, the one you ditched after the scrap with that bloody Minotaur thing? Well, she's been on the 'phone again bitching about the amount of back maintenance you owe her - old cow. What did she ever see in you? And another thing, get this bloody gate fixed before nightfall, otherwise that thieving swine Ajax will be prowling about and you know him, he'll have the garden furniture away and melted down before you can say, 'what sheep?' - just a sodding rag and bone man if you ask me."

"Far be it for me to ask you anything," mumbled Theseus, hands in his braces and foot idly scuffling the dirt.

"What was that?" Hippolyte rounded on him.

"I said yes dear, anything you say dear."

"Humph," said Hippolyte heading back to what, in Theseus' opinion, was her rightful place - the kitchen.

"Miserable old slag," he muttered.

"I heard that!"

"Miserable old bat-eared slag."

Gudong, tschinkle!

The saucepan that had just been ejected, at near light speed, from Hippolyte's rightful place had impacted with Theseus' right-hand temple before ricocheting into the greenhouse and pureeing most of the remaining tomatoes.

That was it, enough was enough. He banged a couple of four-inch round head nails into the gate's sagging top hinge and bent the ends over where they had skewed through the side of the post. Time for a beer, he thought and indiscriminately tossed the claw hammer over his shoulder. *Tischinkle*, spake the greenhouse for the third time that day.

III

THE DIVINE COMEDIAN

Prometheus didn't see it the way the storybooks told it. They had him written up as a total rebel without a bike to ride. According to history, he was the kind of guy who loved himself, liked blowing his own trumpet and stirring things up in the heavens. He was responsible for the change in the God hierarchy because he turned on his own Titan type and assisted the Olympians to affect a coups d'état. He'd made Zeus's immortal life a nightmare with his random predictions and prophecies and had little in the way of humanity about him.

Let's start right there with that novel little idea, thought Prometheus. A bunch of Gods had chained him to a rock and a bird spent all day feeding on his liver. They did that because Prometheus would not tell Zeus, the omnipotent, all-seeing, immortal king of the Gods, what his future was. In Prometheus's viewpoint that meant that omnipotent, all-seeing and immortal were somewhat valueless terms of reference or description. I mean, you would think the king of the Gods would have a pretty fair grasp on the plan and its possible outcomes! Then Zeus goes all petty and schoolyard about it and gets his big buddies to chain Prometheus to a rock to be fed on by scavengers and the history books dare to call him lacking in humanity!

He, Prometheus, had done stuff. If it wasn't for him there would be no humanity. He'd made the clay models and convinced the Gods that blowing life into them was probably a good idea. He'd shown them a few things too, like how to mine precious metals and given them a bit of technology and some guidance in medicine.

With hindsight, his giving them the gift of fire, albeit by default, was probably not one of his smartest moves but on the whole, they weren't a bad lot. They could build their own machines to mine metals to make beautiful representations of the Gods and keep themselves fit and healthy to continue to worship the Gods down the generations of their short lives. Gods liked being worshipped, it was in the job description, what was the problem? Gods were not going to worship Gods because they were, like, Gods and didn't need to worship anything. The Gods didn't have time to worship other Gods because they were too busy playing power games and fighting with each other so they needed worshippers to be Gods to surely? Hence Prometheus's brilliant idea, create a race of worshippers.

Zeus, however, was not so pleased with the outcome. He didn't like the self-awareness that the clay models were developing and their potential to totally screw up his, work-in-progress-without-a-coherent-plan, plan. Zeus particularly didn't like that Prometheus was somewhat of a prophet. He could see things before they happened in the work-in-progress-without-a-coherent-plan, plan. That bastard could see the future and Zeus was none too pleased about that because that was his remit.

Prometheus knew this and he milked it to its fullest extent. Zeus wanted to know what Prometheus knew about his future and Prometheus was damn sure he was not giving that nugget of information away for free!

That narrow mindedness pissed Zeus off a fair amount and in consequence, Prometheus was chained to a rock for some correctional therapy.

Prometheus was an outdoors sort of guy. He liked the freedom to roam the world and be at one with it and the creatures in it, rather than be confined by the chains of a work-ethic-God-king with visions of superior grandeur.

He could put up with this crap though because he knew it wouldn't last forever. The work-in-progress-without-a-coherent-plan, plan, would sort this entire travesty out for him. It was no small wonder to him that he ended up a drug-dependent stoner, you had to have an outlet but there was a bitter and comic irony in knowing that Zeus's need to copulate with Prometheus's creations would lead to his downfall. One day soon, Zeus's son would free him from his bondage and then there would be reparation and compensation, it was time somebody worshipped him. Prometheus was not at all happy with the sodding Gods!

In the beginning there was Chaos – at the end there was Mayhem

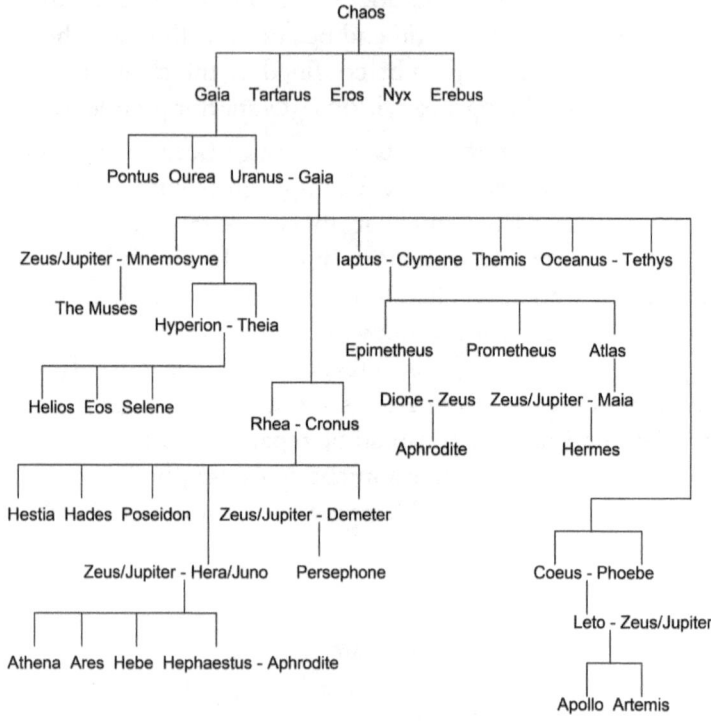

IV

SPLASH OF THE TITAN

Life for Hercules had not exactly been plain sailing, until now that is. It had been fraught with evil, nasty, beastly encounters. Bores, bulls, that shaper changer Achelous, lions, those snotty arrogant horses arses the Centaurs and of course the hound.

Hercules was another who had the rapid uptake capability and he realised, though he may be immortalish he wasn't getting any younger and he should take things a little easier at his time of immortalishness.

So he had tossed a Drachma over the parchment map of a flat world and decided to settle down and retire wherever the coin landed heads up and, here he was, in a settlement on the right bank of the Styx that was rapidly turning into an old folks retirement village.

Boring, boring, boring, bloody boring. The most exciting things to happen here in the last year were Andromache breaking a fingernail while catching a keg from the brewery cart after the horse threw a shoe and spilt the load - but that was just the horse showing off to a couple of oncoming fillies, it very rarely managed to pitch a shoe around the peg anyway and, on that occasion, missed completely as far as the peg was concerned and would have sworn blind that it was aiming for the right-hand door pane of Theseus' greenhouse and that it was, therefore, a perfect shot - and the milkman's cart lost a wheel and, much to Charon's disgust, careered off the stick bridge over the Styx and had its fall cushioned by a recently renovated ferry which it reduced to a mass of floating sticks and, to Charon's great disgust, both milkie and horse survived, which was probably just as well because his ferry was obviously going to be in dry dock for a bit.

That episode had created quite a backlog of unable to pass souls and had certainly livened the town up a bit at nights but the resultant heart attacks had been a bit counterproductive and half the shades didn't even know that they had stiffed it and tried to carry on as normal. It was quite amusing watching them sink into their commodes and fall through their Zimmer frames. The hound had been in its element chasing them around the park but, for all its three heads, it had been left somewhat wanting in the cortical filler department and discerning between ghost and genuine article was not really its forte, the obvious outcome being a bigger backlog for Charon to worry about and he was already paying The Valkyries time and a half on a contracted-out basis.

"Sod it," said Hercules, aimlessly tossing a tree for the dog to chase, "nothing ever happens around here!" A phrase, as most know, well known for its tempting of providence and incitement of destiny qualities.

"Oowefya," groaned a voice about a trees throw away, "all right, who threw that?"

"Me," replied Hercules, not wanting to miss the chance of a good kick up, well, he could use the exercise. "I threw it, what of it?"

"Who is me - I?" Questioned a voice about a trees throw away.

"That's a question I have often pondered myself," responded Hercules, "but I'm not too hot on all that logical, negative positivism, metaphysical, psychological, crap."

"Look, you just hit me right in the left nut with that tree, the least you can do is tell me your name!"

"Ah, gotcha, my name's Hercules, performer of labours to the rich and famous."

"Indeed? The Hercules that slapped a lion and a few horses' arses around there a few years back, one of Io's bunch?"

"Yeah, that's me, what's it to you?"

Being fearless did not necessarily guarantee intelligence and being quick on the uptake did less to guarantee against outbreaks of crass stupidity. Hercules looked over the crest of the hill from whence the voice, and an up-ended tree, emanated.

"Woof woof," barked Cerberus.

"Woof woof,"

"Woof woof," barked the other two heads, catching on to the new game of bark at the stranger, retrieve the tree and drop it again when startled by the other, "Woof woofs."

"Oowfukit," said the voice as the tree caught the right nut. "So you're Hercules? A right scrawny looking article you are too. I could have taken the likes of you with one hand tied behind me!"

"Oy, there's no need to be offensive, that's fighting talk that is and considering you appear to be shackled to the hillside with a rather septic hole in the midriff, I'd be careful what you say. Just because I'm out of practice doesn't mean I can't handle you."

"Ha, fine words but that's all they are, get these chains off me and let's go a few rounds."

With crass stupidity now taking the upper hand, Hercules stamped on the chains and snapped them like the running thread of a hemline two stitches from the end of the run.

"Thank the gods," said Hercules, "some action at last."

Zischpkoor!

Forked lightning rent the air, and a fair portion of the park too, as the man no longer in shackles rose to his feet, which appeared to be a good twenty feet from his head. Hercules, in between dodging lightning bolts, couldn't help thinking that the guy had definitely been shorter prior to standing up.

"Oy you, long fella," bellowed Hercules, "what's your name and what's the crack with all this lightning stuff?"

The giant downshifted a few spectral gears and became something closer to a recognisably human stature and said proudly, "I, am Prometheus."

"Oh shit!" replied Hercules, "now you've really gone and done it haven't you? You've totally pissed the old man off good and proper."

"I know, fun isn't it?"

"Fun! You call this fun, dancing around the local park dodging the best that the Cyclopes can forge in the way of fire and brimstone? Why now eh, why do you have to surface just when I want to retire?"

"Heroes don't retire," Prometheus pronounced, "they go out in a blaze of glory and if we don't get out of here now you might just become the proud owner of an object lesson in the blaze of glory theory."

"All right, hold on, hold it right there," said Hercules standing astride with his fists bunched on his hips. He looked towards the sky and said, "All right Dad you've had your fun, you knew this was going to happen one day, well, looks like today is the one, so just leave it out with the sodding lightning bolts, you're starting to scare the dog and you're ruining spring."

Zischpkoor! Was the reply as lightning split the dog's chase tree into smouldering cinders and sent Cerberus yelping for cover behind his master or, from the dog's point of view, a better conductor.

"Aw, come off it, Dad, this is just a pathetic tantrum display, now turn it in and stop pissing about before I have to come up there and sort you out!"

At this juncture, what with threats in the face of the almighty and all that, Prometheus ducked behind a convenient war memorial obelisk, fully expecting to be savouring the stench of over-cooked Hercules at any moment.

A minute or two later nothing much seemed to have happened and Prometheus removed his fingers from his ears and risked a look at the sky. The rolling thunderheads were gone, along with any hint of lightning and the sun was shining again. Prometheus, partly because it was still a novelty, stood up again - looking a tad embarrassed after depositing a load in the only pair of trousers he had to his name - as a deep voice from nowhere in particular said,

"Sorry lad, things just get on my tits every now and then, don't take it personally."

Hercules turned to Prometheus. "The river's over there, here's a couple of Drachs."

"What's that for?" asked the un-fragrant not so giant.

"Sewage charge, you'll work it out as you go along," said Hercules eyeing up another tree for the hound to play with.

Presently Prometheus returned smelling sweeter, looking wetter and a couple of Drachs lighter. "That Charon," he said, "I knew him donkey's years ago, when he was just the ferryman's tea boy and, believe me, vintage has not improved his disposition, he's still a miserable, arrogant, wet fart."

"Well," said Hercules, "with the possible exception of the fart, I'd say you had a lot in common."

"Now look here, sonny boy, I haven't spent two golden ages and the longest election campaign in history shackled to a hill and pestered by a pesky vulture, just to listen to a snotty-nosed young upstart taking the piss!"

Hercules promptly took hold of Prometheus and threw him the half-mile into the Styx, incurring a heavy fine for excessive pollution dumping, and reached into his pocket for a hankie.

"Snotty nosed indeed!"

V

ONE HERO AND HIS DOG

Paris was still limping after the previous evening's altercation with young Helen, when he entered Andromache's Bar and Bistro - still carrying his chair - for a swift dinner time half. Theseus turned on his barstool, which gave a disturbing creak. "All right Par, how ya doin'?"

"I'm limping to the left and dying of thirst, 'part from that, fine."

Theseus turned back to the bar, to the sound of another ominous creak, and leaned over it.

"Andro? Andro baby we could do with another beer out here. Oy! Shop, we in any danger of service out here?"

"Awright, awright I'm comin!' the kids got 'is big toe stuck in the bung 'ole on the ale keg." replied the landlady.

"So what?" enquired Paris.

"So I can't get the tap in, is wot, so you can't 'ave any ale 'til I get the brats hoof out, is wot!"

"I'll have lager then, I don't like ale with too much body, 'specially his rancid toenails."

Kerdunck!

Paris fell headlong with a large wooden spoon embedded in his left ear.

Theseus deftly shifted sideways on his stool and the ominous creak became the renting sound of splintering timber as the stool finally gave in. His beaker of ale hit the bar top milli-seconds prior to his chin doing the same and in a half-hearted flick-flack, Theseus ended up unconscious on top of the semi-conscious Paris.

Schplunk!

The toe came free, minus its toe nail, to the sound of a deathly wail from Astyanax, followed by a resounding, *tischwack!* as Andromache's now spoonless hand made contact with his right ear.

"Now bugger off out an' play, I've got a livin' to earn," said Andromache, returning to the bar.

"Right lads, what'll it be?" The bar was deserted. "Hmm, that's strange," muttered Andromache, wiping ale off the bar top. Chancing to look over the bar, she noticed the avant-garde sculpture in still life representing how to stir your bar stool.

"That's just bloody typical that is, you come in 'ere pesterin' me for ale, you moan about it bein' flat, 'avin no body, got no flavour, bit short on alcohol an' now look at yer, all yuv 'ad is a sniff at the barmaid's apron and there yer are, pissed owt a yer faces, unconscious. I ask ya, why do I bovver, treat this place like a pub…" she grumbled coming round to the clientele side for a tentative prod with one Doc Martened foot… "yer do. C'mon on yer feet," said the proud owner of the aforementioned apron bending to extract one large wooden spoon with one large wax plug attached to it, followed by a more violent interaction between Doc Marten and uppermost arse.

There followed a series of grunts and expletives from the pile of human detritus on the floor and Andromache returned to her keg tapping.

Five minutes later, two dishevelled, sawdust bedecked faces, brought still life to life and poked up above the bar from the clientele side of the room. Paris looked at Theseus who looked back in a likewise manner. "Nice one These," said Paris. "Ay, Andro, another two pints of that please."

Schliss, Schliss, two pints of full-bodied, toenail free ale schlissed along the bar top and stopped in the outstretched hands of the now fully conscious sculpture components.

There was a resounding thud as Theseus realised that one bar stool appeared to be missing. Paris sat on a convenient seat that he had just happened to bring along with him and after dragging a table over, Theseus sat on it. Paris took long draught on his ale and inquired, "What brings you out for a dinner time beer then?"

"Well, you know how it is, new day, new beer! One has to cope with life's indifferences. My granddad Pittheus died. I liked having a beer with him and listening to all his sarcastic witticisms, this is how he would have handled the event, if in doubt – have a beer!"

"Aahh yes, Pittheus," replied Paris, "a sagacious prank master if ever there were one. Didn't he get Aegeus pissed when he didn't understand the oracle and set him up with your mum?"

"Yeah, that's the one, joke a minute and nonstop humourist. I was at his place one day when Herky came round after some labouring job. I was about seven then. Herc had put his lion skin on the couch and when I came in from school, Pittheus goes, 'shit, oh shit a lion' so I grabbed the fireplace axe and mashed it good and proper." Theseus paused for a snigger. "You shoulda seen the look on Herk's face, brand new winter coat full of axe slashes, fookin priceless. I thought I'd saved everyone and Pittheus sat there with tears rolling down his face pissing himself laughing!

Good times, good times indeed." Theseus raised his beaker and clashed it against Paris' and downed it in one.

"So, what happened to give you the limp Par?"

"Aah, um, woman trouble."

"Woman trouble?"

"Yeah, the telescopic rolling pin."

"What, you mean the bitch belted you in the nuts with it?"

"Certainly did, really sneaky too, I was already down, *dunck, crunch,* absolutely no regard for unsatisfied conjugal desires, left me with no desire for any conjugal desires I can tell you."

"Yes, I remember it well," spake Theseus.

"That diminishes with age," he said as his eyes misted over, or was it glazed over, in an attempt at memory retrieval.

"Hippolyte worked out that, if she belted me any time the request for sex reared its ugly head, I would keep a severe check on the rearing incidents. It works as well, you don't get a lot and the pattern is always changed before it gets a chance to be one but, you do feel grateful at the time that, having got you by the balls and being fully aware of the fact, they don't squeeze them too much. It's a delicate control art that starts, generally, with a smile, then the reeling it in, then a ring, then a cold shoulder and some moodiness followed by the rolling pin phase. This generally gives way to the - we're too old for that silly, platonic is good, hurry up and stiff it, I need the insurance – phase."

Paris sat quietly through this and said, "Do I detect a hint of dissatisfaction with the status of your marital status? I mean, don't get me wrong, I'm not one to pry but are you sure you're getting your leg over enough?"

Theseus smiled and considered that, though Helen was overqualified to be a fishmonger's wife, she would make a damn good fisherman and was at present in the, reeling it into a waiting net, phase.

"My round Par, want another one?"

"Nah, I've got to get this chair back, later mate."

With that, Paris headed for the Odysseus Date-a-Mate and Employment Agency, with one chair in tow.

In the Redundant Future Kings' Department, the clerk said, "Take a seat please."

"Been there, done that, had the free sample," said Paris "Missus doesn't like it, clashes with the drapery," he added by way of an explanation and left the startled clerk wearing a recycled chair.

"God that felt good!" said Paris to no one in particular as he stepped onto the cobbled pavement outside the Employment Agency.

Squelch!

"Oh bollocks!"

Hercules, who had just happened to have walked past the agency door, looked over his shoulder at the sound of the exclamation and thought, rather appropriately, oh shit, to defuse or to vanish? Defuse, he decided.

"Paris, it is Paris, isn't it? We met earlier this week in similar circumstances. Wow, man, lucky boots, really lucky boots, in fact, I've never seen such a lucky pair of boots."

"What," growled Paris, who was on the verge of a severe sense of humour deficit, "is so bloody lucky about having my boot engulfed by a triangulated, curried dog do-do? And I should think very carefully before attempting a reply!"

"Well, it was very lucky you were wearing them otherwise your foot would now be very be-shitten."

Hercules quickly gathered, when a medium dollop of be-shitten took flight briefly prior to splattering around his right ear, that he obviously hadn't thought carefully enough.

Cerberus by this time was a helpless case of side-splitting laughter with virtually no muscle control, which made it much easier for Hercules to pick him up and explain, via the nose up to the ears covered in shit method, that he really would prefer it if the dog would desist from crapping on the pavement.

'Hey - what's it to you?' thought the be-shitten head.

"Just remember, you have three noses and the other two aren't all covered in your own crap - yet!"

'Yeah, I read you, boss,' considered the hound, giving its head a good shake and pebble-dashing a large portion of the frontage of the Odysseus Date-a-Mate and Employment Agency.

"I think he's got it now," said Hercules returning his attention to Paris - who, having just daubed dog-doo all over the strongest man in the world, was wondering what he could possibly do for an encore short of run very fast and very far - and clapped a vice-like hand on his shoulder. "I think we ought to take a stroll down to the old Styx P.L.C. and clean up a bit. I'll cop for the sewage charge, I like a bloke who stands up for himself, come on."

Paris was slightly miffed, he had fully expected Armageddon on legs and a rather fore-shortened lifeline, all courtesy of the be-shitten hero and not so local boy made good. Making the rapid decision that the offer was better than the expectation, Paris strolled down to the river with one hero and his dog.

Meet the Family Part 1

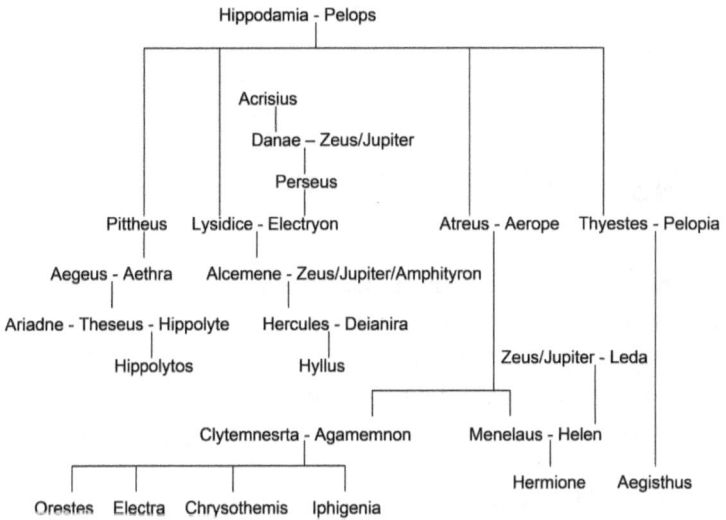

VI

INSURRECTION FOR THE MASSES

As they lay in the sun on the riverbank drying off, Paris and Hercules listened to the wondrous sounds of the countryside. The petrified high-velocity screech of a cat that had recently discovered its place in the pecking order of life by the acquisition of an over-enthusiastic, triple-headed dog bringing up its rear. The *tap-tap-tappety-dumpf*, "oohyafuckinbastard" *smash!* of Charon in pursuit of a D.I.Y. boatbuilding career, along with the footfalls of a recently released pretender to the throne of Jupiter.

"Here Herky," said Prometheus from a safe distance, "that wasn't bloody funny, I mean, I've only just got the hang of standing and walking again, there was no need for the flying lesson so soon. I need to take things at a more leisurely pace at my age."

"So, what do you want Prom?"

"Well, a general election would be a good start! Your old man's had carte blanche for long enough."

Hercules tutted. "Same old song Prom, how many times in life do you have to screw it up to realise, you just ain't omnipotent governing material."

"I aint? Well that's alright then, I didn't intend to drive the boat myself."

"Oh yeah?" inquired Hercules, "who do you reckon should run the show then, Juno, the money-grabbing, jealous, vindictive tart? Or maybe Venus? we'll have another 'peace and love man', deal with her. How about Mars perhaps? He's a hard worker, keeps having a go here and there but he doesn't quite seem to have the apocalyptic vision of old anymore, good for a skirmish but he couldn't run an election campaign. Tossers, all of them, tossers. The backbenchers are crap too, freeloaders all of 'em. They like to have a say or a bit of a, 'hear, hear', but they do bog-all. I mean, Apollo? Diana? Cupid? Stuck up spoiled rich kids the lot of them, got no sodding idea, twats. How can you have an election with an apathetic shower of shit like that on offer?"

"Exactly," said Prometheus stepping a little closer, "look around, the place is full of people, it's their world, and they should run it."

"The people?" Hercules looked back at Prometheus incredulously, "look around yourself, they've been running it for the last three-thousand-odd years, right into the ground generally, couldn't organise a sludge pump in a fertiliser farm, they'd just about - with a little imagination - make the raw material."

"That's 'cos they've had no choice, they weren't in charge. They could always say it was God's fault, destiny would take care of it, they've always had something to fall back on. What they need is a party of the mortals run by the mortals for the mortals."

To Hercules that had a familiar ring, though he thought that the last syllable of the adjective should be the opposite of offs!

"I don't know Prom, why stir it now? It lurches along relatively well, can you imagine what mortals would be like with no disasters to keep them in check? They need to have at least one god to reproach every now and then," said Hercules as he watched the dog crouching furtively behind Prometheus.

"Why? Without the gods farting around, being bored and playing head games and dishing out guilt trips, there wouldn't be any disasters for them to be reproached for. Most of the old boys have had enough, with the exception of one or two die-hards, they all want out, they all feel that they've slaved and laboured long enough. I reckon we give it to the mortals and let them chart their own destiny, make their own cock-ups and be their own gods, give them independence, they're ready for it."

"Hmmm…?" said Hercules, "very eloquent Prom, so let me get this straight, what you're talking about here is compulsory redundancy for the die-hards, yeah? You want to retire the old man without any severance pay, no golden handshake and no consultancy opportunities, right?"

"That's more or less it," said Prometheus, "put very basically."

"So what's it got to do with me?" enquired Hercules, watching the dog kick the grass up with its hind legs.

"Well, I could use your help."

"What, more of it? I've already broken the chains off. Chains, I might point out, that I had no intention of ever bloody breaking. Oh yes, I know the story of what you did to great-great-granny Io. She came to you looking for help with a fly spurring her along stinging her arse and what did you do? You sent the stupid old heifer halfway round the world with the cock-ass story that one of her descendants would free you and off she went with a fly up her arse believing herself to be one of the chosen. It never crossed her mind, in its bovine state, that if you were worth a fart you could get your own chains off and give her a hand by at least swatting the fly."

Prometheus stared at the ground rather like it was the two-foot square piece of coconut matting in front of the head masochist's desk in a Christian Brothers school. "I'll grant you," he mumbled, "the credentials don't look too impressive but destiny and fate have decreed that this is the way of it, I'm just following orders really."

"Fate," snorted Hercules, "blind bloody chance would be closer, the devil looks after his own and all that. So now you want my help?"

"Er - yes, you see between you and I, we can create a new order. A new age where everyone gets a bit, it has been decreed by the fates. Cast in iron and wrought in stone, prophesied and heralded, you, Hercules, were chosen."

"Oh yeah, pure chance, that's what chose me. I don't care if it's cast in stone, wrought in tin and countersigned in Strasbourg, it's a complete crock of shit from end to end."

"I know," pleaded Prometheus, "and we can change that, will you help me, please?"

"I'll think about it, now bugger off, me and Paris here are trying to sunbathe."

Believing something to be preferable to nothing, Prometheus turned to walk away and leave them in peace.

Squelch!

Hercules grinned to himself, ten feet further to the left, Cerberus sat with his heads cocked to three sides and sniggered.

Prometheus fumed and assumed his full imposing height, which could easily cover ten feet in a stride.

"Urraych, urraygh, urraych!" was the howl of pain that echoed around the park, as a godly, sized twenty-five Doc

Mythistrone

Marten boot united the triplicate arses of a mythical hound in searing agony, with one god damn almighty kick.

"Temper, temper," said Hercules.

Meet the Family Part 2

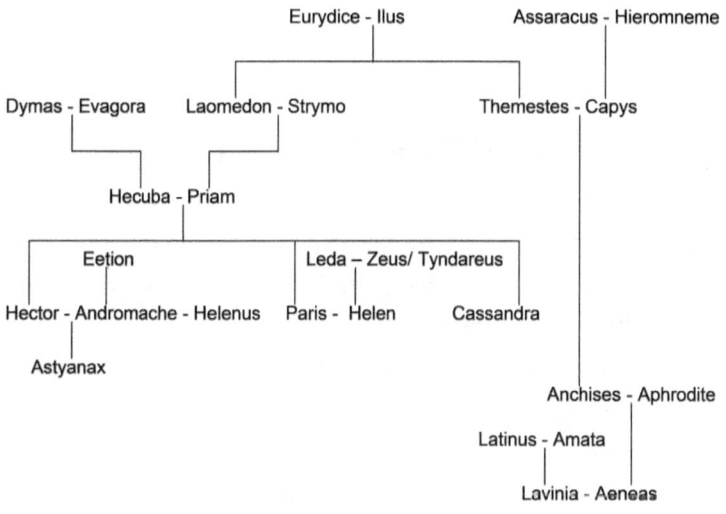

VII

AGENT PROVOCATEUR

"Well," said Paris, "all this sunbathing is rather strenuous and it has, I find, given me quite a thirst. Perhaps you would care to join me in a little liquid refreshment?"

Hercules nodded, "Sounds like a rather pleasant pastime, don't mind if I do."

Whumpf!

The dog touched down again, after a near rendezvous with an orbit courtesy of the animal-loving Prometheus.

"Yes, now that the dog's back, I quite fancy a beer. C'mon boy, here Cerberus, we're going to the pub and no crapping on the pavement, okay?"

Cerberus weighed the options, his master was taking the piss, right? Crap on the pavement, all three holes were probably cauterised for the next six months, he would be lucky if he ever crapped again. If it wasn't for the fact that he'd seen Hercules throw Prometheus half a mile in well under four minutes, he would have sunk a set of doggy dentures into the pert hero buttock that was dangerously close to his right head. Options weighed, the hound trotted, with difficulty, obediently behind his master, after all, the guy had rescued him from a real hell hole.

Hercules put the dog in the beer garden, which did little to attract passing trade at the Bar and Bistro and joined Paris in the bar.

Theseus was still in the same spot Paris had left him in earlier that day and the fact that both pupils were looking out of the same eyeball suggested that the ale was working a treat.

"Hey, Andro baby, give us a couple of pints over here," called Paris.

"Thaas very kind of you 'ole schport," said Theseus, suddenly re-alert.

"Make that three," said Paris.

"No, no, 'sorrite one senuff," said Theseus, as his elbow slipped in his own vomit and he cracked his chin on the bar for the second time in the current session. Following which he belched stopping just short of a repeat follow through and said, "Gotta schtop, 'top drinchin' thaas 'tuff."

Dunck, splush!

Theseus remained bent double, his head ten inches above the bar supported by the rim of his ale beaker, the handle of which - despite his comatose composure - his hand encircled in a grip that would have made a tyre-fitter envious.

They left Theseus to the privacy of his own coma and his own particular aroma and went to sit in the garden, which was now strangely devoid of clientele.

The dog sniggered as it played with, what looked like, the remains of a set of dentures, a blue-rinsed wig and a handbag.

"So, who's the big guy?" ventured Paris in an offhand kind of way.

Hercules looked grim. "That's Prometheus, he was one of the original bunch responsible for initiating this volatile cock-up called life. There were others but one by one they all sold out to the old man, apart from Prom. He believed in the people for some obscure reason and he wouldn't sell his franchise. Well, the old man got in a right pisser over that and nailed Prom to a rock face with chains of adamantine.

All this stuff about Prometheus stealing fire from the gods and giving it to the mortals is bollocks, complete and utter bollocks. Prom was a really cool, laid back guy and one afternoon he was chilling out with some mates and a joint of the finest Thailand could offer and when he was half stoned the joint went out in mid-inhale. So, he struck a match, re-lit it and very coolly flicked the match over his shoulder, end of story - usually. Well - like the Australian bush used to be exquisitely vegetated 'til someone dropped a fag butt - the planet earth used to be a veritable Garden of Eden until Prometheus let the joint go out. Now Adam and the kids were not slow in realising the potential of this throw-away from the gods and, within the first hour the first barby the planet had ever known kicked off.

The gods took second place to the pursuit of pleasure and the old man took it real personal and nailed the stoned titan to the hillside because he wouldn't give up the franchise and let the old man clean up the mess. You see, Prom had the old man by the short and curlies because he knew that one of the old man's kids would turn out to be a real upstart and would eventually give the old git a real good sorting out. So there was the old man frightened to get his leg over and the planet was going to pot."

"Hmmm," said Paris, wiping the froth from his top lip, "so what's that got to do with you?"

"I'm the upstart kid and it's payback time."

"Oh!" spluttered Paris through his ale. "Oh shit! So what are you going to do?"

"I think," replied Hercules speculatively, "that it may be time for a change of hierarchy."

"Oh shit!" repeated Paris, "but then again the old man wasn't too much use to us recently, bloody wooden horse and all that. Count me in, I could do with something to get me out of the pub."

"What do you reckon to local support Par, do you think there would be any?"

"Hard to say, there's plenty around here with good reasons for rebellion, but I mean, we're talking about the big guy here, lightning bolts, roasted where you stand kind of discipline. Most of them are still licking the scorch marks after the Trojans versus Greeks match. They got a right good stomping there, just before the final ram's horn blew and they aren't too keen on the wife since either. Mind you, I can totally understand that, I mean, I know she's a looker but she's very demanding to live with, hell on legs you might say. More of a punishment than a prize. Rumour has it that the big guy's her dad - wow! That would make her your half-sister. We're related Herc, I'm your half-brother in law."

Hercules, who thought he had long ago reached rock bottom, groaned inwardly at the realisation that he was related to Troy's redundant royalty.

"Why," he said, "do I find that out now, after you've squandered everything? Just when I thought it couldn't really get any worse, look what happens. It does. So quit bellyaching about what you have to suffer for the sake of a beautiful woman and get to the point - have we got any remote chance of some back up from the locals?"

"Well," said Paris "not to put too fine a point on it or overestimate the locals and, because I'm good with single syllables, in a word, no! However, if they thought it was their own idea - you see what I'm getting at? I mean, there's a few out of work heroes around about who could do with expressing their anger in a mutually beneficial experience.

Turnus is well pissed off at losing his Missus Lavinia to my cousin Aeneas. Melenaus is about the same over Helen. Ajax is none too happy of late, being demoted to a rag and bone man and there's Odysseus of course and he runs the employment agency too."

"Hmmm," said Hercules pensively, "what we need to do is start a rumour that can't be traced back, get the word out sort of thing."

Inspiration suddenly struck both men simultaneously. "Theseus!" they shouted in unison.

"Yeah," said Hercules, "he's pissed as a fart, he'll remember the basics but not where he heard it from." They stood as one and trooped back into the bar.

Cerberus, again, had the beer garden to himself, where to start? He eyed up the rather over ornate statuary, he sniffed at Mars, who looked imposing, with a big frown and a much bigger weapon.

He took a really savage bite out of a depiction of Prometheus which, if the statue had been the real thing, would have guaranteed the termination of that particular divine genetic line. Honour partially satisfied, he had a quick pee on the leg of Venus and sniggered as the marble foot dissolved and the statue tumbled over breaking the arms off it.

The dog considered this a rather boring garden with a sad lack of smaller furry animals to chase, dissect and digest. Still, make the most of it, he thought, picking up a combination bench and seat and shaking it around acrobatically from one head to another.

Andomache, seeing these canine antics from the back kitchen window was not impressed. "Oy you, hellhound," she yelled hammering the glass. "Put that down or I'll separate you from your heads!"

The dog was startled in at least one head and looked round, completely missing the pass from the offside head, which resulted in the middle head being flattened beneath the table and seat combo.

Cerberus was motionless for a moment then, with a titanic heave he raised his shoulders and shook his heads, the table ascended rapidly and - in keeping with the conservation of angular momentum and parabolic mechanics - descended in a likewise fashion, clipping the five-foot-high wall of the garden and eventually coming to rest with a, *tischinkle*, five feet lower down on the ten-foot-high side of the wall on which Asyanax so loved to play.

Theseus had comatosed his way back to consciousness of a sort. He was awake in at least one nostril, he could hear and most importantly he could co-ordinate his right arm, ale beaker and mouth - not to necessarily operate in the correct sequence but to be in the same spatial reference point at the same time - well, it was a promising start, interspersed with the odd ten-second cat-nappette.

Having moved Theseus to the other end of the bar where the ex-contents of his stomach weren't, Hercules and Paris sat either side of him and chatted amiably over his head. "Couldn't believe it," said Hercules, "this guy in the park says he's going to take on Jupiter."

"You don't say," replied Paris interestedly.

"I do, I just did, said he's going to kick his butt and have a different god."

"What?" said Paris, "all on his own like?"

"Don't think so, apparently some of the local retired heroes've got a hand in it. Eh, three more beers when you've got a mo Andro."

"So who is this guy?" inquired Paris.

"Think he said his name was Prometheus," replied Hercules.

Paris looked over Theseus' head as three fresh ones slid along the bar. "Do you think These can handle another?"

A mop of hair decoratively adorned with diced carrots and assorted sticky bits rose slowly, followed by a nicotine stained index finger. "Corsh I c'handle anovver and I'll tell you schumink elsch too, there's gonna be schum jobs goin' schoon, 'sall husch husch but I'll let you in corsh on account of you bein' matesch an' all vat."

"Here you go," said Hercules depositing a fresh ale flagon before Theseus, "some jobs you say? What sort of jobs?"

Theseus took a furtive look to left and right, then to above. "Right get closcher, gor - schomone whiffsa bit, any 'ow I 'eard thish bloke inna park on about gettin' a crack commando schquad togevver to 'ave a pop at Zeusch or Jupiter or wot eva 'e calls himshelf."

"Naah," said Paris, "you're taking the piss you are, who told you that lot?"

Theseus looked genuinely hurt. "Nah, schtrue, honest, I 'eard it 'sall, I just 'eard it schtop scheret," he said as another cat nap moved in.

"Well, that was easy," said Hercules draining his flagon, "should be all over town by tomorrow morning."

Paris looked at Theseus who was presently occupied with throwing up in mid-nap. "More like afternoon I think, old These won't be conscious for morning let alone recognise it and be capable of spreading rumours across it!"

"Yeah, guess you might have something there," said Hercules, "guess we should get him home eh? It's only round the corner."

They half walked, half carried Theseus to his house as he continued to mumble, to himself mainly, before suddenly erupting into lucidity with a slur.

"D'jew know my granpaw, ole gran daddy Piffeus?"

"Sure," replied Hercules, "I know Pittheus, haven't seen him for a bit though."

"Yeah, well, ya won't be scheeing 'im for a bit longer now on 'count of his bein' dead."

"You don't say?"

"Sho I do, I jusht did. I got no gran pappy now, 's a schame."

"Well it just so happens," said Hercules, "that I just happen to have great granddaddy Perseus on the paternal side, due to a little godly bit on the side episode, so you can have Perseus on permanent loan."

"Aaaw 'sreally consid'rate of ya, 'Erk, fanx man," gurgled Theseus as he misplaced lucidity in its recently discovered form and re-discovered the more comfortable semi-comatose-ness with which he was so familiar.

They left him by the garden wall and continued on their way, Hercules in search of his dog and Paris in search of a feasible excuse.

Hercules was luckier than Paris in their relevant quests. He found Cerberus barking in triplicate at a woman he had penned in halfway up a tree.

"Oy, get here now you miserable hound." The dog reluctantly gave up its harassing of the female citizen and came to heel. "I'm sorry," said Hercules, "he hasn't had enough exercise today what with one thing and another, let me help you down."

The woman was a vision of beauty and Hercules thought to himself that he might well have pulled here, until he caught sight of the telescopic rolling pin with which she deftly pounded the dog's middle head. "You're a bit like my mate Paris, not really a dog lover are you?"

"Paris," she snorted, "you know that good for nothing statuesque idle sack of sodden swan's down then?"

"Yeah, I was just having a beer and a chat with him, went that way," he said, expertly pointing in totally the wrong direction, with a completely convincing attitude, in the way that only a wise and well divorced, but stupid enough to get married again, man can.

"I'll give him bloody beer and a chat, wait 'til I get my hands on him," she fumed stomping off in the direction indicated.

Hercules looked at the dog, whose two outer heads were licking a rising bump on the other one. "I guess that's Helen then, good dog, well done."

Cerberus was now confused but his master was happy and that was all that mattered.

Theseus lurched along with the aid of the wall until he found the dent in it that indicated a gateway. "Ah, aahaa, foundit!" he grunted, pushing, pulling, bumping and kicking at the woodwork which stubbornly refused to move. Realising that he was rapidly getting nowhere, Theseus stopped to catch his breath and reconsider the situation. As he reconsidered, he leant on the other side of the gate which swung inwards very easily and very swiftly, followed by a very surprised Theseus, who stopped only when a crooked skewed nail sticking out of the frame caught in his sleeve and skewered his forearm.

"Ow! Hoo the fook put that there?" he snapped at the gate post. "I know those pissin' hinges were on the ovver side when I wen' out, hoo turned the gate round?" He turned to look at the gate again, "well bugger me!" he exclaimed, "they've moved back again, aah sod it."

Turning towards the garden he beheld, in a pissed up mixture of incredulity and blurred focus, what appeared to be a sacrificial altar. "Well, I know we din't 'ave one of 'em when I wen' out."

Then, paranoia created the, 'I've been here before, déjà-vu, prickly feeling', that it's good at creating, shortly before it strikes. Someone was going to 'chuck the big guy out'. Now, where had he heard that? "A bunsch of commandos or someffing," he mumbled, "can't remember, any'ow, guess they had a bit of a rumble and the altar fell down 'ere, schloppy bastards!"

It was, he noticed as he approached it, a very strange altar; bits of it twinkled. It had a large flat centre and two narrower, higher levels running the length of each side. Along the vertical end axis, a vee-shape protruded spikes into the air at either end. "Schtrange," he slurred, "veaary schtrange."

Kerdunk!

A rather nondescript medium-sized saucepan had suddenly materialised spontaneously and delivered onto him a glancing blow. Hippolyte stepped out of the shadows practising her tennis stroke, with a nondescript medium-sized saucepan racquet, using Theseus' head as the desired object of many a ball boy.

Kerdunk, kadonk, kerdong!

Theseus, much selective amnesia later, awoke, eventually. He looked out of the bedroom window and saw what appeared to be a pub, combination bench and seat upended in what was left of his greenhouse.

VIII

WHAT THE FLOCK

Like so many others of his era, Ajax had a king for a dad. It was commonplace for all the rich kids to play together and develop the deep-seated psychological disorders that would define the enmity of their relationships and frame their future psychotic exploits.

Ajax had been drawn into the Trojan affair on the basis of the 'Helen thing'. It wasn't really his fight seeing as she had buggered off with someone who was not a party to the agreement but, the old boy's network could be very persuasive and if not persuasive then very violent.

There was no doubt that he given a good account of himself on the Trojan gig though. He'd taken on Hector a few times and given him a good hiding. He'd been the one to persuade Achilles to stop being such a baby and get his arse back into the game. He'd pretty much single-handedly fought off the Trojans when they tried to burn the ships. He'd saved the body of Patroclus from the mob of Trojans, which wasn't quite as good as saving his life but, it must be worth a few brownie points. He'd brought Achilles' body back after Paris dispatched him to the underworld or Elysium, again not as good as saving his life but, again pretty good on the brownie point league tables.

Ajax had scored a fair few firsts but they were outnumbered by his second-place scores and, as with every job of work, you're only as good as your last cock-up!

It was the armour that had really pissed him off. He'd won that fair and square. He'd saved Achilles' armour from the enemy but he didn't get to keep it because that slimy toad-spawn Odysseus had stitched him up over the deal with his eloquent rhetoric subterfuge.

That was the final straw, after all his faithful service to a cause that was not his to serve, they had laughed at his strength and martial prowess. They had made him, Ajax, a laughingstock!

He was raving, he was enraged, he was psychopathic and he was well and truly upset! Well he would show them, he would show them all. He would attack them, that night.

He put his plans in motion and set out to claim his revenge, he was going to take out all of their troops. He was halfway to his objective when Athena showed up and poisoned the waters. She drove him insane, which wasn't too difficult a task seeing as he was seven-eighths of the way there and, to his eternal shame, he attacked a flock of sheep.

There was no living this one down, there was no way out, they were already laughing at him and this one didn't even get on the twat league tables and it was the vindictive Gods that had done it!

Ajax had not been treated well by the Gods. Ajax was not at all happy with the sodding Gods!

The Ajax, Achilles & Neoptolemus Bunch

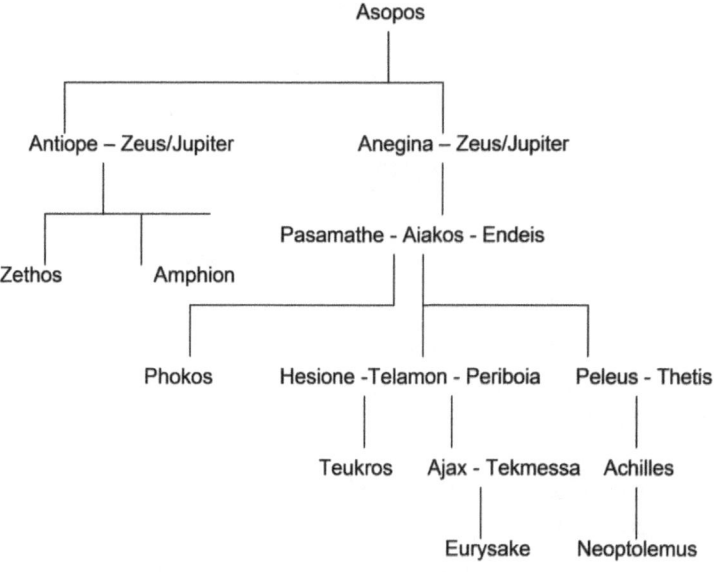

IX

OEDIPUS VEXED

Oedipus had had a hard life. His mum and dad threw him out just after he was born. It was a bit of a tradition at the time really. His old man, King Laius, was a superstitious old git and an oracle had told him that his son would kill him. So when his missus, Jocasta, had a baby boy Laius got all jittery and decided that infanticide was better than murder! It didn't seem to bother Laius too much that there was a touch of murderous intent about his own decision.

Oedipus had his ankles pierced and was thrown out on a Cithaeronian hillside somewhere between sea level and 4,623ft at some point along the road between Athens and Thebes and left to fend for himself. This was not an easy task when you hadn't even learned to crawl and your ankles hurt like hell.

He got lucky though. A shepherd found him and took him home to the wife as a bit of a surprise after her long day on the loom and other duties fitting for a shepherd's wife like, cheese and butter making, sheep shearing and general household stuff like cooking, cleaning and feeding the kids.

She looked at the surprise which, to her way of thinking, was not a pleasant one and said, "We've got enough of our own already, do you think I'm looking for a challenge or something?"

The shepherd said, "I found him on the hillside, I couldn't very well just leave him there. I've been out all day working, tending to the king's sheep while you sit around the house having the easy life."

She tipped her head to one side, as many a sniper would just before a kill shot. "Sitting around the house, sitting around the bloody house? I do everything here, every bloody thing, including all of the childcare, while you are up the hillside importuning sheep. Seeing as you work for the king and you found this kid in pursuit of your un-gainful employment to the crown it's the king's responsibility. So you can bloody well give him the kid!"

Oedipus was duly handed over to the king, let's face it, there were plenty of kings around in those days so finding one was as easy as going to the supermarket.

The king in question was Polybus a Corinthian guy. Polybus did a good job of naming and rearing Oedipus. He let everyone else he employed, including his wife Merpoe, do it!

Young Oedipus was happy in king land and his dad, for he knew no different, wasn't such a bad bloke. Adolescent Oedipus however, was a different matter. Adolescent Oedipus got into hanging with his homies, recreational drugs, listening to drunkards and visiting oracles. After one such drug session, with the hallucinogenic effects still on full throttle, he thought it would be a laugh to go to the oracle for some entertainment.

The oracle had seen all of this shit before and knew exactly how to deal with these kids who thought they'd invented sex and drugs. She frightened them shitless and they left her in peace.

She played well to Oedipus' choice of narcotic. She told him he would kill his father, marry his mother and, have kids with her. That he would destroy the family and ultimately kingdom.

Oedipus had definitely had the shit scared out of him. He packed a bag and left Corinth never to return, well he didn't really want to kill his dad and he really didn't fancy his mum.

As he trudged the lonely road some older arsehole looking for a fight started picking on him. Well, that was it for Oedipus. He'd been on the road for two weeks now and he just didn't need this crap. He took the older guy out like a ninja assassin and left the carcass for the dogs and vultures and headed on, for another two weeks, towards Thebes.

Thebes was an impressive spectacle from the outside. It had the kind of brickwork that only the top brickies could create. The gates, of which there were plenty, had been made by master chippies of timber trades. The joints so tight an engineer would have been astounded and shamefacedly packed up his hundredths and thousandths and left town with his tail between his legs.

However, there was a problem getting in due to a troublesome sphinx in the road pretty much killing anything that dared to come that way if it couldn't answer a simple question.

The sphinx looked Oedipus up and down and thought, it's about lunchtime and you'll do!

"Where do you reckon you're going mate?" asked the sphinx.

"In there," said Oedipus indicating the city of Thebes.

"Fraid not mate." replied the sphinx, "not 'till you get past me and nobody gets past me!"

Here we go again, thought Oedipus, another arsehole on the road. "What do you want?" asked Oedipus.

"An answer to a simple little riddle or you for lunch!" replied the sphinx.

"Ok shoot." said a rather bored Oedipus.

"What's got one voice and becomes four-footed and then two-footed and then three-footed?"

"What a twat question!" exclaimed Oedipus, "every bloke who makes it to old age. One voice, crawls around on all fours, gets up on two legs and needs a stick to walk with when he gets old and after that, it's six feet or four wheels. You need to keep up with the new trends in incapacity aids you do! Now piss off out of the way, before I have lunch!"

"There's no need to get shirty mate, you are free to pass," said the sphinx as she evaporated.

There was a lot of cheering and merriment when he got to what looked like the front gate. Oedipus was lifted off his feet and carried aloft into the city by the citizenry. It was not what he expected but maybe they didn't get many visitors around here!

There was a banquet thrown in his honour and it was explained to him that they had lost a lot of good guys trying to get shot of the sphinx and he was the conquering hero. Then the negotiations started.

Thebes didn't have a king, he was missing presumed dead and the job of kingship was up for grabs to the right calibre of conquering hero. All good so far thought Oedipus and then the sucker punch came. They did, however, have a queen and marrying her was part of the deal.

Oedipus thought for a few moments and asked if he could look her over first. There was some mumbling but no real dissent to the idea. After all, none of them would buy a wife or a chariot without having a viewing and a valid M.o.T. and at least 6 months tax in on the deal.

Mythistrone

The queen had her own reservations when she met Oedipus but, he was young and fit and kind of handsome. He looked like king material and he was the son of a king apparently so there wasn't any training required. She was up for it!

Oedipus thought, she's getting on a bit but still cute for her age and knows her way around Theban bureaucracy. He was up for it!

They were married shortly after and began the job of successfully ruling the kingdom and raising a family.

This all seemed too good to be true to both of them and, indeed it was!

The old crones were gossiping in the town and word got back to Jocasta, Oedipus' wife. She did a bit of digging around and worked out that Oedipus was actually her son, the one Laius had thrown out on the hillside and, that their children were technically his half-siblings. How the hell could they claim state benefit now!

Jocasta fell prey to the old crones gossiping and drove herself up the Theban wall. Eventually, she couldn't handle it anymore and topped herself.

Oedipus thought it was a bit selfish of her leaving him to sort it all out. He became introverted and withdrew from public duties while all semblances of family life and the kingdom fell apart. He was four miles up and, half a mile under, shit creek without a snorkel. He could not bear to look at what he'd created and his boys had taken over and were really cocking things up.

If thine eye offends thee pluck it out, he thought or, alternatively, poke it in!

Oedipus chose the poke it in option. The Gods had exacted a cruel punishment on him and he quit town with his daughter and ended up living with Theseus for a bit.

Oedipus had not been treated well by the Gods. Oedipus was not at all happy with the sodding Gods!

There was this guy called Cadmus – then it got complicated!

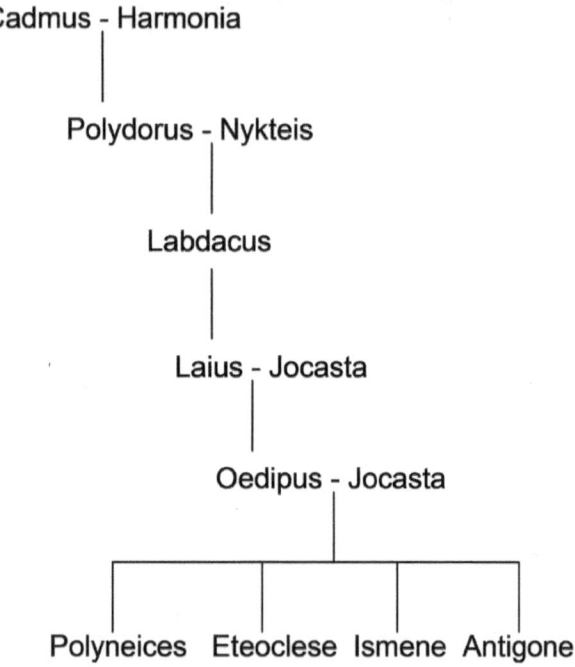

X

IMPOTENT OMNIPOTENCE

The son of Cronus and father of the gods - and a goodly number of mortals too, if half the unfaithful wife stories were to be believed, well, why on earth would they lie? - was not a happy deity. Things were beginning to ever so slightly tick him off. He was sick of life, not its immortal facet, just all the other facets, the day to day boring humdrum stuff.

His kids were a complete pain the arse, whinging and whining at the smallest of hero tasks. For God's sake - or in his case, for his sake - in his day you would think nothing of a skirmish with a raging bull or an altercation with fifty stones of lion and the occasional centaur, followed by the taking out of a hydra or perhaps some Minotaur euthanasia and a bit of Cyclopes extermination, before lunch. Look at them now, he thought, on a par with the mortals, grumbling about inflation, moaning at keeping up mortgage repayments, complaining about the excessive road fund licence and general chariot maintenance, browbeaten by tax collectors and door to door salesmen. The heavens were going to hell.

The planet had gone to pot, in a very literal sense, the mortal stock were a simpering, whimpering bunch of girlies' frilly socks and most of them were on pot or coke or crack or ecstasy. What the fuck, he wanted to know, was up with good old-fashioned booze and fags? They gave you a buzz, they gave you a high and if taken, at times, in moderation, you could follow them up with some exceptionally kinky sex and have a damn good time, no problem. But no, the mortals wanted more and they wanted it bigger, better, faster, longer and more frequently and they wanted it now!

Everything to excess, they were never happy, even at the instant of sublime ecstasy and total brain wipe-out there was something to whinge about. The coke was duff stuff, the condom was too thick, the baby was crying and it ruined the mood, it was too hot, too cold, too bright, too dark, too boring. It wasn't his fault, it was just life, that was how it was, you coped or you didn't and, compared to the slaying of hideous monsters, constant wars, earthquakes and plagues, it was a damn easy ride, all the morons had to do was enjoy it.

Then there were the agnostics, the bloody agnostics who were growing in number by the day and even worse than that, he, the major god of the universe, was noticing their presence in it! The, 'I'm an agnostic but I can't find anything to not believe in,' bunch. Fuck me, every time they refuse to believe in a god there's that many gods around that one is bound to show up and educate them in the error of their ways, along with totally destroying any notion of agnosticism. Even so, even the face of the irrefutable proof of the wrath of God, these twats still reserved the right to not believe in what they can't find to not believe in!

If it had been left to him, there would be no mortal problems, in fact, there would have been no mortals full stop. He'd had the right idea at the time of the first barby - wipe them out, hit them there and then while there were only a few of them to deal with, don't let them proliferate, learn from the rabbit cock-up, so to speak.

And what happened? That twat Prometheus dug his heels in, he wouldn't give up the franchise, he wanted to save them, his creations, his babies. But I showed him, thought Jupiter, that bloody flood shot him a flanker. There he was nailed to a rock and powerless. I, Jupiter, had it all worked out. Deucalion and his Missus would survive, as mortals go they were respectful and just about worth it, let them repopulate the place and we'll get it right this time. The wanker on the rock had to stick his oar in though didn't he, got one of his mates to instruct that bloody zookeeper Noah to build a boat on the sly and stuff it full of animals.

I mean, how can you create utopia with that cesspit for a genetic pool? Some very psychologically disturbed animals came off that boat, cocked the whole thing up altogether.

Even so, they were on opposite sides of the world, a whole fucking planet between them, loads of room, loads of peace and quiet and what happens when they meet? Mutual respect for fellow creatures? Not a bit of it, they have a bloody war that's what, each one wants the other one's half, why? I mean, Judas bloody Priest isn't half a planet enough for anyone? No, not them, they have to wipe out the enemy because his flag's a different colour, his skin's a different colour, his grass is greener, just because he's bloody well there and then they start amongst themselves about how best to knobble the enemy, they split, they fracture, they blame God! Then they make some new gods and give thanks to Prometheus for the gift of life and now he's free, my own son, my own flesh and blood has betrayed me. Well fuck 'em, fuck 'em all, they want Prometheus, they can pissin' well have him. I've had enough, I should just retire and wash my hands of it and let them get on with it without any divine assistance and see how they like it, in fact, not see how they like it. I don't want to know anymore, don't want to see, hear, smell or in any other way sense them, complete waste of a perfectly good planet, bollocks to 'em.

Thus were the thoughts of Jupiter as he thundered along the collonaded corridor. "Juno? Juno you old tart? Pack the celestial suitcases, we're outa here!"

"Oh, that's nice dear, are we having a holiday, I do so love a good, get-away-from-it-all, holiday. Have I got time to get the decorators in before we go and a couple of decent designers? Minerva's good and Arachne and they could do with the work. I thought some new tapestries in the main hall and a few drapes and hangings along the colonnade and the airing cupboard could do with a good dose of woodchip and magnolia, oh yes, and the outside loo needs whitewashing again."

"What?" said Jupiter, in a way that echoed around the hallowed halls and stirred up a few tornadoes in Midwest America. "Decorators? We're leaving, moving on, not coming back, understand?"

"Well that's just typical that is," said Juno exasperatedly, "something's got on your tits hasn't it? So you just expect me to drop everything and follow you. Well, I have an immortal life too you know. You always make all the decisions, you never consult me, I am your wife you know. It's supposed to be a partnership, give and take and all that, you never give a thought to my feelings. You just swan around here all day long, acting like you were God or something!"

"I am bloody God, I made it all, I own it all and it's crap, all of it, crap. Now stop faffing about and get the bags packed!"

"No." said Juno stiffly.

"No!?" bellowed Jupiter. "No!? What do you mean no?" he rumbled as Japan became the beneficiary of a tidal wave.

"It's pretty self-explanatory," asserted Juno, "but if you insist, it means I'm not doing it, I don't want to, I want to stay here, I like it here, after an eternity it grows on you and all my friends are here."

"Friends? bloody hell woman, you are the biggest, most powerful goddess there ever was, you can make new friends!" exclaimed the king of the gods as a hurricane removed most of Northern Russia and deposited it in Alaska. Or at least that's what the papers said.

"Prometheus tried that one once and, if I remember correctly, you were none too pleased at the outcome," said Juno knowing exactly where the deital sphincter was located and how best to apply the business end of a brass-shod winklepicker to it.

Well, that was it, Hawaii had perhaps four minutes to batten down the hatches before it became a constituent of the Atlantean continent.

Juno ducked down with her fingers in her ears. "Yes!" she said to herself, "oh yes, this is going to be a good one, the prat's going to reach critical mass any second now." She gave a mischievous little smirk and waited.

Jupiter quaked, as did much of the Midwest, he fumed, along with Etna and Vesuvius, he raged, and so did every weather front that ever existed and finally, he blew a substantial cortical fuse.

"Prometheus, bloody Prometheus, that bastard is the bane of my immortal life, he's the coffee stain on my cream shag-pile carpet, the woodworm in the grandfather clock, the con-rod that's sticking out of the engine block, the duff wheel that won't swivel on the shopping trolley, he's, he's - words fail me!" he thundered, hefting a large oak dining table and propelling it the full length of the colonnade, the impact of which laid waste to a significant area of Central China. He shook his fists and thunderbolts rocked the universe. Snooker on a planetary scale ensued. Comets and planets interacted in a manner that destroyed orbital paths and totally screwed up any concept of night and day. He bellowed and ranted until the veil of many a temple was rent in twain and a good many other subdivisions. He was in a right pisser.

Juno kept down out of sight, which wasn't difficult considering she was bent double splitting her sides laughing. Eventually, he began to subside and Juno broke surface with tears of mirth rolling down her face. "Temper, temper," she chided in between fits of laughter, "look, you've broken the Ming vases." Her hands were clasped about her midriff the laughter hurt so much. "Try not to fart, you'll blow yourself inside out." At this point she was on her back beating the floor with her hands and feet in an effort to control her hilarity.

Jupiter had a sneaking feeling that his display of ultimate might was falling somewhat short of the mark regarding having the desired effect. This resulted in him becoming very moody, miserable and sulky. He turned and headed towards his private back room bar and its solace producing product, viciously kicking seven bells out of a mop and bucket which had the poor taste to be in the way.

Monsoons mysteriously descended upon a large tract of middle Yorkshire - but no one could tell the difference.

The thing about the Olympus residence was that it existed simultaneously in at least two places at the same time. There was the earthly residence and there was a god's celestial dimension. There was a temporal shift aspect to the place which allowed the gods to move around the universe but it was a highly restricted portal facility and not for the abuse of, such as pulling a hangover sickie in another star system.

However, there was a glitch in the system that allowed rapidly moving small objects at the correct angle to pass through the portal. It generally applied to airborne insects and it was never a problem genetically as all organic matter never survived the transit past the energy exchange stage of its atomic structure into separate atoms.

The bucket was now moving at a hell of a rate, bat out hell with a nitro afterburner rate and, relativistically speaking, it was comparatively small and not really organic in the genetic sense. The bucket would normally have taken, as the laws of physics usually dictate, a parabolic course to the point where it interacted with an obstacle, such as the wall of the house or, in the event of an open door or window, terra firma. In this case, it interacted with a temporal shift portal at precisely the correct angle, just prior to interacting with a low class, devoid of life and atmosphere, large planet. It interacted at incredible velocity, thereby indicating a double unforeseen glitch anomaly with regard to exit acceleration and in doing so, created a wide variety of asteroid belts and comets.

Jupiter stomped on sulking all the way to the bottle of temporary oblivion and completely failed to notice the two-mile-wide chunk of newly-created comet that was charging its way, in a large elliptical orbit, toward the River Styx' locality.

Juno's laughter finally subsided, and she made a cup of tea, lit a fag and 'phoned Minerva and Arachne and dished out a few instructions involving Persian threads and some assorted chintz. She left a message on Michelangelo's answering machine regarding the outside loo and sent a hierofax to Cheops and Rameses detailing structural changes, a wall removed here, break a window out in the main hall, a couple of pillars there and some ornamental arches for the rose garden.

Now to take care of her overburdened husband, after all, it was a tough task running all of creation. What he needed was a break. Get away from it all for a bit.

She called the Druids on the gateway to the stars hotline, which was of course a free 'phone number and arranged a quick vacation on the Alpha-Centauri System with all of the tours, cruises and a few quiet intimate dinners. She wanted the full five-star supernova treatments, sod the expense.

XI

MARRIED BLITZ

Menelaus had it easy. He was the son of a king and then King of Sparta himself. So he could pretty much do what he wanted and generally did!

It was all tripping along quite nicely, some debauchery before breakfast, a bit of warmongering before lunch, a smidgeon of rape and pillage before dinner and then off down the pub to talk shit with the lads and in his own Neanderthal way break a few heads over a few flagons.

He was basically a caveman with a crown and he liked it that way. If he saw a problem he hit it and maimed or killed it. That was fine until the 'Helen thing'.

Menelaus spotted her and instantly fancied a bit of that. The trouble was - so did every other bloke. They came from far and wide to win Helen's hand in marriage. She had suitor kings showing up at all hours and forming a queue at the back door.

Being well balanced in the art of dealing with horny blokes and having the advantage of being the most beautiful woman in the world, Helen had no problems playing them off against each other. It made good evening entertainment watching them knock heads outside the walls, from the safety of her tower bedroom.

Tyndareus, technically Helen's old man because he didn't believe his wife Leda's story about the gods giving her a baby, was getting a bit pissed off with it all.

Tyndareus also watched the nighttime antics outside the wall, mainly from the disgust at lack of revenue, point of view. Every bloody night they were drinking themselves stupid, fighting with each other, pissing and throwing up on the walls, throwing takeaway wrappers all over the place, after they had decorated the windows with the takeaway and general social delinquency. These arse-wipe kings would not be doing this in their own back yard.

It was, in Tyndareus' opinion, ruining tourism. Nobody could get in or out safely, you couldn't get holiday insurance to cross the suitor zone, tour operators had blacklisted it, the press were having a field day with it and the gift shops were going bankrupt. It had to stop and it had to stop now!

Tyndareus summoned his daughter Helen to his presence, a summons she complied with a day and a half later, and laid down the law.

"Stop pissing around and pick one of these twats or leave home." This, to Tyndareus, was a strategy guaranteed to get her out of the family home one way or another. Problem solved either way!

Helen, knowing how to get the old man's back up, said, "Ok pop, I'll have Menelaus."

Tyndareus looked her in her unblinking eyes and said, "You are supposed to be a child of Zeus and the most beautiful woman in the world and you could have anything you want anywhere you want it and you want that ginger headed prick? You want that complete waste of genetic cesspool leftovers, that ignorant pig with the manners of a swamp rat and the intellect of a dried turd on the flagstones?

That's your best shot, the one that everyone else already hates?"

"Yes, daddy." She defiantly replied.

Tyndareus rubbed his chin and thought, call the bluff. "Ok my child, it's your choice. I will make the announcement at first light tomorrow."

"Shit!" Muttered Helen under her breath but she would not lose face and back down now, that would be inappropriate behaviour for a future monarch and she definitely intended to be a monarch.

Helen reckoned that the other guys would take Menelaus out and solve the problem.

The next morning Tyndareus gathered the suitors together and told them that a decision had been reached in the, who gets into his daughter's knickers stakes. There was utter silence as Helen watched the proceedings with impunity flavoured with mild boredom.

"Gentlemen," he announced, using the term loosely. "It has been so nice having all of you kings and future kings around the place but all good things must come to an end.

Now I appreciate that all of you wish to marry my daughter and you have indiscriminately slaughtered members of your own ruling classes in pursuance of that aim. I now propose a treaty to which you must all agree. You will all agree that whoever Helen chooses to marry will be totally and completely supported by all of you in the event that any other should try to steal her from her chosen suitor."

There appeared to be general consent and Tyndareus' clerks were now circulating amongst the suitors getting signatures to that effect.

As soon as he got the thumbs up from the head clerk, Tyndareus announced, "My cherished daughter and the apple of my eye…" for he had no notion of how much trouble apples were going cause in the future, "…Helen has chosen to give her hand to Menelaus of Sparta in marriage, a union to which you are all now duly bound to uphold upon pain of death."

After she had finished spitting out feathers, Helen stood there, with glazed eyes and mouth open. She couldn't believe it. Her dad had stitched her up!

Thus began Menelaus' 'Helen thing'. It was a thing that didn't last too long. Shortly after moving to Sparta, Helen apparently buggered off with the Trojan Paris.

Menelaus threw all of his toys out of the pram and rounded up the other suitors bound by their agreement. He went, as all good kings do, to war. He went to war with the Trojans and got his arse well and truly kicked for a good ten years and won a totally hollow victory.

Menelaus had not been treated well by the Gods. Menelaus was not at all happy with the sodding Gods!

XII

A DAY IN THE GARDEN, A NIGHT AT THE BOOZER

As his hangover dissipated, Theseus decided to put a day in on the garden. It could do with a bit of a tidy up he thought and that was definitely preferable to pursuing the things he should really be doing.

Astyanax was hanging over the garden wall innocently beheading begonias with his catapult when Theseus emerged, looking rough and squinting at the sunlight. "Ay? Ay, mister?" he called, "can we 'ave our bench back please?"

Theseus looked up at the snotty-nosed kid and, considering the request to be reasonable enough, consented. Two minutes later Astyanax was lying face down in the Bar and Bistro's garden wearing a rather splintered, glass impregnated, combination bench seat.

"S'pose you fink that's ferkin' funny?" squealed Astyanax. "Mum, Mum, help, the old git next door's lost it, post-traumatic stress disorder, club shock, 'e's off 'is ferkin' trolley."

Tischwhack!

"Ow ya bitch," said the sandwiched kid.

Tischwhack!

"An' you can stay there 'til you learn some respect, I've told you not to bug Theseus 'aven't I? He struggled for the likes of you…"

"I know, I know, two wars, a Minotaur an' a bloody 'angover," droned the weighed down brat.

Tischwhack!

"Oochyafuc…"

Tischwhack, tischwhack, tischwhack!

"Hiya These," called Andromache, "sorry about 'im, ain't been the same since my 'ector got killed, kid needs a father to impose some discipline, I can't 'andle it all on my own, I ain't 'ard enouff."

"Yer bloody 'ands seem 'ard enouff to me," wailed Astyanax very unwisely.

Tischwhack!

"Any'ow These, fanks for the bench back, you can borrow it anytime you like, must run, got customers." Andromache winked and vanished from Theseus' view and the whimpering of Astyanax gradually diminished.

Theseus got stuck into the greenhouse reconstruction project and five hours later had achieved something that very closely resembled what a train driver - with a degree in sociology, following a fail-safe instruction leaflet in a D.I.Y. kitchen unit pack - would have created in a bank holiday weekend.

Hippolyte, who had been watching in amusement from the comfort and safety of the conservatory, which had been built one weekend by a sociable friend of theirs who drove trains, brought him a cup of tea. Theseus, catching the reflection in what was left of the glass, instinctively ducked and stepped on the garden rake, which in defiance of gravity, rose to the occasion and belted him one behind the left ear.

Hippolyte, who was fighting hard, though rather unsuccessfully, to contain her laughter, handed him the tea, complimented his construction and dashed for the kitchen before doubling up in fits of unshackled hilarity.

Theseus picked up the rake and indiscriminately hurled it, javelin fashion, into the air.

"Ouch!" came the response from beneath a combination bench seat on the opposite side of the wall. Theseus sniggered, drank the tea and decided that it was time for a beer. Well, it was the weekend, not that that really made any difference to his consumption, it just altered his social outlook and he tended to take the wife with him.

At the kitchen door, he was met with, "take your boots off, I've just mopped, get yourself cleaned up, I'll be ready by then."

Theseus took his jumper off, shook it out, sniffed at it, turned it inside out and put in back on again, he was ready to go.

Two hours, three changes of skirt, four pairs of shoes and an extensive makeup job later, Hippolyte re-appeared looking like she'd made an attempt and announced, "Ready! Where shall we go then?"

"Well," replied Theseus, "I thought we'd have one at Andro's, just to get in the mood and take it from there."

"Oh, so we're going to spend the night in Andro's? What a pleasant change."

"Look, don't start, you don't have to come, you do have a choice you know," grunted Theseus, wondering if now would be a good time to duck. No, it was safe, she never touched a saucepan with new nail varnish on. "They've got a singer-musician-comedian-poet act on tonight and happy hour's been extended, it'll be a good night."

"Ooower, alright but he better be an improvement on last week's offering. I mean, a bunch of wandering minstrels who'd wandered a million miles looking for a smile from their mother, who probably wouldn't recognise them anyway, what with all that black and white paint on their faces, well it's hardly a gripping story, not what I'd call entertainment any road," she said with a flourish of neck scarf.

"They weren't all that bad," pleaded Theseus.

"No, no not all that bad, I suppose that's why you and Paris wedged two of them headfirst down the best pan in the ladies is it?"

"Yeah, well," said Theseus, matter of factly. "That's 'cos men drink more."

"Oh, I see, that excuses you taking a duff act or two and upending it in the ladies loo, does it?" glared Hippolyte.

"No, what I meant was, men drink more so they need to pee more often and we didn't want the men's loo blocked with bloody wandering minstrels, did we? It takes too much time and energy trying to pee 'round them when there's ale to be drunk. Stands to reason, girlies don't drink seriously, ergo they don't need to pee so often, so they can take longer about it and generally do!"

Hippolyte now broke the habit of a lifetime, as was attested to by the resonant echoing, *Kerdong!* that suddenly resonated and echoed around the kitchen. She bent her fingers on to her palm, looked at them, blew on the tips and smiled sweetly. It's good for him to get taken by surprise every now and then, she thought, it prevents complacency, keeps him on his toes. "Let's go then!" she smirked.

Andromache's Bar and Bistro was, as usual, being patronised by a selection of local roughnecks and minor criminals with the odd smattering of out of town roughnecks and minor criminals. One face stood out from the crowd of associated criminalia, that of Odysseus. Not because he was in any way lacking in the criminal offences qualifications department, more because he never came here unless he was looking for something.

Theseus went to the bar and ordered a beaker of ale for himself and a half with a lemonade top for Hippolyte.

"'Ere ya are These," said Andromache, "Oddy's payin', sez 'e aint seen yer for a bit, reckon 'e must be lonely 'cos 'e wants to 'ave a chat wiv yer."

"That's a shame," said Theseus, "and it had been more or less a good day so far. Strange what you see when you haven't got your bow and arrows with you! Still, if Oddy's buying, that's his first round in a lifetime, might have some curiosity value."

"Nah!" replied Andromache, "'e ain't payin' 'imself, 'e just ripped some outa towner off over there wiv the three mugs and disappearin' conker trick."

"Typical," snorted Theseus, "parasite."

Hippolyte was already loading coins into the one arm bandit in the corner when Theseus showed up with her lemonade top.

"Thanks luv, get a couple of bingo cards, will you? I'm on a winner here, I just need a battle-axe, an invincible aegis or a severed head for a tenner."

"Bloody addictive them machines are, cost a fortune to run and when you do win you pump it all back in again."

"Theseus," she replied quite firmly, without removing her gaze from the machinery. "Bugger off and get the bingo cards!"

"Yes dear, of course dear, anything you say dear, never met anyone who cost me so dear, dear," he muttered as he walked away.

Kerchink! went a nearby bottle now drained of beer, which was standing in in lieu of a saucepan, as Hippolyte sniffed haughtily and said, "I heard that!"

As Theseus pushed through the socialising felons, he met Paris, who bought him another beer. Not wanting to appear ungracious Theseus drank it and returned the favour while conversing at great length about sod all. "Anyway," asserted Theseus, "I've just got to go and get some bingo cards, back in a mo…"

"Evening boys," said Hercules, walking up with another beer each, which, not wanting to appear ungracious they drank and returned the gesture.

Six beers later the issue of bingo cards surfaced in Theseus' memory and he stumbled towards the ticket seller and purchased a handful of cards, stumbled to the bar and purchased another one for himself and a half for Hippolyte and went in search of her.

There she was the other side of the room yapping to Celaneo and a bunch of old harpies. As he lurched in her direction Odysseus stood up out of nowhere. "Theseus my old mate," he cried, taking the beer from his hand. "Thanks, should have got yourself one as well, oh you have, very wise drinking halves, keep a clear head, good idea. Take a load off, have a seat."

Theseus sat down, "less of the old," he said, "in fact less of the mate too, now that I come think of it." he added, realising as he spoke that the worst thing he could have done after six beers was to sit down.

"So, how's retirement treating you?" inquired Odysseus.

"What's it to you?" replied Theseus remembering the duplicitous nature for which Odysseus was renowned. "What're you back in town for?"

"And it's nice to see you too," said Odysseus. "I was just remembering the old days when we helped each other out on the odd heroic expedition and I thought, it's time I called in on some old friends again, you know how you do?"

Theseus, whose right eye was beginning the short trek towards his other one, looked at him in quizzical inebriation, "so let me know if you find any 'cos I seem to remember that you spent most heroic expeditions hiding behind anyone who was bigger or winning."

"Tactical, that was all tactical, to gain the advantage by subterfuge."

"Yeah," said Theseus, "trouble was none of us could ever work out what the advantage was or who it was for. Apart from your own, it was very difficult to decide whose side you were on."

"I was always on our side," said Odysseus.

"'S'that so?" said Theseus, having trouble keeping track of exactly where the conversation was going. "Often wondered, guess that's alright then, s'long as you were on our side."

"In fact," proceeded Odysseus, "I heard a rumour the other day that something might be about to kick off round here and thinking of my old friends, possibly in need, brought me straight back."

"Awww," said Theseus who, having just approached the line where six beers meant good fun and total coherence as long as you kept going, had rapidly stepped over it by sitting down. "'Ats really nice 'at you care, so where's the match?"

"What match?"

"The one you just shaid about."

"I didn't say anything about a match."

"Shor you did, you shaid there was going t'be a kickoff around - er – shomtime," slurred Theseus, thinking that he had been alright until he'd had to drink Hippolyte's half. "Shorry 'sa bit - um - constipated, 'fad a few."

"You're constipated?" inquired Odysseus.

"Chertainly not, whash it got to do wi' you any'ow? 'S complicated, 'sa lemonade, shee? I was fine 'til I had the lemonade, 'sbloody dangerous shtuff. Whaas yer name 'gain, oh yeah, Odysseus. Well y'know what Ossydeus? You'll never believe what I heard in here t'ovver night. Scheems as 'ow vares gonna be schum kind of hush, husch commando manovr - manouve - manvour - operashion round here."

Odysseus couldn't believe it, this was exactly what he wanted, sometimes things just came to him free of charge and if it wasn't free, it soon would be because Odysseus never paid for anything that didn't double its profit in the first two seconds of ownership.

"Shee," continued Theseus, "'sa guy inna park shee, an' 'es avvin a bit of a tiff wi' Jupiter over frankincense or sommat. Jupe wantsh it but 'e ain't sellin' sho Jupiter put 'im in nick and 'es 'scaped and out for revenge. 'Slookin for commandos I fink wantsh to give Jupiter a kickin'!"

"Very interesting," said Odysseus, calmly considering the commission involved in the recruitment and supply of bonafide, out of work, hero/commandos, "so who's the guy in the park?"

"Schecret!" said Theseus, "'sall very husch husch an' Promeffus' is playing a low-key role fer now - oopsch!"

"It's okay Theseus, the secret is safe with me, I only want to help, don't you worry about it, here let me get you another beer."

Tischwhack! The right hand of Hippolyte made full contact with the right ear of Theseus from behind, as he snoozed on the table. "Where're my bingo cards you pissed up fart?"

"Right 'ear dear," he spluttered, pulling out some crumpled beer-stained documents and poking them in a roughly rearward direction and returning to semi-consciousness.

Odysseus did not return with the offered other beer, which was totally unsurprising, totally predictable and totally unnoticed.

Homers act went down quite well, she had a new brand of musical poetical humour never before experienced in the Bar and Bistro and Theseus featured highly in many of the jokes, generally in the honoured position of comatose butt of.

Paris was still sniggering over the Trojan story - the bit about Achilles being a hero had him bent double with mirth and Priam as a fair and honest king was beyond credibility and, that brave bit where the Trojans set the Greek ships on fire, everyone knew that was Achilles in a right pisser, trying to cook chips after a few skinsful when the oil went up and the prat threw a bucket of water at it and nearly torched the fleet - when he went to wake Theseus from his coma.

Theseus was obviously having a good dream if his reaction to Paris' interruption was anything to go by. He jumped bolt upright in full combat mode saying, "Sorry, sorry, I fell asleep, I thought this was my room, where's my trousers, I never touched her… honest, I thought she was the wife," which, luckily enough, was said out of earshot of the said wife's ears.

"Take it easy," said Paris "I've been there too you know, time to go home, the bar's shut."

"What already," said Theseus, "what about the comic poet, been cancelled has it?"

"You slept through it, but you enjoyed it, well we enjoyed it, largely at your expense."

"Oh," replied Theseus, "well I've got a few flagons in the greenhouse, want to come back for a bit?"

"Yeah, splendid idea, I'll just go and get Hercules, hang on a mo."

"Theseus dear," came the ringing tones of Hippolyte.

"Oh shit!" he uttered as the paranoid silent fear surfaced in his newly conscious state, "er, I can explain," he began but was cut short by the sensual tones of his wife saying, "honey, do you mind if I stay here with the girls for a bit? Andro's having a girlie stay back."

Theseus, ever rapid on the uptake, replied very rapidly, "yeah sure love, no problem, I think I'll go and turn in for the night, you have a good time and don't rush back, see you later."

Theseus wandered off outside and waited for Paris and Hercules. "What a stroke of luck," he announced as the other two joined him. "Andro's having a sexist stay back, just when we needed it."

"How else is she going to make the bingo cash prize back for next week?" said Hercules.

"The stroke of luck," declared Paris "was that Hippolyte won it this week."

"The cocky, devious witch," said Theseus, "always an ulterior motive up her sleeve, I buy the cards, she spends the winnings and it's always a woman that wins in there too, it's all highly discriminatory if you ask me!"

"We didn't," responded his two associates in harmonic stereo, "where's the beer?"

Arriving in the greenhouse, Theseus moved what there was of a prize tomato, singular, out of the way and withdrew from a hole in the ground beneath it, a sack full of flip-top flagons, each of which was full of beer. Thus, re-began the dedicated craft of serious drinking with feeling, the loss of which was the general aim.

Some flagons and a copious amount of verbal diarrhoea later, Paris announced. "The trouble with women is 'at they don't think right, they don't think like men do."

"Yeah!" Theseus cut in, "they don't think logically, well no, they do think logically, but it's not logical logic, not like what blokes think. I mean, when you fix your chariot, you know that the axle goes into the axle pinion clamps and the wheel fits on to the splined end secured by a washer and a split pin or left-hand thread nuts. Now your woman thinks, vile machines, squash the flowers, rut the roads, squeak and break down. So when they come to fixing one, you get something like, this pole goes in them holes, I think, and then hammer it in and then put the round things on the end with them curly hairpin bits or some backwards nuts. Then they find the splined ends are in the middle and they get all upset and run off crying and such like about it being a useless contraption and having a mind of its own."

Paris, who had been listening attentively, said, "'sright, there isn't a machine that breaks down that you can't repair, you can always fix it - but women, when they break down you're shagged, well no, you probably aren't, that's the first thing to go during a breakdown but try as you might you can't fix them, which brings us full circle. Why can't you fix them? Because they aren't logical that's why."

Theseus sat staring and misty-eyed, having a little coma-ette in preparation for the major after flagon comatose. Hercules snapped his fingers in front of Theseus who jumped and said, "yeah, schtrange creatures women, I mean, you fhink you 'ave trouble, look at Odysseus. Ten bloody years bein' schipwrecked an' generally pissed about by gods an' stuff an' when he comes home to Penelope, who should be dyin' for it after that long, what's 'e find her doing? Interviewin' suitors an' weavin' bloody tapestries. Got no time for him has she, says she developed a life of 'er own while he was gone an' she ain't prepared to give it all up now, so Oddy's put all his efforts into the agency and travels a lot to keep out of 'er way."

Paris and Hercules swapped furtive glances and Paris inquired casually. "So what's Oddy up to lately?"

"Oddy?" said Theseus, after a full pint from his flagon was transferred to his digestive tract in one gulp, "'sgot shum bee in 'is bonnet about 'avin' a match roun' 'ear schomware an' 'slookin' for a hero team to play for Promeffus 'gainst a gods eleven or somfink like that. Schounds like a twat idea to me, don't know where 'e dreams 'em up from!"

Paris and Hercules smiled in a conspiratorial kind of way. All they had to do now was sit back and watch for a while.

"Well," said Hercules, "I'll have to make a move, I promised to take the kids out tonight!"

"Going anywhere good?" inquired Paris.

"Clubbing probably," replied Hercules.

XIII

TURNUS NIL - AENEAS WON

Turnus was different to so many others. For starters, he was not the son of a king or a god for that matter. He was a warrior, a legend in his own back garden but not in his local pub. He had been the driving force behind many a failed onslaught against the Trojans. He had a right bee in his bonnet about those guys. The main reason was that his testosterone was leading him into poverty.

Lavinia was the woman in question. He wanted her but the dumb cow didn't appear to reciprocate she seemed to want a fluffy Trojan git by the name of Aeneas. It made his blood boil, that bunch of jumped up royalty got anything they wanted. Paris got Helen because he fancied her and didn't give a toss about her husband, Hector was doing well in the conquering and questing arena. Priam had the biggest bestest fortress the world had ever seen and loads of treasure. Aeneas had already had Dido the queen of Carthage and now he was having the woman that was meant for him and, just to rub salt in the wound, she liked it!

This was just not fair. Aeneas wasn't even real royalty, he was the son of a prince so he was just a bit related, a cousin at best to Priam's kids and yet he got the full might of Trojan protection. That bloke must have had pictures of the sheep or the donkeys or something!

Whatever, that whole family pretty fairly pissed him off, lording it around like they owned the country, which incidentally, just to turn the screws a little more, they did. To Turnus, they were the most dysfunctional family imaginable. Look at the mother Hecuba, she had fifty kids. Fifty kids! She'd spent her life shagging. They were all apparently fathered by Priam, a likely story indeed, mind it would explain why the bloke always looked a bit washed out on his rare public engagements. They were rare because he was too busy shagging no doubt. He was too knackered to even go out and defend the kingdom. He left all that war and butchery stuff to the lad Hector.

Turnus had to admit that Hector was a force to be reckoned with, he was a proper warrior, the one redeeming factor in that twisted family. He can't be one of them thought Turnus, probably adopted or stolen! Paris was a pretty boy of questionable sexuality, just a shag bandit that one. Helenus was another pretty shagger boy. There were some girls as well. Cassandra, total retard, what was her problem? No sex and confused to hell and back, a right mixed bag of neurosis, psychosis and witchcraft. She heard voices in her head and spoke to them and understood them but couldn't make anyone else understand. A definite case of multiple personality disorder with a side serving of pure bat-shit. That was just four of them, there were another forty-six of the misfits out there in varying stages and degrees of lunacy.

It didn't matter, Aeneas was the one, the Nemesis. He'd taken the bleeder on far too many times and he always lost because the Gods were never on his side and now the sneaky shit bag had married his girlfriend and it was his own fault. He'd started all the rumours about Aeneas and Lavinia so that he could have a couple of wars and be a hero, be a king, it wasn't fair everyone else got to be a king or the son of a king or the son of a god.

What did he get? He got his arse kicked sideways and handed to him on a broken toilet seat because the sodding Gods - and even worse, the Goddesses, yeah even the women Gods were in on his total disgrace - favoured the royal arse wipes.

Turnus had come from nothing, had no heritage to speak of, had nothing left and nothing to lose, Turnus was not happy with the sodding Gods - or the interfering sodding Goddesses!

XIV

PATRICIDE LOST

Neoptolemus had been a bad lad from a very early age. His parents could do little to keep him under control and, consequently, they didn't.

He had grown up considering his father to be a cross-dressing transvestite and had some sort of axe to grind with that. This view was a bit rich coming, as he did, from a society that considered most sexual persuasions to be normality. However, in his head, that was the reason for his own brutality.

His dad was Achilles, the biggest badass in history and there was no way he was going to screw with him. As a consequence, he took it out on just about everyone else.

He had done things that were just not polite in royal or any other society. He was half responsible for dragging Philocetes into the whole Troy thing just to get some arrows on the scene. He had convinced Odysseus that he should be in on the wooden horse incursion and got his own way on that one.

It was when he got out of the horse that he really got into some excessive revenge on people who just weren't guilty of what he was killing them for. He took out Priam and sacrificed Polyxena after generally creating carnage around the city first.

Then there were the women he'd womanised, whether they'd wanted or not and those he had gained by lies and deceit.

It was entirely his dad's fault for not being there, he blamed the parents because that was a societal and socially acceptable normal default position. The old man had got himself killed being a hero and poor Neoptolemus never got a chance to stand up to him. Never got the chance to punch his dad out and show him that he could give as good as he got. Apollo had made sure his dad died and he was left being a first-class arsehole and he knew it. He didn't want to spend the rest of his life being an arsehole. Apollo deserved a right good kicking too!

In Neoptolemus' misguided, sociopathic, psychopathic, twisted mind he had not been treated well by the Gods.

Neoptolemus was not at all happy with especially one of the sodding Gods!

XV

DE-STRESSING DEITY

Jupiter found the atmosphere and environment around Alpha-Centauri very relaxing. Alpha Centauri B was the place to go. It was only 90.7% of the terra suns mass so not quite so hot in high season and only 44.5% of the luminosity so no need to pack UV sunshades and all that tanning lotion. If you wanted it really hot, you could take a short stay cruise to Alpha Centauri A.

The real benefits, however, had nothing to do with the location. No getting up in the morning and chasing gods around to get the sun out and the tides turned. No presiding over minor gods bickering with each other over which cloud to send to which Bank Holiday and most definitely no D.I.Y. or terraforming.

Juno smiled as she watched him unwind with celestial bowls, followed by a quick frame of galactic pool and a dip in Alpha's own Milky Way before coming to lie beside her on a spiral nebula sun lounger to bathe in the cosmic rays.

There were so many things to do here if you really wanted to. Spiral arm surfing, black hole rim free boarding, solar wind parascending, galactic tide jet skiing and comet skeet shooting. The last one though was considered by many a celestial busy-body-job's-worth as a galactic pollutant and NIMBY wimps were trying to secure a universal ban on all ballistic pastime occupations. Most responsible participants cleaned up after themselves, it wasn't too taxing to have to pull a wormhole over and vac the place up when you'd finished. Checking that it was a black hole transit connection wormhole before use was always a good idea, otherwise you just ended up indiscriminately showering a NIMBY in its own back yard and strengthening their 'ban it' cause. It didn't do any harm, no planets were destroyed or damaged by the sport. In fact, there was a reasonably logic opposition sector that considered the removal of comets to be a good thing. They were unpredictable, they had varying velocity and erratic course deviation influences. They were a menace to celestial public health and spread diseases. Extermination was the most effective way of controlling these potentially planetary destroyers and it could be done for free if it was considered to be a past-time, participants would finance it for themselves!

The other option in this resort was slob out, do nothing and watch the universe go by with the occasional dip in the Milky Way and a star cluster cocktail beside the spiral nebula sun lounger.

"We should do this more often dear, it's lovely here. Completely unspoilt, no indiscriminate microwaves, no inappropriately loud music, no carbon dioxide excess, no dioxin poisoning, no extortionate radiation levels, no PCBs, no epoxy resins, no smog, no dog crap on the street, no nitrogen run off, no algal blooms, no genetic mutations. In fact, there's no genetics at all, which, now that I think about it, probably explains the lack of all the rest."

"Indeed," responded her husband as a large star quaked ominously and he turned over to get an even tan. "They've got to go!"

"Who's that dear?"

"All that carbon, DNA genetic concoction of Prometheus', they're a liability to everything, including themselves."

"Now, now dear, we're on holiday, no talking shop, but I do wonder what the children are up to while we're away."

"Inefficiency probably," said Jupiter absent-mindedly, "they'll have forgotten to take the sun in or left the moon out over day or have forgotten to turn the stars off. You know what they're like left alone, pathetic, next to useless, they miss every opportunity going for godly retribution and acts of gods. They're a disgrace to the godhead profession, absolutely totally fucking useless, I don't know what I keep them for!"

Nearby, the large star went Nova. "But you're right dear, enough shop talk, it only annoys me." He stretched out and snoozed. The star settled into an unsteady binary union with an older black hole.

Juno lay back thinking about the alterations at home on Olympus, the window in the big hall gable end would make such a difference to the ambience of the room, airier, brighter, it would create new light play in the dull, dank, corners up that end. Perhaps she'd get Michel to knock up a couple of busts, when he'd finished the loo of course. Yes, the loo definitely needed painting out, the mildew in there had become quite embarrassing of late. She anticipated having some high-class alterations to return to, which was nice because it steered the mind away from the inevitable depression one suffered on returning from holiday to the same old stuff. If you weren't careful, things could get awfully boring and stuffy in a short eternity!

She mused over the wonders that Arachne and Minerva would have produced between them. They were such gifted girls when it came to tapestries. What they couldn't do with a loom and a flying shuttle just couldn't be done and positively creative with a few yards of satin and filigree and a bucket of dye. Yes, it would be good to get back after this holiday!

XVI

IT'S ALL GORGON TOO FAR

Being the son of a king was easy. Being the son of a God was a little more complicated. There was a lot of expectation to live up to on the one hand and on the other hand, there were the detractors, the ones who hinted about his mother's morals. They never hinted to his face, the hypocrites with illegitimacy for a family tree, they just made sure their scandal-mongering gossip got back to him. Perseus would hear things like, 'pregnant by Zeus eh?' That's the excuse they all use for an unexpected up the spout-ness. Yeah right, maybe it was child abuse when she was locked up in the bronze room by her father - we always knew there was something not quite right about that guy. She's daddy's girl that one and no mistake.

It was never quite clear where the rumours started but it was always the same old fish wives and bar room tramps sharing their sagacity with all and sundry. Most of it was water off a duck's back to Perseus but he didn't like his mother getting all the hard press. He often considered that if the Zeus story was true, then Zeus would have to face some reckoning one day!

When he thought about it, which wasn't too often because he was basically having a pretty happy life, the story had questionable ingredients. His granddad, Acrisius, was a bit of a worrywart, as well as being the king of Argos. I mean, he visited oracles for guidance, what kind of way was that to run a kingdom? Surely if you were the king you were doing the running of the kingdom, not the soothsayers! Whatever, Acrisius had taken it upon himself, in a moment of indecision, to consult Apollo's oracle. The oracle had told him that one of his daughter's sons would one day kill him and he believed it. In order to circumvent the oracle's prediction Acrisius had locked his beautiful daughter, Danae, in a bronze room, for an awful lot of her productive years.

Being a dutiful dad all the same, he used to visit his daughter in her freedom-deprived-imprisoned-but-with-all-mod-cons status. On one of his visits he found Danae holding a boy child that, according to her, she had conceived by Zeus who descended upon her in a golden shower through a crack in the ceiling.

Perseus had two problems with this. First, Acrisius was a king, money was not an issue, skilled tradesmen were not in short supply and any who worked for a king knew full well the price of failure. Why, in that case, did a palatial residence have a crack in the ceiling? Second, what the hell was Danae's old man doing for the nine months previous that he didn't notice his daughter was up the duff?

Anyway to cut a long story short, far too long after that was a possibility, Acrisius lost the plot a bit. He put his daughter and her son in a large chest and had it thrown into the raging sea. His thinking presumably being that he didn't kill them, he gave them a chance and the rest was up to the Gods.

The chest washed up around the island of Seriphos and a bloke called Dyctis, a fisherman, who was incidentally the brother of king Polydectes, hauled it to safety and freed mother and child and offered them a place to live.

Dyctis managed to keep the existence of Danae and Perseus pretty well under wraps for a number of years. The problems started when his kingship of a brother set eyes upon Danae and decided that she was going to be his port of entry.

Polydectes did all the usual stuff, sent flowers, chocolates and asked for a date. Danae always respectfully declined. This kind of rebuttal did not go down well with a king who had street credibility and a reputation to uphold and Polydectes decided that, by fair means or foul, he was going to have that woman. The major problem was the not-so-much-a-kid-these-days son, Perseus. Perseus had grown up big and strong and devoted to his mum. He didn't much like Polydectes and he didn't hide the fact. That really bothered Polydectes. This little shit was not afraid, so he was a danger!

Polydectes hatched a half-arsed plan. He told folks that he was going to marry Hippodamia and that every citizen must donate a horse in honour of his bride to be because her name meant horse tamer. This said a lot, from Perseus's point of view, about how Polydectes viewed himself. However a royal decree was a royal decree and Perseus did not even have a horse, let alone have one to contribute. Perseus was no slouch though, he saw what was going on and he went to Polydectes and explained the situation to him in terms of, I haven't got a horse what else would satisfy you?

Polydectes metaphorically rubbed his hands together in glee and thought, 'got you, you little shit!' He looked Perseus in the eye and said, "The head of the gorgon Medusa would do." He considered that one to be a suicide mission which would clear the way for him to have his evil way with the boy's mother. What he hadn't allowed for was Perseus having a bit of clout in the God echelons. Perseus said, "Yeah ok mate, anything you say."

After a couple of day's trek, Athena and Hermes showed up with directions to where the goods Perseus needed could be found. That was another black mark for the Gods as far as Perseus was concerned, they were Gods, they could have just given him the goodies instead of pissing about with a trail for him to follow.

This was not cutting the long story short, he realised. Right, cut to the chase, he thought. He'd gone on the trail, got the magic bag, got the invisibility hat, got the adamantine sickle sword, got the polished bronze shield and got the flying shoes. He'd got lucky with the gorgon trio, they were asleep when he rocked up. He slashed the head off the mortal one, Medusa, stuffed it in the magic bag and headed off home.

On the way home, he saw Atlas struggling with the weight of the world on his shoulders. So he showed him the contents of the magic bag and watched him turn into a mountain. He'd done the guy a favour and hit step one on the Godly retribution stakes.

Further along the way home he took out the sea monster Cetus, as it was about to devour a good-looking woman called Andromeda and, got himself a wife in the process. Not a bad day's work that one!

He returned to Seriphos and introduced that mother bothering king, Polydectes, to the contents of his magic bag and then decided he deserved a beer or two.

Some celebratory games ensued with all and sundry displaying their martial prowess and Perseus, being a bit the worse for beer, decided to leave the sharp stuff alone and opted for a discus. As he expected, he cocked it up. Halfway through his third spin he slipped a bit and so did the discus, right out of his grasp. It flew towards the crowd, most of whom flew in sideways directions to get out of its way. Unfortunately for Acrisius, who was making a side bet at the time and didn't see it coming, the discus gave him a right vicious belt on the foot and the ensuing tumble down the rubbish-strewn temporary seating deprived him of his life.

Perseus smirked, the oracle didn't see that one coming, he thought. Serves him right, fancy throwing your daughter and grandson into the sea and hoping to get away with it!

Business was more or less sorted in Seriphos and Perseus went to see his mate Megapenthes and did some dealing and set up his own little city called Mycenae. There in his own city, he and Andromeda had one daughter and six sons.

The sodding Gods had made him work hard for it. Perseus was not happy with the sodding Gods!

XVII

DIPLOMATIC DUPLICITY

Odysseus, being a mean, calculating, double-dealing, underhanded, two-faced tosser, decided to go for a walk in the park on the calculated likelihood that he would probably run into Prometheus. He reckoned that if there were some God bothering going on, he had a right to a high ranking position in the proceedings, where he could lead from behind and get his own back for all that shipwrecking, Siren temptation, Cyclopes encountering and general monster-bashing he'd had to endure at the hands of certain gods. The best position for reprisals of this nature, as far as he could see, would be from a well-guarded rear administration type of set up and where better to hide behind and administer from than a pissed off semi-God giant with a chip on its shoulder?

He wandered around the park until he spotted a likely looking ravine with a cave at the end of it. The cave was all the more likely looking for having a rather large, hungry-looking vulture, perched over its entrance. Odysseus, who had met with many a strange creature in his day, was not the type to be deterred by something as irrelevant as an overgrown crow and he brazenly approached the cave.

"What do you want?" rasped the vulture, eyeing up what appeared to be a possible apéritif on legs. It wasn't dead yet but that was a small insignificant detail which could be easily remedied.

"I seek Prometheus," replied Odysseus, wondering if he could still take the eye out of a vulture with a longbow at a hundred yards.

"Yeah, I used to but I'm really sick of eating liver, he's in there," croaked the vulture, Nodding its beak backwards under its left wing. "Don't tell him I told you!"

"Would I? I'm nobody. I was never here okay?"

"Suits me," said the vulture.

Odysseus could see little in the darkness and rapidly stubbed his toes on a large boulder which, judging by the accompaniment of vulture sniggers, had been strategically placed to achieve just such an effect. Being incredibly crafty himself, Odysseus immediately ducked, just before a sizeable portion of tree trunk moved pendulum fashion over the spot he had just been stubbed on, at very high velocity. As the timber thudded against the opposite wall, the sound of unrestrained vulture laughter came to Odysseus who, still being crafty, rolled sideways at the double and avoided a large array of double-pronged spikes on a rack that descended at supersonic speed in an arc from aloft. The apparent intentions being that the spikes would impale anything left standing, scoop it towards the entrance and eject it in a general Styx-ward direction.

The vulture by now was helpless with lunatic fits of laughter and fell from its perch in uncontrollable mirth, hitting the floor of the ravine with a whump and flutter. Beating its wings and kicking its talons, along with spasms of hilarity, the bird managed to right itself, still convulsing with laughter. It turned, fully expecting to see prepared apéritif, freshly diced and skewered and said, "Aawukk?"

"That wasn't very fucking friendly," said Odysseus, "you could have warned me."

"I could have," replied the now miserable vulture, "but where's the fun in that? Oh well, win some lose some I guess!"

"Is there," said Odysseus, firmly imprinting the vulture's image on his memory cells for possible future revenge, "anything else I might possibly like to know about?"

"I suppose so," cawed the vulture. "Otherwise you nearly died for nothing, be really stupid to risk all that if you didn't want to know about something."

Odysseus found himself wishing that somebody would hurry up and invent hand grenades. The vulture did a little Saint Vitus waltz and ascended from view in a flurry of feathers and scrawny fluffy bits.

Now more accustomed to the interior gloom, Odysseus continued on into the cave. Ten cautious steps further on a very big voice asked, "Who are you?"

"Oh, nobody really," replied Odysseus.

"So what do you want nobody?"

"I want to have a chat with Prometheus. I think we could do each other some mutual good."

"Is that so?" echoed the voice, "and do you intend to carry on with this nobody crap? I mean, it's not very inventive really is it? It's not like you haven't tried this approach before is it?"

"Aaah, you heard about that one then, did you?" said Odysseus.

"Heard about it? The whole bloody world's heard about it! You wound that poor guy Polyphemus up to breaking point, which granted doesn't take too much when you're dealing with a Cyclops, and told him nobody was there and then when he'd had a few joints you poked his eye out with a stick you nasty little shit."

"Yeah, well," said Odysseus, "he had it coming, I mean, he was eating the crew, you want to try rowing a triple-decker with no oarsmen for one, gods throwing sodding lightning bolts around for another and that race of bloody moronic one-eyed prats slinging rocks around for a third. With that sort of pressure, he's lucky I only poked his eye out I can tell you!"

"Touched a raw nerve there, did I?" said the big voice. "I knew Polyphemus, he was a good mate of mine, we often got stoned together, it increased my workload no end when you poked his eye out, he couldn't skin up any more, had to roll all the joints myself after that. How would you like to join your ex-crew?"

Odysseus thought frantically for a moment. "Would that be the ex ex-crew, or the still living ex-crew?"

"Don't get cocky with me," said the big voice, as twenty feet of early vintage giant materialised out of the gloom holding an equally giant rock in one hand. "I am Prometheus and like I said in my second question but with more adjective emphasis, what the fuck do you want?"

"Point taken," began Odysseus. "I have a reputation for being somewhat of an enabler and organiser."

"You have a reputation for being a devious, double-crossing, two-faced little git," said Prometheus, "now get to the point."

"You don't mince words do you?" replied Odysseus in a rhetorical sort of way. "I have heard that you may be in need of a few good blokes for a bit of a revolution."

"So what?"

"Well, I can get them for you without anyone being any the wiser," said Odysseus.

"What's in it for you," asked Prometheus suspiciously.

"Just a little well overdue pay-back of a purely vengeful nature, and a possible position in the new organisation," replied Odysseus.

"Sounds pretty straightforward," said Prometheus, "sounds like what I'd expect from the likes of you. So what I'm offering is this. You get the squad together and if they shape up okay, maybe I'll let you live. If they don't, you join your ex ex-crew or perhaps I should just cut to the chase and reunite you with the crew now!"

The rock wobbled perilously in his hand and Odysseus made his already brown underwear a little, well a lot actually, browner.

"Just my little joke," boomed Prometheus, "but don't fuck with me okay?" The rock wobbled more and impacted with the cave floor, leaving two millimetres between it and Odysseus and his new aroma.

"D-d-don't you w-w-worry about a t-t-thing," stammered Odysseus. "I'll s-s-sort everything out.

"Good, now sod off, you're stinking the place up. I'll be in touch."

Prometheus watched him leave, smirking as he rolled, ducked and said, "ouch! Who moved that bloody boulder?"

Two things intrigued him, firstly that the word was on the street so quickly and secondly why was it on the street with Odysseus? Hercules wouldn't be taken in by Odysseus surely? So who was pulling whose string here? Not that it mattered anyway as long as Jupiter didn't get hold of it too soon.

Odysseus stumbled out into the sunlight squinting.

Schplatt!

Dead centre on the top of his head he experienced an impact of a warm trickly nature. The vulture circled laughing. Odysseus stood there speechless, for a change, wishing for the invention of ground to air missiles and shook his fist at the carrion capering overhead.

Schplatt!

Right in his left eye, the warm trickly impact recurred. Odysseus fumed, he was covered in shit at both ends, he had been directed by a piss-head ex-hero, threatened by a giant and now, to cap it all, that scavenging winged parasite was laughing at him from on high and crapping from the same vantage point. He stomped off towards the Styx with the intention of adding to the environmental pollution of hell's waterway.

XVIII

THOR'S RIGHT AND THE HAMMER DWARVES

Unlike most of the others, Thor was not the son of a king. He was the son of a God and, if the hype was believable, he was also a God himself. Thor had never been happy with the God tag. He saw himself as a bit of a socialist, always championing the cause of the underdog. He was a strong lad and so far he hadn't met anyone stronger, which did tend to leave him feeling a little bit intellectually short of his full potential.

When he was younger he had by no means been the sharpest spanner in the cantilevered cart-box. The other Gods and their giant offspring were constantly taking the piss out of him and playing practical jokes on him and it really got on his tits! It made him short-tempered and generally resulted in the antagonist having some portion of his cranium united with the nearest tool to hand in the forge or the barn.

Eating and drinking were his favourite pastimes, especially the drinking one. He'd had a bit of a session the previous night, which didn't confine itself to the previous night, and he was hanging badly. He had the over-hang from hell going on. Knowing he was due to give a chapter and verse pep chat at a socialist charity benefit gig in a couple of hours he thought he'd better straighten up a tad. To which end he was having a swim in the chilly waters of a shady glade in Midgard a few miles uphill from the town boundaries.

It was a sunny afternoon and things changed for Thor that sunny afternoon. He got out of the water and his iron gloves and boots were missing. There was some sniggering in the bushes but nothing to be seen. Assuming it was the other godly offspring farting about again Thor knew his pressure valve was about to be sorely tested and, tested without any available clobbering instruments within easy reach. He stomped his foot and gagged on the pain from the thorny briar which had had the audacity to place itself between where his foot was and the intended destination of his indignant stomp. As he hopped around trying to remove the offending thorns the sniggering bushes turned into pissing-themselves-laughing bushes.

That was it. The other giants were laughing at him again. His steam valve was about to blow a seal when Dwarves rolled out of the bushes still chuckling and started jumping around like circus acrobats.

Shit, now what? He couldn't hurt them, they were just little guys having fun and supporting the underdog was what he did. Then, strangely out of place for him, he smiled and the head of steam evaporated with the valve seal intact. These little guys were funny and harmless. He'd just learned a lesson, if he could smile at the dwarves he sure as hell could smile at the giants and that would leave them with a steam vent problem. A problem they couldn't vent because they knew Thor would win if they aggravated him because he wasn't aggravated.

One dwarf approached him with a stool and he sat on it but was still twice as tall as they were! Two more dwarves approached him carrying a boot each and one of them removed the thorns from his foot. Then two more came carrying an iron glove each which he duly donned. Honour seemed to be satisfied for Thor and he was about to take his leave when two more dwarves approached carrying a very spanky top of the range majestic sledgehammer.

"We have crafted this for you, it has power that Zeus himself would be envious of," said one of the dwarves, "we chose you because you are the protector of the downtrodden."

Thor picked up the hammer, that it had taken two dwarves to carry, in one hand and assessed its balance. This was some piece of artwork. He swung it, hefted it, spun it, swivelled it, threw it up in the air, threw it over his shoulder from behind and caught it in the other hand, bounced it off the ground, bounced it off a tree, threw it as far as he could throw and every time it returned to his hand like the yet to be invented Aboriginal boomerang, if a kangaroo didn't get in the way that is!

The other dwarf sniffed and wiped his nose on his sleeve and said, "Learn its ways and don't fuck up, we are not happy with the sodding Gods and we're pretty sure you aren't either!"

As far as Thor was concerned Zeus was just another equal among giants in the ongoing battle of wits for supremacy and if Zeus needed equalising then Thor was happy to be the instrument of some equalisation.

He was not happy with the sodding Gods!

The Big Hammer

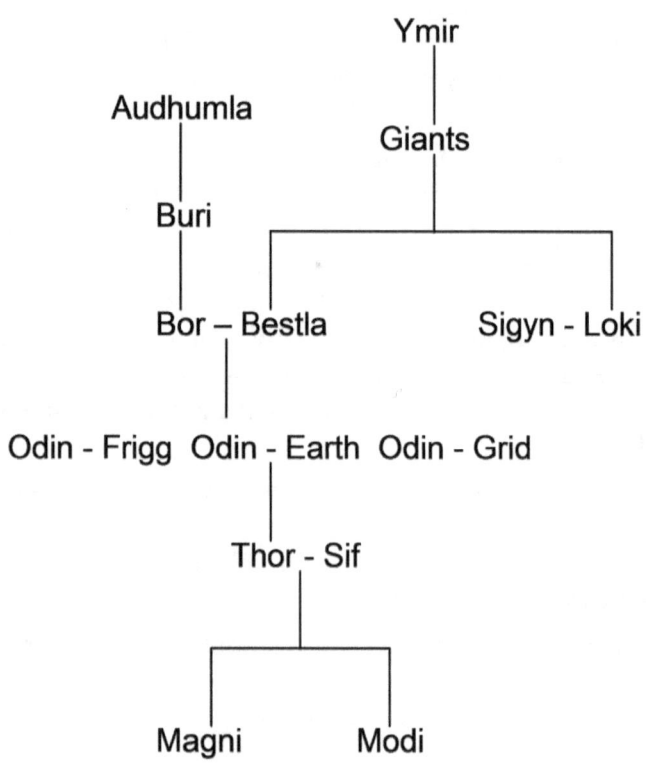

XIX

IT'S THE ONLY WAY TO FLEE

Camilla, like so many others, was born at an early age and didn't remember the occasion herself. She relied on her daddy, Metabus, for the details and she was a right old daddy's girl in the early years.

Daddy came from Volsci where, surprise surprise, he was a king - until the locals dethroned him. He'd had to do a runner with baby Camilla in his arms and with a shed load of well-armed Volsci hot on his heels. It was looking like a walk in the park until the river got in the way of his strategic withdrawal. He was in deep do-do, he could swim the river but not with the kid weighing him down and he couldn't just leave the kid to the mob behind him.

Metabus was not really a religious man but he suddenly developed belief. The only member of the God line-up he could remember ever having been interested in was Diana, mainly because all the paintings and tapestries showed her up in a light that delighted most teenage boys. She would have to do. He prayed to her, he promised her everything he had, which wasn't much at that point, one spear and one daughter!

He had a plan and he wanted divine sanction on the idea so he promised Diana that Camilla would be dedicated to her for life if she saved the child in this endeavour. It was quite a bold move, telling a goddess he secretly fancied - who would obviously know that anyway due to the nature of the God squad and its monopoly on omnipotence - that these were the terms of the contract she would sanction. Especially as it was going to cost him bugger all as he was passing the obligation on to a daughter who was too young to have any say in the matter. This was typical kingly behaviour, even for a de-throned one!

Metabus considered he had covered all the angles and set to the task. He wrapped and swaddled one of his only possessions, Camilla, following which he bound her to his spear shaft, his only other possession and he took reasonable care in selecting a spot on the opposite bank of the river. He hurled the spear and its infant passenger at the chosen and, Goddess sanctioned, target. It was a perfect throw and the spear embedded in a large oak tree with the cargo still attached and up out of harm's way. Metabus went headfirst into the water and swam to the other side and retrieved Camilla.

There were some landmark achievements in that flight. Camilla was the first person to fly by manmade propulsion means. She was the first to fly across a river. She was the first to nosedive, crash land in a tree and survive the first-ever passenger flight. She was the first to not have to log a flight plan. She was the first and probably only person to have a Goddess for an air traffic controller. She was the first and probably only passenger to not have to put up with checking in and the overpriced luxury of duty-free goods. She was the first and only one to not have to pay landing tax, fuel surcharge or excess baggage charge. She was the first to not have to pay transfer fees. To add to that, as if that were not enough, she was also the first woman to do all of that as well!

Metabus remained true to the terms of his contractual agreement and he began to teach Camilla every martial method of cunning and warfare at his disposal, as soon as she was detached from his spear.

Camilla learned rapidly how to handle all manner of weaponry and also one other very important method of self-defence, how to run like all the devils in all the hells were chasing you. She could run across water without disturbing the surface and over the top of a field of grain without breaking a single grain bearing stalk, ensuring that she would be fully ecologically friendly in the instance of famine or food shortages.

Camilla grew up worshipping only one Goddess but - after watching her daddy's demise at losing everything and dedicating his life to rearing his daughter, after giving her the benefit of an initial in-flight training session - she was not at all happy with the sodding Gods!

XX

THE VIKINGS ARE HERE

Down at Andromache's the nightlife was just kicking off when a cartload of out of towners, on a day trip, arrived. They were ready for a beer and prepared to stay the night. To the casual onlooker, they were a bit of a strange-looking bunch. Women and men with long hair, mainly blonde, parted in the middle and plaited to around waist length. The blokes were discernible only by the large and imposing cow horns in their hats and the waist length plaited beards, though for gender purposes, the horned hats were a more foolproof identification indicator than the beards.

They all seemed to be well tooled up with a variety of blades, axes, staffs, chains and miscellaneous instruments of indeterminate purpose that would have looked very much at home hanging from a chrome bar over a butcher's meat block, or deep in the bowels of a drain cleaner's tool bag.

They were laughing and chatting and seemed, for the most part, friendly and by halfway through the evening they had usurped the hired minstrels as the night's entertainment.

They had drinking songs the likes of which no local had ever come across. They juggled knives while drinking and alternately slicing fruit into it between drinks. Two of them juggled four ale beakers, six knives and five cow horned hats between them. By the end of the evening, martial equipment of every description had undergone an introduction to flight and the air was thick with assorted military and domestic paraphernalia.

Hercules looked on impressed, thinking that there were a few handy blokes in that collection. Paris flirted with the single women, and the not so single because he was good at that too, in the travelling group. Theseus snored on the bar. Cerberus spent the evening in the garden barking with alternate heads at a discarded cow horn helmet propped up on a spear. Andromache offered the travellers four rounds on the house to come back the following night and entertain some more, after rapidly knocking up some sharp fly posters and dispatching Atalanta, the runner, to various post boxes, public loos and 'phone kiosks with said posters and a bucket of paste. Well, the takings were up, these people certainly drew the punters and nothing got broken.

Smiling her 'good night's,' Andromache dispatched them all to a boarding house on the crossroad at the far end of town which was run by her sister in law Cassandra.

Cassandra had tried to make a living as a prophetess but she had been too obscure with her predictions to be believable and had finally given it up after predicting a hoard of buried treasure. A prediction which she wisely kept to herself, knowing full well the unjust nature of the laws regarding treasure trove, preferring instead to buy a disgustingly large house on the crossroads on the outskirts with her find, rather than give the state a free meal ticket. She predicted that this would be a good move because as trade expanded, it would make a good boarding house. The prediction business, she now found, was so simple when you were filthy rich and dreams were affordable. So she bought off Clytemnestra, her captor's wife, after the Troy episode, faked her own death and got Clytie to dispatch her husband

Agamemnon. This done, she was a free woman, she assumed the surname of Cross and became the limited company known as Cassandra Cross Incorporated.

Business had been rather slow for Cassandra Cross Inc. so far this year and Cassandra was delighted with the arrival of a luxury cartload of tourists. Lucky she had had the foresight to get extra supplies at the hypermarket last week, there was still some of the old magic left in her yet, she thought.

She asked them to sign in, just to keep the register up to date and informed them that there was a residents' bar, a sandal re-thonging and overnight laundry service, that breakfast was served between 07.30 and 10.00am and local tours could be arranged via the Odysseus Date-a-Mate and Employment Agency.

Most went straight to bed. Two decided to indulge in more ale. Cassandra had a rather prescient feeling that they were up for a right good session and moved herself to the other side of the bar. "Evening folks, what can I get you?"

"Just a skin of house white," said the man, "and a couple of goblets please."

"Would you care to join us?" asked the woman.

"Well?" said Cassandra, "I shouldn't really but just the one won't hurt I suppose."

Cassandra didn't like to drink too much because it tended to make her waffle a lot and brought out the prophetess in her and that tended to frighten the guests.

"So, you folks travelled far?"

"Oh, we've seen a bit of the world in our time. We organise these trips and we like to go along on the odd one just to check on the service we supply," said the woman.

"My name's Camilla by the way and this," she indicated the man, "is Thor."

"Well it's nice to meet you both, I'm Cassandra," said the proprietor and shook hands with them. "I really must turn in now, breakfast's not far away. Help yourselves to the bar, just make a note on the slate and I'll charge it to your bill." The amount of which, she felt, was predictable.

"I'll say goodnight then."

"She seems nice," said Camilla.

"Yeah," replied Thor, "maybe we could use this place again."

Four skins of wine and an incredibly horny feeling later, they went to their room in a fumbling, drunken stagger, determined to get laid, sort of way. They stumbled in and Thor slammed the door shut as quietly as possible with Camilla's back as they tore at each other's clothing. Camilla smirked and looked up sideways raising one eyebrow and said, "In the tradition of all the best poets, I need a pee." Thor reluctantly released his grip and Camilla dashed for the bathroom.

Two minutes later, Camilla stood there in her full battle dress with one breast bared, as was her tradition in battle, looking ever so tantalisingly slightly like raw sex appeal.

Sizzkadumpf!

The battle axe sailed through the air and embedded in the oak door a couple of millimetres below where Thor's manhood dangled after the optimistic removal of his codpiece. He now understood the dangers of unprotected sex, as did Camilla when Thor's 10lb throwing hammer shattered the leg of the four-poster by way of a reply.

Thor smiled unsheathing his 25lb pump-action sledgehammer from its back sling and brandishing it in a menacing manner.

Camilla pouted and tutted but secretly, all feminism aside, she loved a bit of foreplay and, withdrawing her right hand from behind her, proudly displayed her latest acquisition. A 9mm, fully automatic, quadruple bladed uzi-mace. Thor's grin broadened and he rose to the occasion, this was going to be the shag of a lifetime.

They hit the four-poster together, destroying the remaining three legs in the process and immersed themselves in the pursuit of pleasure.

Four hours and no sleep later, Thor stood on the balcony of his room, raised his hands to the sky and announced to the world in general, "I am Thor!" in a loud and resonant voice. Camilla raised herself up on one elbow and replied with a mock lisp, "You're thore, I'm tho tender I daren't go for another pith." At which point the earth moved again but in a more discernibly physical way this time as a shower of meteorites touched down around the town.

"Hmmmm…" said Thor, "that's a bit ominous."

XXI

REVENGE IS A DISH BEST SERVED IMMEDIATELY

Thyestes was a nasty abominable piece of shit. When he was a kid, he and his brother, Atreus, murdered their half-brother on their dad's side because their mother, Hippodamia, thought it would be a good idea.

Atreus ended up in charge of Mycenae when king Eurystheus messed up on a rape and pillage mission and got himself killed.

Atreus decided to sacrifice a lamb and while he was out interfering with his flock he found one with a Golden Fleece. Well, obviously that lamb had to die! He slaughtered it and gave the fleece to his wife Aerope for safekeeping.

Thyestes had got far too friendly with Atreus's wife, Aerope and she was still hot to trot for Thyestes and she had given him the Golden Fleece. Thyestes, being a nasty abominable piece of shit, saw the opening for some revenge and agreed with Atreus that the true ruler of Mycenae should be the owner of the Golden Fleece. It shot Atreus one right up the chocolate spangler when he told Aerope to go and fetch the fleece. She came back empty-handed after making a show of looking everywhere and then Thyestes pulled it, like a rabbit from a hat, out of nowhere and told Atreus to get out of what was now his throne and make himself scarce.

Atreus wasn't going to take it lying down though. He now wanted re-revenge. He negotiated a deal whereby if the sun went backwards in the sky Thyestes would give up the throne. It turned out that Atreus had a friend in Zeus and he managed to pull off the deal and get his throne back and, obviously, he banished Thyestes from what was now his kingdom.

He was, however, still not happy, it sort of took the shine off having a throne when the penny dropped and he realised that his brother had been bonking his wife. He was the usual 'last one to know' kind of husband and when he worked it out he was a smidgeon irritated and by way of re-re-revenge, invited Thyestes to a barbeque. Now some would say it was a bit over the top as far as revenge goes but, he cooked Thyestes' kids and fed them to him. It was just another day on the House of Atreus Ranch!

That was nowhere near the end of the aggression between the sparring siblings. Thyestes, because he was a nasty abominable piece of shit, was really pissed off with his brother's last move and wanted some serious re-re-re-revenge. Thyestes fell back on oracular guidance, any port in a storm sort of thing. The oracle told him that if he fathered a son with his own daughter the son would slay Atreus. This was serious disturbia stuff and he liked the idea! He knocked his daughter, Pelopia, up and left her with Thesprotus, one of his king mates and buggered off to Delphi to let the dust settle.

Atreus was in a bit of a pickle after the barbecue, public opinion was riding high against him and Mycenae was falling apart around him. He too opted for the oracular path to enlightenment. The oracle told him to bring back Thyestes and all would be forgiven. It has to be said that this was not much of an oracle if it was a prediction for future success!

Atreus went to see Thesprotus and while there saw Pelopia and assumed she was his daughter and asked to marry her. Thesprotus didn't want to cock things up but knew that it was already too late for that anyway, things could not possibly get any more screwed up surely!

Absolutely nobody was getting anywhere with the art of oracular future foretelling. In the street, word got round and the general consensus was, did either of these guys take running a kingdom seriously? It was a subject postulated upon in many a drinking establishment.

Atreus married Pelopia. He married his niece who was up the spout with his, nasty abominable piece of shit, brother's kid. She had a son and called him Aegisthus. The poor girl lost the plot completely, all this incestuous stuff was too much to handle and she abandoned Aegisthus in the woods and fled with what little sanity she had left.

Atreus had the kid found and raised him as his own and sent his other sons, Agamemnon and Menelaus, to find Thyestes. They were successful and Atreus imprisoned Thyestes and sent Aegisthus down to the dungeon to kill him.

In the interim Aegisthus had found Pelopia and was in full command of the facts. He farted around a bit just to look like he was carrying out Atreus' instructions and then took out Atreus, so that sad oracle proved to be reliable! This was not such a good idea though because Thyestes, the nasty abominable piece of shit, was now back on the throne!

His first kingly duty was to banish Agamemnon and Menelaus. They quite happily buggered off to Tyndareus' place, everybody has a king mate somewhere. This place just happened to be Sparta and they brought the whole Spartan army back to Mycenae to show Uncle Thyestes who was boss.

Thyestes was banished, leaving room for yet another sequel. Menelaus married Helen and the Spartan throne came with it. Agamemnon married her sister Clytemnestra and took the Mycenaean throne in with that deal.

Thyestes got bored with the whole tit-for-tat royal chess game and washed his hands of the whole affair. He retired from public life and opened a restaurant. Thyestes, the nasty abominable piece of shit, didn't give toss about anyone or anything and he didn't give a green-wet-Monday-morning-after-a-weekend-of-ale-and-curry, fart about the Gods!

XXII

MORTAL-ISH ELEVEN TEAM SELECTION

Having decided that this was a singularly important recruitment drive, Odysseus opened up the Odysseus Date-a-Mate and Employment Agency personally.

This came as a great surprise to the clerk who, in ten years of faithful conscientious service, had never been late for work once. Well, just the once actually and, by some very warped sense of divine humour, it just happened to be the one day in a lifetime that the boss decided to open the shop himself.

The quick-thinking clerk waltzed into the main office, where Odysseus was ransacking a filing cabinet, in between mouthfuls of coffee and lungfuls of nicotine.

"What time do you call this then?" inquired the clerk. "I was expecting you back about ten years ago."

Odysseus looked up and smiled, "Good attempt," he said, "you can stay late and make up the time."

"Oh yeah, make up the bloody time? Would that be the time that you rarely pay me for or would that be the time that you intend to give me time and a half and a pay rise for?"

"Don't get cocky with me sunshine, where's the file on heroes in this pathetic mess you call a filing system?"

"It's all on disk now, I made a few changes while you were away," replied the clerk with a trace of a smirk.

"Well get it off disk, whatever that is, and on to my desk, pronto!"

"What's the magic word?" asked the clerk.

"The magic words," said Odysseus pointedly, "are Pee Forty-Five, now get on with it!"

The clerk walked away amidst great mutterings of an ungrateful - contract shy, illegitimate, mother loving, tight fisted, double dealing - sort and plonked himself down in front of a PC screen of ancient design. He hammered a few keys and input the password 'Cyclops'. The printer began to spew out a list of heroes that had, at one stage or another, passed through the agency.

Odysseus strained his synapses to the extreme in the meantime and busied himself preparing adverts for the local popular press. He considered that Theseus' inebriated notion of a match was a good one and, after stripping out the inebriated associations, decided to run with it. He couldn't do the complicated stuff on a computer but he was ok for the odd bit of script processing with, on special occasions, two fingers.

Following a large number of expletives, Odysseus decided that this was not to be a special occasion!

> 'Calling all the heroes.
>
> Are you bored? Are you at loose end? Short of leisure time entertainment? Do you miss the good old days when men were men and lions were wrestling partners?
>
> Do you need some excitement back in your life?
>
> Well, look no further!
>
> We have a selection of cupboard skeletons in need of a good airing, demons requiring laying to rest, mythical monsters and a wide variety of lightning bolts in need of dodging.
>
> This is a sporting opportunity you will not want to miss.
>
> Call the Odysseus Date-a-Mate and Employment Agency today.
>
> Don't delay, only a limited number of places available whilst stocks last.'

Odysseus looked at the advert and was happy with it. It had just enough pizzazz to attract the, limited-intellect, built-like-a-brick-shithouse, hard-as-granite, type of person he required. The kind of hero that would take on anything, not ask too many questions and be happy with glory or death in the line of duty as opposed to wages.

The advert was rapidly dispatched, via Atalanta the runner, to appear everywhere that mattered.

The clerk appeared with the requested hero list and Odysseus scanned it, marking out the better possibilities. He would wait and see how many of the names listed called the agency and whittle it down to those he had already chosen. He knew what he wanted but he had to make sure - because, no matter how thick the hero, it likes to think it runs its own destiny - they thought it was their own choice and decision initially.

The clerk who, like many before him, was not slow on the uptake put two and two together and realised that it was time to dust and extend the Kings, Queens and various assorted royals section on the extreme right. There was, he knew from bitter experience, nothing like a, 'hero wanted', advert for bringing all the inbred, leftover, club-footed indiscretions of royalty out of the woodwork, cellar, sewer or cesspit, especially in peacetime. They, despite their individual but held in common peculiarities, loved being public figures of adoration and awe, particularly when there was no danger to them.

The clerk looked sidelong at Odysseus. "Are we about to have a war by any remote chance?" he asked his employer.

"What on earth could possibly make you think that?" said Odysseus.

"Well," replied the clerk, "it's the little things, you know? Like a giant in the park, a lorry load of all singing, all dancing, Nordic nutters at Cassy's place, a bit of a commando recruitment drive, you being back in town and a meteor shower. To me," continued the sarcasm ridden clerk, "they are all very clear indications that you are not planning a town picnic and gala day, right?"

Odysseus had to admit that when you put it that way, it did look rather obvious and the clerk was, after all, a smart lad, that's why he got the job. Odysseus decided to come almost clean. "We're going to have a little sports day with the gods," he said.

"Bollocks!" replied the clerk. "You're going to take them on, aren't you? Sports are just tribal warfare on a pitch without the weaponry. You're planning to have a pop at the Olympus boys you sad old toe rag. You want some revenge and you're going to get the heroes to do it for you."

Odysseus was on his feet and across the room with the clever clerk propped against the wall a foot and a half above floor level, by his neck, all in one neat tidy movement.

"You breathe a word of that outside this establishment and you'll never work in this town, or any other for that matter, again. Got that?"

"Eaa, ess, Sir," choked the clerk followed by, *schwumph!* as he slid down the wall and stopped only because the floor got in the way. "There's no need for violence," he croaked, massaging his neck. "It's me who'll end up doing all the interviewing, I just want to know if you want the thick as pig shit, hard as nails variety of hero or the dignified, benevolent, profile of Adonis with a ploughshare chin, type. Judging by your reaction, I guess you've just answered in the thick as pig shit department."

The remark was, for all its rhetorical cunning and intellect, totally wasted on Odysseus. It passed at an altitude so far in excess of his head that it would take a radio telescope to find it.

It was about an hour later after he had left the agency, that Odysseus realised that the clerk had called him thick as pig shit. He was going to have to watch that chap, he thought, because if there's one thing a devious, two-faced employer needs to be careful about, it's a devious, two-faced employee with aspirations.

He pasted a few fly posters around the town and dropped into a little Greek restaurant he knew called The Basted Brat, run by Thyestes and his girlfriend. "Thy, me old mate," said Odysseus, "how's life in the catering trade then?"

"Oddy!" he exclaimed with an inflection of suspicion. "Fine thanks, just fine, haven't seen you around for a bit, must be an occasion in the air for you to be back in town."

"Yeah, the occasion is I'm hungry and you sell food," said Odysseus.

"I see the short sense of sarcasm is alive and doing well," replied Thyestes, handing Odysseus a menu. Odysseus scanned it suspiciously knowing that something was not quite right but not quiet putting his finger on what it was. He made a mental note, Thyestes had got off with a lot over the years and he deserved some poetic justice! However, right now dinner was the issue on hand and Odysseus returned his attention to the splendid and exotic menu.

A-la-Horse-Cart:

Chicken Jowls Diane

Beef Surprise Especial

Exotic Crayfish on Lemon Island

Collar of Llama in Thyestes Imperial Sauce

Liver in Steamed Turkey Estouffade Raclette Infusion Acidulate

To Take Away:

Swan Sarnie

Boil in the Bag Tiger Trotters

Steamed Tripe

Extras:

Gravy

"Well," said Odysseus, "this bill of fare has gone uphill a bit I must say, no more of that kid stuff then?"

"Nah," replied Thyestes, "it was a good gimmick there for a bit, but they always cook up smaller than they look so after the wife got arrested I dropped it from the menu - and her shortly afterward."

"So what's the Beef Surprise Especial?" inquired the two-faced customer.

"That's magnificent," Thyestes assured him, "you'll love it and I promise, if you're not amazed you don't pay," he said, scribbling on his pad, "anything to drink with that?"

"Just a half skin of the house red."

"Certainly Sir," said Thyestes heading for the wine cellar, throwing a towel over his shoulder and calling to the kitchen, "One B.S.E. for table two."

Odysseus enjoyed the meal and, picking his moment carefully, went to the toilet after dipping his fingers into the open till unnoticed on his way past it. He returned to his table and followed lunch up with a cappuccino coffee and a roll-up and paid Thyestes. This was unusual and worried Thyestes. Odysseus very rarely paid for anything. "Guess the beef was alright then!" he whispered to his girlfriend, who was busy cashing up as Odysseus left and headed back to the agency.

As he'd expected, there was already a queue of hopeful potential heroes, sporadically broken by tried and trusted heroes, outside the agency. He waited while the clerk opened up after lunch and the gathered job seekers filed in, in what to Odysseus looked like a re-enactment of the first race riots around Troy's back gate. He smiled fondly at the memory of how he had personally instigated most of that civil unrest and its ensuing carnage. He let the clerk sort out some of the wheat from the chaff and entered his office by the secret back door.

Two days later they had it down to a short list of twenty and Odysseus conducted the final interviews personally, which culminated in the official Mortals Eleven team. This comprised of a bunch of underhand deadbeats that read like the who's who of the criminally deranged but for some reason commanded a modicum of public respect.

Ajax the son of Telamon, Oedipus the patricide, Menelaus the son of Atreus and ex-husband of Helen, Turnus ex-adversary of Aeneas and ex-husband of Lavinia who had moved in with Aeneas after the Troy incident, Neoptolemus son of Achilles the Trojan executioner, Thor and Camilla who just happened to be in town at the time, Hercules son of Jupiter and all-round labourer, Paris husband of Helen, son of Priam and all-round good looker, Theseus the gardener and Minotaur oppressor and finally Perseus son of a shower of gold, possible great grandfather of the all-round labourer, honorary grandpappy to the Minotaur oppressor and all-in Gorgon wrestler.

Odysseus, wanting to be fully involved but not personally involved, had called in one of his old mates as coach and trainer but he was currently tied up with a Hydra, some serpents and a lot of slaying overseas and couldn't start for a week or two - or ever, if the overseas trip didn't go well.

The lads and lady would get restless waiting that long and Odysseus decided to start their training, but from a distance, by calling a meeting at the amphitheatre which looked out over the parklands.

"Good morning gentlemen and lady. This is just an informal get together so that you can get to know each other and have a bit of a warmup session. The sports equipment is over there," he indicated towards the rear left, "and the martial equipment is over there," he said, indicating to the rear left again. He paused for his little ice breaker joke to sink in and quickly noticed that it did not receive even the merest flutter of an amused grin.

"Yes, well, moving on, horses and chariots will be here this afternoon…"

"Er, hang on a mo," said a large ginger-haired bloke with a big beard who looked like he would have been more at home in the Scottish Highlands.

"Yes Menelaus, what is it, you have a query?" said Odysseus.

"What I do in my own time behind closed doors is my business you cheeky bastard, so sod off with the innuendo!"

"What?" questioned Odysseus.

"I'll give you what," said Menelaus straining against Neoptolemus and Thor in an effort to get at Odysseus, "you insinuating that I might be gay or something like that?"

"No," said Odysseus, realising the level of intellect he might well be involved with here. "What I meant was… Do you have a problem?"

"With what! What are you trying to say?" raved Menelaus.

Oh fuck, thought Odysseus, and this is before we even start. "You said hang on a mo, I assumed you had a question, a query, a problem."

"Oh, oh yeah," said Menelaus shrugging Thor and Neoptolemus off, "you said the sports stuff is over there and then you said the martial stuff's over there too. Well I don't want to get married and those bits of broken stick with chains and nails sticking out of them don't look very much like sports equipment to me. They look more like a bunch of broken weapons with bits missing, are you taking the piss or what?"

Odysseus found himself wishing for the invention of saints so that they could preserve him. Calm down, he thought, you don't want them for their intellect you want them for their muscle.

Paris looked at Hercules in disbelief "How?" he said.

"How what?" asked Hercules.

"How did a nation of arseholes like that ever get through the gates of Troy?"

"Life is strange," said Hercules, "but it wasn't them that got in, was it? It was that knob-shiner down there," he said, nodding towards Odysseus, "he was the brains behind the architect behind the large equestrian stuffed full of soldiers."

Paris suddenly saw Odysseus in a new light, "you mean the wooden horse of Troy, the one my arrow bounced off, was his idea?"

"Oh yeah, a little-known fact and that's not all he does with horses either."

Paris was still staring at Odysseus.

"Well I know he trains them and trades them and rides them."

"He certainly rides them," said Hercules, "in more ways than one."

"What?" said Paris, turning to look at Hercules. "Surely you don't mean…?"

"Surely I do. I remember one night out on the battlefield we had to call the heavenly healer Apollo and the company veterinarian to remove him from a horse that, according to him, backed on to him while he was having a pee. I mean, how many people do you know that stack five helmets up and stand on top of them to have a pee, with a hard-on? The vet' tried desperately but in the end, he had to put the horse down, too psychologically traumatised to be any good in battle afterwards. It took Apollo a week to get the smile off Oddy's face."

"At least," said Paris, "with Menelaus you know where you stand, you know your family pets are safe. Reckon I owe Oddy baby a bit of a sorting out then."

"Patience Paris," said Hercules, "he'll get what's coming but not just yet, we need him for a bit longer."

"We do? For what?"

"We need him to organise this shower and as liaison officer with Prometheus. Don't want to get our own hands dirty, do we?"

"You crafty bleeder," said Paris.

Odysseus could see that this was going to get out of hand if he didn't do something fast. "Gentlemen, and lady, I appreciate that the equipment is perhaps a little Spartan," realising as he said it that mention of Sparta, with so many of Greek origin about, was perhaps not the most diplomatic turn of phrase, "but I assure you that this situation will be remedied within the week so try to make the most of it for the present."

At which point he mumbled something about a prior appointment and beat a hasty retreat, which was something he was expert at, to a hail of apple cores, soft drink containers and one catcall in particular from the region of Menelaus, "Fuck off - horse shagger!"

Hercules looked at Paris and grinned very broadly. "See, told you so."

Sisyphus the rock and roller and Odysseus the duplicitous

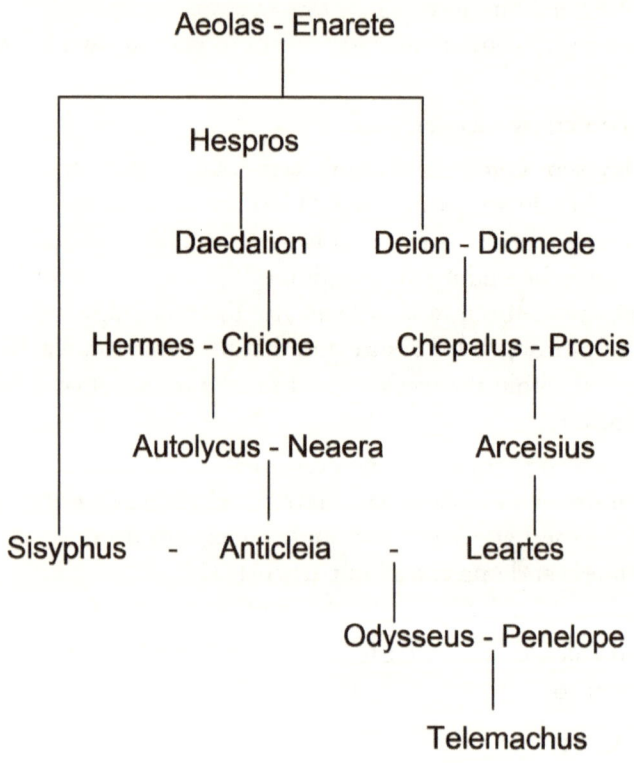

XXIII

MY KINGDOM FOR A COACH

The agency door burst open and a walking apple core, known to many as Odysseus, bolted in and slammed it behind him. The clerk looked up very calmly and did a superb job of not noticing his boss' predicament.

"What are you looking at," growled Odysseus.

"Harrumph me? Nothing Sir, Sphutzz," coughed the clerk.

"Get Jason on the 'phone - now!" rasped Odysseus.

"Sure thing boss, no problem," replied the clerk who, if the hacking, hawking, choking, spluttering sounds were anything to go by, appeared to be having visible trouble with something that seemed to have got stuck in his throat. "Just let me-he-hee get a drink of wa-ha-hater." The clerk stood up with the pressure of concealed laughter becoming uncontainable and dashed for the toilet.

He managed to get inside and prop the pedal bin against the door before collapsing in spasms of uncontrollable hilarity. Tears rolled down his face as the vision of Odysseus issuing orders, with apple-cores sticking out of his ear and nostril, floated before his mind's eye. As his mirth subsided his mind saw the soft drink container stuck over Odysseus' left foot and the straws protruding from his hair and beard oozing little beads of brown, orange and blue sticky stuff and the gut-wrenching laughter returned, he slid down in the corner amid fits of uncontrolled laughing while slapping the palms of his hands indiscriminately at the floor.

Finally regaining his composure after a few false starts, he stood up, washed his face and looked in the mirror. "Well," he said to his reflection, "the money's shit but the laughs are fucking good!"

The clerk returned, re-seated himself and dialled the number for Jason; after two minutes of ringing tones he was about to put the 'phone down when a high-pitched voice said, "Ellow?"

"Hello," said the clerk, "may I speak to Jason please?"

"Jason?" rasped the old crone voice, "you'll 'ave to narrow it down a bit more than that, every soddin' kid around 'ere for the last ten years has bin called Jason."

"Jason of Argos," said the clerk.

"They're all from bloody Argos!"

The clerk drew a long breath, "Jason of Argos, the boat builder, warrior and all-round general slayer of serpents, Hydras and the like."

"Oh, that one. E's not 'ere, e's down the boatyard, they got the Argo in dry dock peelin' off Nereids an' Nymphs from the front bumper an' chippin' off barnacles an' stuff. You'll 'ave to call 'is mobile, oow wants 'im?"

"Odysseus," said the clerk.

"That good for nuffin' bag a rusty spanners, wot's 'e want 'im for? They ain't goin' to give that bloody fleece con a go are they?

"I'm sure I don't know what you refer to madam," the clerk managed to get in edgeways.

"Madam, madam is it indeed? I'll give you madam, it's that tosspot Odysseus, leadin' our Jason astray, tryin' to flog dodgy golden fleeces and skip import taxes."

"That's all very interesting," replied the clerk, making a notation in a little black book, "but I have not been fully briefed on the nature of their business. Who am I speaking to?" he added exasperatedly.

"Me? I'm 'is Mam, an' if you get 'old of 'im tell 'im to stop pissin' about with that bloody boat and get back 'ere an' tidy 'is room up. I've never seen such a bloody mess in all my born days, all swords 'n' spears 'n' stuff clutterin' up the corners, bloody snakes 'eads an' Hydra teeth lyin' about all over the place, the wardrobe is jam-packed full of serpents' skins an' there's bloody sheepskins hangin' about all over the shop. It's a right bloody pig sty it is, the fings a movver 'as to put up wiv, you wouldn't believe it. You know the ovver day, 'e comes in, bold as brass. Soddin' great dragons 'ead under 'is arm, drippin' green stuff all over the kitchen floor 'e's a bleedin' liability 'e is..."

The clerk held the receiver away from his tortured ear and let it fall into the wastepaper bin.

The smart move here was obviously to use the technology available to him. He initiated a Person Locator Extrapolation Band Scan which came up positive, he had a location. The clerk decided to use the hero magnetic wave communications network called, Terra Wave Assisted Transfer, a system that made Email look sadly antiquated. He turned to his screen and typed in Epsilon-Mu, which was affectionately known as E-Mule and in a matter of seconds, he had Jason's online location but no reply. The only option left now was the old reliable, he typed in Tango-Echo-X-ray-Tango and typed a short message – 'Call me!' He waited two minutes and a call back came on his computer. He slipped a disk into the computer, retrieved the 'phone from the waste bin and swapped the conversation to the more conventional telecommunications mode of contact and transferred it to the extension in Odysseus' office.

His boss hated the 'phone but he hated the computer even more and the clerk thought it wise, given Oddy's present demeanour, not to wind him up further by making him chat via computer. That sorted, the clerk set about creating a new screen saver involving a caricature of Odysseus and some apple cores while idly pondering the use of acronyms - that were generally backronyms in his opinion - in communications systems.

Odysseus picked up the 'phone, "Ouch!" he said, lowering it and removing the offending apple core. "Jason my old mate!" Odysseus commenced.

"Well, you've got the first bit right," cut in Jason, "what do you want Oddy?"

"Why do you always assume I want something?"

"Well, so far in life you have never subscribed to the, 'it's good to talk', theory. Like, you never call to pass the time of day or anything of that nature, so I don't have to be Plato to work out that you want something, so come on, out with it."

"It's not quite like that," said Odysseus. "I may just be able to put a very rewarding contract your way."

"Rewarding eh? Rewarding how? Are we talking vast riches beyond the dreams of financial independence, rewarding or the more common character-building inducing of the feel-good factor, rewarding?"

"Oh, definitely a rewarding financial package," lied Odysseus, "on completion of the contract."

"Don't bullshit me Oddy, straight cash, no treasure maps, no hidden lost cities, no golden fleeces or dragon's hoards, I want honest to goodness legal currency, or no deal."

"Of course," Odysseus lied more, "the prospects for large returns with a possible world domination scenario, interested?"

"Yeah okay," said Jason, "what's the job?"

"I think," replied Odysseus carefully, "that it would be best if you come down here and survey the situation for yourself."

He knew that if he could just get Jason there, the rest of the deal would probably work itself out.

"The boat's in dry dock at the moment, probably relaunch around the end of the week. I'll think about it and get back to you. Have I got any back up on this one?"

Ha gotcha, thought Odysseus. "Indeed you have, eleven high profile, high calibre heroes, they're a damn good team."

"And no Hydras?"

"No," said Odysseus, "No Hydras."

"Or Cyclopses?"

"Definitely not."

"And no dogs?"

"Er - not as such, no," said Odysseus, stalling in frantic thought.

"What's that mean?" snapped Jason.

"Well," stumbled Odysseus, "let us define exactly what you mean by dog."

"You know bloody well what I mean, four legs, one at each corner, one tail, fur coat, big mouth, lots of teeth at the sharp end, wears a collar and barks a lot."

"No, most definitely none of those," said Odysseus, relieved that political rhetoric allowed one to lie so honestly.

"All right, I'll look it over Saturday morning," said Jason.

"Excellent," replied Odysseus, "perhaps you could throw a few fleeces in the hold, just in case."

"In case of what?"

"Err, in case you don't want the job, then you could pop down the market and flog a few skins and make the trip worth the bother. They're the kind of merchandise that moves well around here."

"Yeah okay," said Jason, "good thinking Oddy."

Odysseus sat back satisfied as a couple of straws slipped from their perch in his beard and fell down inside his shirt, not a bad day's work, he thought smugly and called to the clerk, "Get Atalanta in here, I need her to run a message down to the amphitheatre."

"What's the message?" asked the clerk.

"New coach arriving Saturday. Informal chat at Andromache's Bar and Bistro tonight at eight."

Having completed the request of his boss, the clerk shut up shop for the day and decided to go for a stroll in the park. He needed a failsafe, backup plan B and Prometheus was just such a backup merchant if played carefully. It was, after all, his team and he had a right to know about possible customs and excise activities that might affect his business venture, especially if it shored up the clerk's aspirations!

The smarter of the newly formed heroes eleven arrived at seven on purpose and, by the time Odysseus arrived, had amassed a considerable bar tab for him. Well, if the deal was as good as Oddy had made out at the interviews, then it could easily handle an expenses account.

Odysseus, with vivid memories of his last meeting with the team, paid up - and rapidly withdrew the credit card from the bar before it was noticed that it was well out of date and covered by the Municipal Bank of Troy - and called the meeting swiftly to order, mainly in order to limit the damage to the newly formed expense account which he had a feeling would come back to haunt him.

"Lady and gentlemen, as you know you have all been hand-picked for this task because you are the best there is." This was met with various, "Hear hears" and, "Get on with its." Odysseus waited for these to subside and continued, "And as the best there is, you deserve the best there is, so I have personally, at great expense secured from next Saturday forward, the services of a number one coach in the personage of Jason of Argos."

There following something that had been unknown since the two minutes before Jupiter had breathed life into Prometheus' clay models, complete silence. This was followed by something equivalent to the volume of the life-giving thunderbolt that followed the two minutes.

"Wot, that twat?" came first, "He couldn't train a plant to grow."

"Here we go again," followed that, swiftly backed up by, "Bloody tin pot organisation, cutting the corners already," from a female voice.

"That's all we need, a fucking Hydra shagger!" The voice belonged, obviously, to Menelaus.

The meeting rapidly descended into complete disorder, as became apparent when the first aerial, half-eaten, porkpie caught Odysseus just below the left ear, rapidly pursued by a selection of chicken bones and boiled, gravy sodden, Brussels sprouts.

He ducked as a leg of lamb, which still appeared to have the rest of the sheep attached to it, came at him from the west and, very unwisely, looked up again just in time to see Menelaus receive it full in the face and slide down the east wall a moment prior to the interaction of a westbound gateau with his own face.

Sensing that the meeting was not going quite as envisaged, Odysseus concluded that it would be prudent to do what he was best at and affect a strategic withdrawal. It was to be a withdrawal that was aided by four pairs of heroic hands, this also, was not as he had envisaged. He hit the double-action entrance doors at mach four and continued on taking most of the frame with him, to the delight of Cerberus, who had yet again been left in the garden and welcomed the company.

The company, unfortunately, wasn't very mobile, due to large amounts of concussion, but it was covered in some really yummy food which should obviously not be wasted.

Odysseus came round about an hour later to find a bunch of dogs licking his face and he froze until the image resolved itself into three dogs with one body.

"Gertcha," he grunted, giving two heads a damn good forearm smashing as he got to his feet and jumping three feet as the third head attached itself to his left buttock with a resounding snap.

Odysseus glared at the hound and snarled, the dog sniggered, and Odysseus turned on his heel and stomped off left foot first towards the agency.

Squelch!

"Aww fuck it!" He turned back and embedded a heavily shit laden foot in the dog's still recovering rectal sphincter.

The dog howled mournfully and inside the bar the Norsemen quickly picked up the cue and began to sing.

"Bastards, bastards all of you, you'll get yours!" Odysseus bellowed and took off right foot first.

Squelch!

Cerberus, having moved to a safe distance, sniggered some more.

XXIV

ROCK AND ROLL RESERVE

Hercules was up at the crack of eleven-thirty on the Saturday in question and thought it might be worth a stroll along to the first training session with the new coach.

Halfway across the park, he saw Paris and Theseus looking at the apex of a hill on the far side of the ravine that contained Prometheus' cave. "Hiya boys," said Hercules, "what's over there that's of interest then?"

Paris pointed about a third of the way along the ridge. "Something's going on up there, just watch for a minute."

The trio watched and something large and curved suddenly bobbed into view. It was hard to tell if it was rocking back and forth or up and down. It resembled a panic-stricken moon on an elastic band having severe difficulty in rising.

"I've often wondered what's on the far side of that hill," said Theseus as the sound of grunting and great labour came to their ears followed by a low rumble and...

"No, no, you fucking bastard, not again!"

"Shall we go and have a look?" inquired Hercules.

"What about the training session?" questioned Paris.

"What about it?" said Theseus.

"Let's go and check it out," said Hercules, "Cerberus, here boy, come on."

A sound that sounded rather like, *Aaeckrrusch!* rent the air, as the marble at the base of the monument on which the dog had just relieved itself crumbled and vaporised and Cerberus came obediently to heel.

Paris looked at the dog. "You've got to stop him doing that. Every bloody statue in the park has got bits missing out of it from where that bloody hound has pissed on them. I mean, the bloody archaeologists will think we had a war here or something."

"He's only a puppy," said Hercules, "it's all new to him, he's just having a bit of fun."

With that, three men and a triplicate dog set off for the far side of the hill. Wanting to avoid the amphitheatre - and Prometheus - for the moment, they decided to walk around the hill rather than across the ravine and climb up it.

Two hours later, walking diagonally up the far side of the hill, they crested a rise and could see in the distance something rather peculiar.

"Here," said Theseus, bordering very closely on supreme understatement, a border which he promptly stepped over and went straight on across. "There's a bloke over there shoving a bloody great rock up the hill."

"No shit," said Paris.

They watched as the man, dressed in a loincloth, leaned into the task. His arms and legs bulged with rippling muscles, which could only be the product of a hard manual life, veins stood out vividly on his neck and forearms as he systematically pushed and stepped the boulder up the hillside. The three watched as he rocked and worried it over obstructions caused by the irregularity of the ground.

Cerberus bounded up behind the man and playfully licked his leg. The man jumped out of his skin in surprise, lost his footing and watched in dismay as gravity took over the operation and the boulder.

"Aww shit! An' I had it that time," he groused, lashing out at the dog and sending it promptly after the boulder. Then he saw the three approaching men. "Is that your sodding hound?"

"Er, yes, more or less," replied Hercules, "you'll have to excuse him, he's just a puppy."

"Yeah, well if he ever does that again he won't live to achieve dog hood!"

Hercules looked the guy up and down, impressed with his physique and thought to himself, this bloke could be useful. "What exactly are you trying to do with that rock?"

The man looked at him incredulously and said quite simply. "Push it to the top of the hill."

"Why?"

"Aah," said the man. "The universally insoluble question, why?"

"Great," said Theseus, "another bloody philosopher, just what the world needs."

The man cocked his head towards Theseus. "Do I detect a hint of sarcasm there by any chance?"

"Yeah, you could say that," replied Theseus, "and that's not all you'll detect if you don't give my mate Hercules a civil answer to his polite question."

"Hercules?" responded the man, "aha, well it's a punishment imposed on me by Jupiter which, to be honest, I consider to be a bit over the top for the crime in question."

"So what did you do?" inquired Theseus.

"I just fiddled a few hands of poker and fixed a roulette wheel in one of the temples, got done for deceiving, fifteen to life on the rock."

"So what happens when you get it to the top?" asked Paris.

"Buggered if I know, bloody thing won't stay there will it, every time I let go it's off down the hill again, rather soul-destroying really. Still, I suppose that's half the point of the exercise but I nearly had it then - honest, I did."

Hercules - feeling slightly at fault seeing as, technically, it was his dog's arsing about that had ruined the attempt - offered some assistance. He turned to the others. "We could help couldn't we lads? Won't take long with four of us on it."

Paris and Theseus looked at the boulder and then at each other. "Did he say we?" asked Theseus. "You mean we've trudged two hours round a mountain to get out of a training session that's looking more and more inviting by the minute?"

"I suppose you could call it field training," said Paris.

"I suppose you could call it bloody stupid and pointless," said Theseus, "or fell running with weights."

"But I guess as long as we're here we might as well give it a go." chipped in Paris.

"Now you're doing it too," said Theseus.

"I am?" said Paris. "What?"

"That collective 'we' thing," answered Theseus.

"That's the spirit!" said Hercules. "Discussion and teamwork."

Hercules and the man did most of the pushing and an hour later the boulder was right on the apex of the hill. Paris and Theseus wedged a selection of sticks and smaller boulders under it and it balanced precariously on the crest.

"Free!" said the man. "Free at last after countless aeons, I can never thank you enough." he jabbered.

A great weight had been lifted from him, so to speak. In his delight and relief he leaned against the nearest available rock, which also happened to be the only available rock, which, as it happens, just happened to be the one they had so laboriously pushed up the hill.

There was an ominous creak as the boulder reached apogee and surrendered to the gravity on the opposite side of the hill and took off in the direction of Prometheus' abode.

"I don't give a toss." said the man, as the boulder hit the back end of the ravine with earth-shattering force and adopted a change in its vector. "The job was to get it up here, no one said how long for!"

At this point, Prometheus stuck his head out. "Oy! Who threw that?" he said, turning and seeing the boulder bearing down on him from higher along the ravine. "Oh shit!" he exclaimed, rapidly withdrawing his head back cave-side with his question unanswered.

The boulder continued on crashing through trees and bushes like something last seen on an Indiana Jones film set. It hit a smaller harder rock and bounced once.

Kerrunchsposh!

"Ouchyafuckinbastard!" shouted the skeletal figure of Charon, standing beside the Styx, looking very wet and shaking a bony fist up towards the hill, after watching a very large boulder skim across his cowl and land on his brand new shiny boat two seconds after he had launched it.

Hercules grinned, sniggered a bit and burst out laughing, which had a viral effect on the other three, who were soon rolling around helpless with laughter too.

"D-D-did you s-see the look on his face?" Paris managed to get out.

"Wh-wh-which w-one?" cried Theseus.

"Both of 'em," laughed the man, "scared 'em both shitless!"

Hercules subsided and said, "So what's your name mate?"

"Sisyphus," said the man extending his right hand.

"Well Sisyphus, we could use you, you want a job?" inquired Hercules.

"Might as well, I've got bugger all else to do."

"This is Theseus and Paris," Hercules indicated his colleagues, "and this," he said, patting the dog, "is Cerberus."

"Woruff," said Cerberus.

"Woruff, Woruff," said the other two heads trying vainly to keep up with the main one.

Sisyphus leaned over and stroked the dog, "Guess I've got you to thank for getting me out of this rock and roll life. I haven't been very nice to people and gods in general, but I love animals."

Cerberus looked sideways at him with the two other heads, wondering what exactly he meant by that.

"Oh, that's great, another one," said Theseus, voicing the dog's reservations. "Menelaus is really going to like this."

"So what's the job?" inquired Sisyphus.

"Come with us and meet the team, check it out for yourself." replied Paris.

XXV

THEY'RE OLD FRIENDS FOR A REASON

The scene in the amphitheatre was one of great strangeness. Thor and Camilla, noticing the deficit in the weaponry department, had commandeered everything available from their touring clientele in exchange for free ale at Andromache's place, the final figure to be added to Odysseus' expenses account of course.

The air was full of moving items, haberdashery of all descriptions had taken flight. Javelins crisscrossed the air above the amphitheatre as those thrown from east to west were intercepted, or more usually weren't, by those thrown from north to south. Large medicine balls made of lead and leather severely endangered the superstructure of the theatre by regularly impacting with foundation blockwork. Well balanced throwing axes whizzed through the atmosphere and, with an accuracy that would be hard to equal, missed the target every time, choosing instead to come to rest somewhere in the vicinity of Odysseus followed by, "Oops, sorry! He he he."

Discuses ricocheted from pillar to post, to seating area, to innocent bystander. Maces were whirled with such ferocious acceleration that had their chains broken, they would have been in danger of achieving escape velocity.

Cerberus, wanting to play Frisbee took a running leap at one discus and was mightily surprised to find it so hard and so mobile and rapidly let go of it as a significant number of teeth in number three head snapped and splintered.

Neoptolemus, the son of Achilles and donor of the discus, pissed himself laughing shortly before scaling a convenient marble pillar to escape the other two heads which, unlike number three, had fully intact and functional dental faculties.

Feeling somewhat deprived, Cerberus cocked his back leg beside the pillar and sniggered as the pillar, followed by a sizeable chunk of cornice and discus thrower, discovered and attained terminal velocity.

Paris looked at Theseus, sharing the unspoken consensus that if the situation were hopeless it would be an improvement. Both looked to Hercules, who grinned and pronounced, "Perfect."

"Perfect! Perfect!" exclaimed Paris, twice. "These twats couldn't hit a barn door with a banjo."

"This is true," said Hercules, "but as a diversionary tactic they could be very useful."

The four plus dog made their way to the refreshment tent, which was miraculously intact, and introduced Sisyphus to some of the team as they came to get refreshed.

Sisyphus, being older, knew most of them by reputation and some personally and decided to conduct his own introductions while Hercules, Paris and Theseus had a snack and a chat.

Sisyphus, sporting a large handful of vol-au-vents, canapés and coffee, wandered around watching the various attempts at martial training, stopping here and there to renew old acquaintances. "Hey, Oedipus me old mate, long time no see! How's your old man these days and your mum, Jocasta wasn't it? Or was that your wife? Well, same difference I suppose, anyway great to see you again, you're looking good."

Oedipus turned sightless eyes in the direction of the voice and scowled. "Who let you out?"

Tschunk! Tisch! Schwick!

"Oomfph! Eniff!" The distraction had left Oedipus open and his sparring partner had gone for it with a large stick, applying it first end on to the gut, followed by a damn good smiting to the back as he doubled up, rapidly pursued by a semi-circular cut back to the rear of the knee joint for a total collapse.

Oedipus lay on the floor trying to stare up. "Nice one Sis, now bugger off, haven't you got a rock to roll, or sommat?"

"Oops, sorry," said Sisyphus, "see-er-em-catch you later," he muttered, continuing on his tour of the amphitheatre.

"Ajax!" said Sisyphus waiting for him to turn, yes, both eyes intact. "Good to see you, how's life treating you?"

"Fine," grunted Ajax, "I'm a bit busy right now."

Swoosh! A large and dangerously spiky mace passed within an inch of his right ear and removed a substantial portion of shoulder pad.

"You'll have to excuse me."

"Okay," said Sisyphus, "how's the sheep farming going by the way?"

Ajax stopped dead.

Swoodunck!

The returning mace didn't and caught him right in the middle of his forehead severely denting his borrowed Viking headwear.

His sparring partner, Turnus, lifted his visor and glared at Sisyphus. "I could have taken him, you didn't have to do that!"

"Do what?" asked Sisyphus.

"That sneaky sheep thing."

"Sheep thing?"

"Oh," said Turnus, "you don't know do you? Well, after that Troy thing Odysseus won Achilles' armour from Ajax. The big guy couldn't take it, he went really hyper and took out a flock of sheep and goats, real commando precision, a joy to behold, clinical slaughter, never seen accuracy like it, bits of sheep all over the place there was. So - we don't mention the sheep around him, okay?"

Ajax came round mumbling. "Didn't mean it... Thought they were Trojans... Milling around they were... Taking the piss... I didn't mean it... It was an accident... misunderstanding... I wasn't well at the time."

"It's okay," said Turnus, "go and have a cup of tea and a sit down."

Turnus turned back to Sisyphus. "See what you've done? He'll be no good for the rest of the day now you prat, no sense of fair play, no social conscience!"

Sisyphus moved on rapidly to another face he recognised "Pyrrhus, how's it hanging? I heard about your old man, tough break."

Pyrrhus turned and hissed through his teeth. "Don't call me that. Round here I'm known as Neoptolemus." He pushed Sisyphus to a less populated part of the training arena. "Half the people 'round here haven't got any family left 'cos of my old man and it wasn't a tough break, Achilles was a twat he just kept on pushing it. He did bugger all but sulk when Agamemnon took that good-looking slave bird

Briseis off him and then when he got her back he didn't bloody want her anyway, so what's he do? He goes out and single-handedly blitzes two-thirds of Troy and gets himself shot in the foot. I didn't even know him, I came out here to see him at his job. You know? Surprise him like, and there he is already planted when I get here. Some father figure eh? Then I find the locals want to string anyone who had anything to do with him up. So I changed my name and moved here. So don't cock it up, I'm doing just fine okay?"

"Yeah, sure," replied Sisyphus. "Take it easy, see you later."

Bur-rup! Bur-rrurp! All heads turned at the call of the ram's horn, which sounded much like one would with the ram still on it, to see Odysseus, his longbow across his back and a quiver of arrows at his shoulder, standing three quarters of the way up in the high seats, well out of range of anything throwable. "Now that we're all here I'll give you an update on our mission, for mission is definitely what it is. You, the gifted, have been assembled here from far and wide to create a team that would be capable of taking on even the gods themselves. You are heroes, er, and heroine, of a calibre sadly no longer available in today's world. You are the best of the best…"

"We know all that bollocks!" shouted the voice of Neoptolemus.

"Yeah, you told us all this crap in the pub if you remember," added Perseus.

"Vividly." breathed Odysseus to his clerk and right hand man, who - having some slight inkling of what might be to come - was standing to the left and turned sideways to his boss, shuddering and stamping his feet with his arms clamped firmly across his belly, in a drastic attempt to conceal the maniacal laughter that was desperately trying to escape as visions of the aftermath of his employer's previous team chats flashed before his mind's eye.

"Yeah," bellowed Turnus, "an' where's our new coach and trainer?"

The clerk took a couple of stumbling side steps and collapsed down on to a rocky seat still holding his belly, his eyes streaming with the effort of concealing his hysterics.

"Aah," said Odysseus, "there's a slight technical hitch there, which will be shortly resolved, er, em, my assistant here has all the details which I'm sure he will be willing to share with you.

The clerk's hysterics were suddenly cured as he realised that the spotlight had just been cleverly transferred on to him. The devious git, he thought, nothing for it now but the truth.

The clerk got to his feet. "Well team, it seems that Jason is being held by Customs and Excise while they conduct an investigation into the contents of the Argo's cargo hold." said the clerk with a slight smirk and just a hint of a snigger disguised as a cough. "It seems that he had a little side deal going and the Customs boys are interested in why he was carrying a shit load of sheepskins and ready mixed gold leaf extract in handy aerosol cans. It's only a rumour of course but it seems that a few years back Jason met a seafarer who had been at sea for nearly ten years after doing something in the equestrian field. The seafarer told Jason that he knew of a place where he could make a real killing on the Golden Fleece market and de-stabilise the national bank in the process and for a fifty per cent share the seafarer would share his information. The seafarer, at present, is still unknown," he said, with a sideways glance at his boss, "and would probably be in deep do-do if Customs ever discovered his identity."

"Herrhawk, ufsnkh," spluttered Odysseus in a small choking fit. "Thank you that will be all for now, I'll take it from here." Then quietly to the clerk. "Haven't you got paperwork to attend to?"

"Eah?" said the clerk, equally as quietly. "No boss, finished it earlier today."

Odysseus gave him the kind of look that would make a cockroach flush with embarrassment at existing. "Best to find some more - now. Before you end up typing your own notice and pee-forty-five, get it?"

"Oh, oh yeah, I get you," said the clerk as the corners of his mouth began to twitch towards a smirk that was having trouble containing itself as a smirk. "So, Customs and Excise, that's the office five doors down from ours, right?" said the smirk, swiftly passing through puberty and growing up to be a grin of broad dimension.

Odysseus raised his arm with the intention of verily bestowing a right good forearm smash upon the clerk and the assembled team drew a collective breath and fell silent, ready to observe what was, obviously, their first serious training session.

Odysseus, caught like an axe murderer in a lightning bolt on a dark night upon the heath, stopped in mid smash and smoothed the clerk's lapels down and dusted his shoulders and muttered. "Take the rest of the day off, we'll talk about this tomorrow." As the clerk trotted off laughing raucously he added to himself. "Li'l bastard'll want a fucking partnership for this one."

Returning his attention to the team, he said, "What you have just seen here is an object lesson in how to obtain the opposition's undivided attention and hold it. That will be all for today, carry on men."

"Excuse me!" came the ringing tone of Camilla's voice.

"Eh, oh yes and lady too of course," said Odysseus, backing towards the exit as the crowd looked skyward towards a large and imposing shadow.

Schplatt!

The large and imposing shadow resolved into the figure of a large and imposing vulture which, if it had had a constipation problem, certainly didn't have anymore.

Odysseus shook a bedroppinged fist at the bird. "I'll get you for this you shit factory!"

"In your dreams pal," squawked the vulture, "Prom wants to see you pronto, awk, awk, awk."

The entire team were now rolling about in helpless laughter and Cerberus wondered whether he could make it to the exit in time to dump another surprise outside it. His heads had a quick conference and decided to reserve the option, no point straining oneself at this hour of the day the hound concluded.

XXVI

TITUS INFATICUS

Odysseus approached the abode of Prometheus with a certain amount of trepidation. In part at the thought of what exactly the gormless Titan might be requesting his presence for but, more immediately, with great concern for where that mouldy old aerial shit factory was. Vultures, he knew, were not really attack birds but this one had vintage far beyond what could reasonably be expected of any self-respecting scavenger. It had to be a millennium old if it was a day and it was a devious, obnoxious, sneaky, bastard and Odysseus hated it with a severe passion. He and the bird were too much alike to share the same planet, there must be retribution.

Odysseus decided to climb higher to get a better vantage point and a good view of the entrance to Prom's cave, somewhere all the better to spot a devious, obnoxious, sneaky, bastard from.

Meanwhile, the devious, obnoxious, sneaky, bastard was one step ahead and had already secured a similar vantage point to the one Odysseus was now looking for. From this vantage point, the vulture saw all.

It watched Odysseus scrambling around moving ever higher, it had noted the longbow earlier at the amphitheatre and had no intention of becoming a victim of aerial repercussions at the hands of this twat! The vulture circled round to a position that put the sun behind it and came to rest around sixty degrees uphill from Odysseus. It watched from behind as Odysseus settled himself and knocked an arrow on to the bowstring. Odysseus then reached into his satchel pocket and removed a dead rat which he threw towards the cave entrance. So that's how it is, thought the vulture. It looked Odysseus square between the shoulder blades and rasped, "Aaawwkkkk!"

"Shit!" muttered Odysseus, turning to locate the sound and seeing nothing but blazing sunlight. He shaded his eyes to get a better view and the vulture stuck its head up and stared him square in the eyes and winked at him. Odysseus loosed off an arrow and, just as the vulture had predicted, it fell short. Odysseus rapidly knocked another arrow on to the string. The vulture knew he wouldn't make that mistake again, even with the sun in his eyes and it came out into full view just a little higher up and capered around like a dancing puppet. As soon as it heard the creak of the tensioned bowstring it went ballistic, straight up and the second arrow hit the rocky face a split second after it vacated the position. Odysseus had the angle of inclination firmly locked in now, "dumb fucking scavenger!" he mumbled as he expertly withdrew and knocked the killer arrow to the bowstring.

There was a trickle of small rocks from the impact of the previous arrow which suddenly became a full-scale landslide. It engulfed Odysseus' vantage point and rapidly sent him sprawling downhill and rolling through relatively fresh cow shit and goat shit. He thrashed around frantically for anything to slow his descent and luckily his longbow snagged on the overhanging branch of a, well lightning roasted, dead tree. He dangled precariously over a cart left there by the park keeper, its contents were greenish-brown with threads of straw through it.

"Aaawwkkkk!" said the vulture from slightly higher up in the tree.

"Fuck!" said Odysseus from slightly lower down in the tree. The vulture dropped down a couple of branches and pecked a few times at the branch supporting Odysseus. "You scrawny carrion bag of horse shit," growled Odysseus, feverishly trying to climb hand over hand up his longbow.

"Horse shit for you!" said the vulture, giving the branch a final peck. The branch for its part gave a sharp crack and Odysseus plunged down into the waiting cart of horse manure. The wheel chocks dislodged with the impact and the cart took off down the hillside until one wheel hit a boulder. The cart flipped end over end disgorging Odysseus and sending him flying into the mouth of Prometheus' cave.

"Aahh Oddy," boomed Prometheus, "nice of you to drop by, even if you are stinking my cave up. Don't you ever take a bath?"

Odysseus looked up from his prone and crap covered location and said, "Fuck right off!"

"Now is that any way to greet your employer? You really have to work on your people skills in your line of work. Speaking of which, how's the team shaping up?"

"Pathetically would be a close approximation."

"Never mind, Jason will soon get them up to scratch."

"Aah, there's a slight technical drawback there," replied Odysseus.

"How slight?" inquired Prometheus, swelling menacingly to one and a half times his present ten feet.

"He's having a little difficulty clearing Customs, something to do with his cargo manifesto."

"Can't you sort it?"

"Er, it's a bit delicate if you catch my drift, I'd really rather not get involved."

"Sounds to me like you already are. Do I detect a hint if a little something on the side going on here?" said Prometheus reaching a stature of some thirty feet.

"Ehm, not exactly, it's very complicated and would take too long to explain," said Odysseus awkwardly.

"Oh, I see," mused Prometheus, "so by that, I take it, you infer that there is an explanation?"

"Oh yes, yes indeed," said Odysseus, in a relieved way, assuming he had evaded this one.

"Well?" echoed the voice of Prometheus. "It just so happens that I'm not too pushed for time this millennium, so let's hear it!"

"Umpghaa," came the reply, "er - ahem, it's difficult to know where to start exactly."

"Let me help you here," prompted Prometheus, "how about a shipwreck a few years back?"

"Shipwreck?" questioned Odysseus, trying to display cautious innocence.

"Yes of course, silly of me, not much of a clue, considering you wrecked so many. Okay, the one where you inadvertently lost all your crew and company and washed up on the beach at Argos."

"Oh," winced Odysseus, "that one."

"Yes, that one, where you met a young fresh-faced chap who had just taken out a hydra and was sporting a natty new Golden Fleece hunting jacket that looked like it might be worth a few bob."

"Aah, you know about that then?"

"Indeed, I do," said Prometheus, swelling ever closer to the roof of the cave, "and a good deal more."

"Well yes, I, er, may have happened to mention that I could find an outlet for such superb tailoring, er, if there was a way to get them to my lock-up. But if I did happen to mention it, it was only in passing, you know? A kind of offhand comment, like you do. I never really expected anything to come of it."

"So offhand that you left Achilles' armour as a deposit?" fumed Prometheus, "and sort of offhandedly signed a contract for forty thousand of them?"

"Look," pleaded Odysseus, "I didn't know he would be twat enough to try and ship the whole lot in one go did I?"

"Ship the whole lot in one go?" thundered Prometheus, "The whole forty thousand counterfeit Golden Fleeces that you may have happened to mention perhaps?"

"Er, yes," muttered Odysseus.

"So, it's your fault," raved Prometheus, "that the team doesn't have a coach? So now it's down to you," he said, stamping his size thirty Doc Martens and rattling the whole cave, "to finish the job and get these boys ready. You got that?"

"Yeah, but they seem to have taken a dislike to me," whinged Odysseus.

"Not half as much of a dislike as I'm about to take if you fail." bellowed the irate giant, raising his fist and thumping it down on an outcropping of rock, which crumbled and dislodged an extravagant amount of the roof, which hit him on the crown of his head rendering him unconscious just before his forty feet of bodywork hit the ground awkwardly.

"Time to leave." mused Odysseus, rapidly heading for the cave entrance and out into the sunshine.

Schplatt!
"Aaawwkkkk! Aaawwkkkk! Aaawwkkkk!"

XXVII

HERESY

Having watched half a day's training and done a little weightlifting himself, Hercules was satisfied that the team was going nowhere, Odysseus was a laughingstock and Jason, the new coach, was going to be detained for some time.

This, he considered, was just the right time to launch a takeover bid, which would leave Odysseus in charge and, forever in his debt. His plan was to get his lieutenants, who didn't know yet of their promotion, together and let them in on a few particulars. To which end they were all having a quiet drink in Cassandra's residents' bar.

Paris, Theseus and Sisyphus were having a few hands of poker and more than a few beers. Thor and Camilla were watching Cassandra farting about with the Ouija board which was predicting good profits for the evening and some possible Armageddon scenario involving sheep and gold on the stock market.

"Ladies and Gents," said Hercules. "We appear to be on the precipice of a new world order. We've all had a good dose of the gods at their playful worst and I don't think there's one of us who hasn't got good reason for wanting to get shot of them."

The assembly looked at each other. "Bloody hell, Herc," said Theseus, "don't you think that's a bit stiff?"

"Not at all These. They've been running it into the ground. Imposing dogmatic beliefs like fear, guilt, worship and inhibitions, making everyone work harder and endure hardship for the prospect of a happy afterlife that, rather like a company pension scheme, might exist when you need it. So what do you do when you get there and you find that there is none of either there? Ask for a rebate? Petition the gods? Fuck me, three-quarters of the population spends three quarters of its guilt-ridden life doing that. Saying prayers, going to services, offering sacrifices, being good, being kind, being nice, being faithful and why? Is it because they are good or kind or nice or faithful? Is it bollocks, it's because they're shit scared of the consequences that might be imposed by the gods they worship and sacrifice to if they don't behave that way. The same gods that are so good and so kind, the gods who gave them life and then let most of them spend it in a state of guilt while trying vainly to achieve a state of grace by working, worshipping, enduring hardship, plague, disease, acts of gods and general piss-taking by every divinity they choose to adore in blind faith. Let's face facts here, these gods are not exactly proving to be that good for us." At which point Hercules stopped for a breath.

Paris leaned back and crossed his legs on the corner of a table and drew a long breath. "Well, when you put it like that, you make a damn good point. Apart from the bit about them giving us life, I thought that one was true."

"Oh, come on Par. Every bloody religion that ever was or ever will be has a Prometheus guy fucking about with clay models. They all had a flood and a few plagues and a couple of miracles. All of them have got some kind of father and son set up at the top, one to take the flack and one to worship if you can't get on the good side of the flack-taker. Neither of them are about to actually consult with, so the masses wander about in blind faith believing that when the shit hits the fan there'll be a second coming to bail them out. The disasters get bigger each time they happen and the second coming never comes and they say, 'that's life'- bull shit! This is life, we make it, we run it and we cock it up. Well, I reckon it's high time we took the reins and drove our own boat."

"Wow!" said Thor, looking at Camilla, "some kind of heresy or what?"

"He's certainly on a roll," replied Camilla, "and from the absence of lightning bolts and divine retribution, I'd say he probably has a point."

"Yeah," said Sisyphus, "and he puts it across bloody well too, lacking a little perhaps in eloquence and finesse but definitely not short on direction or content, way to go Herc!"

"So what you're saying," struggled Paris, "is that all the plagues and floods and stuff weren't acts of the gods, right? Like they would have happened anyway, even if no one praised, or failed to praise, the gods?"

"That's a fair part of it," replied Hercules. "How did you meet Helen?"

"I went on one of those, avoid the duty on booze, cheapo trips to the continent and I saw her with a paper bag full of apples chatting to her girlie mates in a marketplace. Anyway, the bag burst and golden delicious rolled all over the place. Having drunk all the incoming duty-free, I offered the empty bag to put the apples in. They all picked up a few and put them in the bag and we got to chatting and she ended up coming back with me. Her husband was none too pleased though, but I was young and horny and we fancied the pants off each other."

"Right," said Hercules, "and as a result, Troy got a right good kicking."

"Yeah well, that's not my fault. I fancied a shag and she was game too!" said Paris defensively.

"Exactly," said Hercules, "That's how it went, you fancied her, she fancied you, but when the history books tell it, it'll get all distorted. You'll have stolen a princess after three goddesses in disguise promised you wondrous things, gave you golden apples and said, 'pick one', and the Troy deal will be divine retribution because you chose Helen instead of them and it'll all be the gods' fault."

"Right," said Paris, "when in reality it was just that the other three were, quite understandably, jealous and went and stirred the shit with her husband, who just happened to own an army. I couldn't win, could I? Whatever I chose there would have been three spurned women standing about in a pisser. I was the son of a king, I could have had anything they were offering anyway, all I did was fancy a gorgeous woman."

"Fuckin' 'ell," said Theseus. "You mean that there ain't no gods, we made 'em all up?"

"Sort of," replied Hercules, "I don't doubt that some force is behind the whole life syndrome but it's the same force for everyone, people personify it, make it like themselves but wiser. I mean, you went out and with extreme prejudice terminated a minotaur but you didn't do it because you feared some god or other, you did it because you wanted to impress a woman and get laid, didn't you?"

"Sure did," replied Theseus, "cost me a bloody fortune in divorce settlement and maintenance though."

Sisyphus looked uncomfortable. "Are you trying to tell me I spent aeons pushing that sodding rock up that sodding hill for sodding bugger all?"

"What did you say when I asked you what happened when you got it to the top?" asked Hercules.

"Buggered if I know," replied Sisyphus.

"Precisely, that's precisely what you said," smiled Hercules. "How many times did any God come and have a look or check that you were still doing it?"

"Er, now that I come to think of it, at least, never."

"But you still carried on, firstly because you feared the reprisal of some vindictive God but later because it became a thing of pride and frustration, you couldn't allow it to beat you, it ruled you by making you want to dominate it."

"So," said Sisyphus, "the more we aspire to find out what the gods are, the stronger their hold becomes?"

"That's about the size of it," replied Hercules. "The more that believe the stronger they get."

"Well if you know all this," queried Sisyphus, "what was the crack with all those bloody labours of yours?"

"Yeah well, I was young and impressionable then. I wasn't frightened of the gods but I did want to show them how good I was. However, after number eight I thought the gig was wearing a bit thin, you know? Like I'd performed eight gigantic humanitarian tasks and nobody seemed to give a toss either way, gods included. They just kept coming up with more labours. So, still having dedication to the tasks, like Sisyphus and his rock, I kept on performing but now I was looking for evidence of the godly hand in affairs.

I followed all the clues and everything led back to this king bloke called Eurystheus who reckoned Juno told him what to do. So I decided there and then that the whole thing was a crock of shit and I was going to get even.

Vindictive gods were one thing but a vindictive stepmother was another altogether. She's got to be stopped or every bloody stepmother that ever there was will be trying it on."

"Sounds good to me," said Theseus, wondering if he could extend the theory to vindictive ex-wives as well.

"So what about them two?" he asked, indicating Thor and Camilla, "why bring a couple of foreigners into it?"

"For precisely that reason," replied Hercules, "they are foreigners. Camilla gave up these gods and she's had a good look at Thor's bunch and she's worked it out for herself, right?"

"Right," agreed Camilla.

Hercules continued, "Thor has got no fear of our gods, he's got his own who he thinks much more formidable and, from what I hear, has had a pop at them on more than one occasion, right?"

"Dead on," confirmed Thor.

"So he's a sort of independent who can't be swayed or got at by our bunch."

"You're a clever, sneaky bastard Herc," said Paris, "but I like your style, I'm in, lead on Mac-Hercules!"

The joke went unnoticed as Shakespeare had not yet been invented to interpret it.

"Kick some divine ass eh?" said Thor. "I'm game."

Camilla said nothing but smirked crookedly and nodded.

Theseus looked at Sisyphus and shrugged. "Could be a laugh I suppose, beats sitting at home looking at the wife all night, I'll give it a go!"

"Okay," added Sisyphus, "I'll have some of that, let's face it, it won't be the first time me and a god had a difference of opinion. What about her though?" he indicated Cassandra.

"What about her?" said Hercules.

"Well, she's been here all the time, she knows too much, maybe we should neutralise her."

Cassandra spoke up. "You Sisyphus are not finished with rocks yet, get yourself a hard hat, there is much in the universe that you do not understand. There is more to being a prophetess than merely profiteering." The look in her eyes was glazed by more than wine and Sisyphus wisely backed off.

"Cassandra is trustworthy," said Hercules, "her prophetic power is unbiased. She may not wish to be with us but she is not against us, or we would not be meeting here."

"Thank you Herc, I didn't know you cared," said Cassandra mischievously and dished out more ale and drew Hercules to one side. "Attend to your wardrobe."

"What?" said Hercules. "Have I got another DIY Bank Holiday coming up?"

Cassandra continued ignoring the interruption. "Wear nothing that is not your own, Juno interacts with Sagittarius."

"Bloody hell Cassy, do you have to be so obscure with all this prophesying stuff?"

"I just tell it how I see it," she replied.

"So where do we start?" asked Paris.

"We take over the team," replied Hercules, "and get Oddy out of the shit but leave it looking like he's still in charge."

"Beware!" said Cassandra, "of Greeks bearing gifts."

"He's already done that one, you dopey bint," said Theseus.

"Yeah, and people never learn and history repeats itself," said the dopey bint.

XXVIII

MANAGEMENT RESTRUCTURE

The clerk looked up as Paris entered the Kings, Queens and various assorted royals department. "Aah yes, Paris of Troy and what can we do for you today?" he inquired, wisely declining to offer Paris a seat.

"I'd like to update my curriculum vitae," replied Paris.

"I wasn't actually aware that you had one," mumbled the clerk.

"There's an awful lot that you are not aware of!" growled Paris.

"Indeed?" said the clerk. "Item one, acute hearing, I suppose that could be useful, hardly the stuff of a high-profile CV though, what else? Furniture removal perhaps?"

"If I remember correctly," replied Paris pointedly, "I wasn't too bad at furniture re-delivery either!"

"Quite," winced the clerk in a visible manner, "shall we start again?"

"Smart idea," agreed Paris.

"Good morning Sir," began the clerk, "I understand that you wish to update your CV."

"That is correct," replied Paris.

"Just bear with me while I run through your details, now let's see. Aah, Paris, son of Priam, heir to the throne of Troy, presently unemployed. Previous experience includes attending the court of King Priam, advising on boudoir colour coordination schemes, looking good and womanising."

Paris glowed with pride, that certainly sounded like the Paris his people had come to know and love, especially the women who, if they flashed an accidental ankle in public, spent the following two months trying to fend him off, or more likely, attempting to introduce him to more of themselves once he had got the initial taste for them, in the forlorn hope that keeping him interested would secure marriage into royalty.

"So what would you like to add to this?" inquired the clerk.

"Well," said Paris, "it seems a shame to ruin a perfectly good CV but one must keep up with the changes in the employment market I suppose. Troy was, as you know, a very large city, well known, amongst other things, for its athletes and their martial prowess and their bi-annual games."

With a supreme effort, the clerk managed to stifle a snigger of derision. "I see and you, er, you were a regular participant?"

"I was indeed, mainly in the archery and bowman skills department. My real work was behind the scenes, organising equipment and prizes. Coaching the teams to a standard fit for competition. I kept the morale up and nurtured the team spirit, that sort of thing."

"I see," said the clerk, now somewhat more attentive, "and you were efficient in this capacity?"

"Efficient! Efficient? Bloody hell, when it came to proving it the boys gave a damn good account of themselves. Kept them Greek bleeders out there on the beach for a good ten years! I'll say I was bloody efficient and we would have come first if it hadn't been for some very sneaky, underhand, devious match-fixing," snarled Paris.

"Point taken," said the clerk, "and I suppose second place isn't that bad. Would you mind waiting here for a minute while I consult my section head?"

"No problem," replied Paris. "I take mine ground with two sugars and milk and a couple of digestives wouldn't go amiss either!"

"Excuse me?" said the clerk.

"What for?" said Paris.

"No I mean - aah, ah, nothing, would you like a coffee while you're waiting?"

Strange, thought Paris - how a language with one common root can become so confusing - as the clerk left the room.

"Hey, Oddy," called the clerk.

"That's Mr Oddy to you!"

"Well excuse me," replied the clerk with more than a hint of sarcasm, "but it just so happens that I have the answer to all your team problems."

"Oh, is that so?" responded Odysseus with equivalent sarcasm.

"Well, if you're going to be like that about it I'll just go and send him home," said the clerk with a flick of his head.

"Who?"

"Who what?"

"Who are you going to send home?"

"Only the one guy in the world who can get you out of the shit you've got yourself into after the, er, Jason incident," smirked the clerk.

"Don't push it pal," warned Odysseus, "what have you got?"

"Oh, nothing much," replied the clerk absently, "just the guy responsible for training the Trojan boys for their big one and, he's unemployed."

Odysseus felt like the clerk had a good hold on his scrotum and was rapidly applying pressure to it. "Hmmm," hummed Odysseus, perhaps a tad of an octave higher than he normally hmmmed.

"You sure about his credentials, public schoolboy, royal descent, institute memberships, etcetera?"

"Yes, yes," droned the clerk impatiently, "he's even got his own four by four chariot with optional twin hoof differential lock, roll cage, bull bars, tinted screen, quad sound system, two-ton winch and javelin rack; he's perfect, a gift from the gods and all that."

"I've had gifts from the gods before," said Odysseus suspiciously, "they have six hands, they give with one and take back forever with the other five."

"Look," said the clerk sternly, "the way I see it, you're two miles up and two fathoms under shit creek with no snorkel and no paddle. Put this bloke in the job, retain overall control and blame him if it fucks up!"

"Hmmm... I like it," mused Odysseus concluding that the clerk was going to have to meet with an unfortunate accident when this was all over, just to keep his delusions of grandeur in check.

"Okay, sign him up."

"Don't you want to interview him yourself?"

"No, not at present. If you wish to aspire to promotion it's time you took some responsibilities on. I'd like you to handle this one," replied Odysseus, firmly believing that if there was one thing better than having someone to blame, it was having two someones to blame. Backup strategy was always a good idea.

The clerk left mumbling, "Responsibilities indeed, who's he think runs this place, bollocks to a partnership, I'm having the whole fucking lot!"

Paris looked up from his coffee as the clerk re-entered the room and calmly re-seated himself. "It seems that we may have a vacancy to which you would be aptly suited," he began.

"More like grossly overqualified, I'd say," interrupted Paris.

"Er, yes, quite so but the post will require an exceptional ability to demonstrate transferable skills in a learning by doing environment, with possible job progression and an attractive company pension scheme."

"You mean," said Paris, "that it's a shit job, with shit pay, high mortality rate, little job satisfaction and applicants are few and far between and, because of the jam you're now in, anyone will do?"

"Oh, come on," pleaded the clerk, "I'm really trying here to conduct matters in a semi-professional, semi-civilised, with the appropriate level of protocol, manner. The least you could do is play the game."

"So sorry dear chap," replied Paris, "very crass of me. It sounds like an excellent position with low initial remuneration, leading to staged incremental increases dependent on proven practical abilities and results with a generous pension package should retirement age be attained while continuously employed in the service."

"Exactly," beamed the clerk handing over a job description which was all in small print. Paris, feeling a sneeze coming on and not being able to resist the temptation, let rip, "Aah, aahtishitjobyooh!"

The clerk raised one eyebrow and slanted a sideways glance at Paris. "Sign here please and present yourself at the amphitheatre at eight a.m. tomorrow; Odysseus will introduce you to your new colleagues on site."

Paris managed to get outside before hysterical laughter consumed him. Suddenly he was pinned against the wall and his face became very wet as three tongues lavished attention upon it. Paris lashed out viciously with his right foot.

"Gerrowtovit, ya dumb brute!"

"Eruff," *Sploshlashp!* Responded the dog, followed rapidly by "Eruff," "Eruff," *Sploshlashp! Sploshlashp!* The other two were improving, they were catching on quicker, synchronicity was closer.

"I guess you got the job then?" asked Hercules, applying his right hand to the scruff of Cerberus' collective neck and hauling him off Paris.

"Of course," replied Paris, "what did you expect? When are you going to get that pooch under control?"

"Aaw c'mon Par, he's…"

"Only a sodding puppy, I know," Paris interruptingly finished for him. "So what do I do now? Teach them to defend a fortress? Show them how to womanise?"

"Now," said Hercules, "you do nothing, just show up, get them going with a bullshit pep talk and let them carry on as they are."

"I thought the general idea was to train them," said Paris.

"It is," replied Hercules, "but not quite in the way that Oddy expects."

"So, pep talk? A bloody pep talk!" rasped Paris, "about what? What am I going to pep them up about?"

"The truth," said Hercules, "tell it to them straight. Whatever you say they won't believe it anyway but in the long run you'll get better results and more respect for the truth."

XXIX

A NEW BROOM

After making a supreme effort, which had Helen wondering if it might be a good time to call a priest or a doctor or a divorce lawyer or something, Paris presented himself at the amphitheatre at eight am.

The scene was much as it had been on his previous visit. The sun was partly occluded by the tea strainer effect of much aerial haberdashery and objet d'art. Horses and chariots were strewn about in odd places and anything that wasn't presently airborne was forming piles of twisted metal that closely resembled the contents of a bricklayer's tool bag.

Camilla and Thor were idly juggling snub-nosed hatchets between them in a clearing off towards the edge of the spectator stands. Ajax and Sisyphus appeared to be ten pin bowling with a lead medicine ball and some shop-soiled Viking helmets. Oedipus stood close to where Paris observed from, resembling something from a low budget, blindfold, martial arts production, designed to display swordsmanship. He ducked, turned, swirled, slashed, hacked, sliced and flowed with the lucid fluidity of a Spanish restaurant sink drain after a heavy night.

"Oy you!" raved Turnus, "why don't you watch what you're doing with that sodding thing? You'll have somebody's bloody eye out you will!

"Sorry," said Oedipus, "couldn't see you there."

"*Schkedunkh!*" spoke a substantial chunk of ex-chariot axle as Turnus shared one end of it with the blind ex-king.

"Prick!" he muttered, discarding the axle stub in the general direction of some innocent onlookers.

"Strike!" shouted Ajax as the innocent onlookers made like dominoes and imitated the domino effect. "Nice one Turn."

"Fuck off!" replied Turnus, hefting a fifty-millimetre soft-tipped javelin at a distant chariot which, micro-moments later, was sporting a hole the size of a match football.

"Bit touchy today, ain't he?" observed Sisyphus.

Gerdoynng! Gerdoynng! echoed a gong, the size of which would have impressed even Bombardier Billy Wells (look that one up!)

Odysseus stood even higher up than last time and considerably closer to the exit too. "I'll make this short as time is of the essence. Due to the pressure of work at my agency, I have been forced to re-deploy my own skills elsewhere and, while retaining directorship of you fine body of men, er, and woman, I shall no longer be operating in a hands-on capacity."

"Hooray!"

"Bravo!"

"Hear-hear, sod off!"

"'Bout bloody time too!"

Odysseus raised his hands for calm and quiet to return, which it did, shortly after a catapult full of bovine aftermath zinged through the air and impacted with his lower left jaw.

"Your new trainer and point of contact with the company has been appointed and I shall be leaving you in the very capable and professional hands of a man with a proven track record, a man known personally to most of you already."

Menelaus, feeling a heckle coming on called, "We don't want that serpent shagging twat Jason!"

Odysseus, ignoring the interruption, continued. "Lady and Gentlemen, I present Paris of Troy Land, recently re-assigned but extremely proficient at his job."

"An' what job exactly would that be?" shouted Perseus.

"Yeah," joined in Menelaus, "yeah," he said, for once lost for words, "er, um, wife shagger!"

Neoptolemus looked at him and said, "Well, it's a start, at least he doesn't shag animals."

"Oh, I wouldn't say that," responded Menelaus, reflecting briefly on his briefer marriage and suddenly shouting, "Cow shagger!"

Oedipus smiled and muttered, "Good old Menelaus, always on hand with some witty repartee."

Odysseus, in predictive mode, could instinctively feel where this was going and after finding himself attached to two more nuggets of a slightly younger vintage cow shit, looked round frantically for Paris while edging ever backwards.

Suddenly, very suddenly the air was split by a terrifying noise.

Gerdoynngfitzsputaireechzing!

The, bigger than anything Billy Wells every saw, gong, took on a molten appearance and more than a fair amount of topspin as it exploded in a shower of sparks and abruptly parted company with its retaining frame in a vaguely Odysseusward direction.

"Holy shit!" gagged Odysseus, who managed to duck just prior to achieving the second part of his exclamation, as the molten disc whizzed through the space that his head had, a split second previously, occupied.

The team turned as one to see a strikingly handsome figure standing atop a sheared off marble column holding a large gilded bow and a quiver full of hollow-point armour piercing arrows.

"Aah good," said Paris, "now that I have your attention - I don't think we'll be needing that anymore. I've never been in favour of working to the bell, flexibility and flexitime are so much more civilised concepts. For those who don't know, my name is Paris, son of Priam and I'm here to kick arse and womanise and, having mistakenly, perhaps, brought a wife along with me, one is well and truly taken care of. The other, however, has a wide and varied range of opportunities to offer and I could use your help in the pursuit of some of them."

"Bugger me!" said Menelaus.

"What, again?" queried Oedipus.

Menelaus ignored the honest question thinking it was a vague attempt at sarcasm and continued, "you gotta hand it to the cow shagger, he certainly knows how to make an entrance," he said, almost in admiration.

Odysseus, who was at that moment crawling through the fire escape exit with squelchy pants and the top of his head seared into scalplessness, thought the entrance was perhaps a smidgen over the top. He was torn between brewing retribution and relief that the teamwork thing was at last off his back. "He'll get his!" he mumbled to himself and scuttled off towards the Styx.

Hercules nudged Theseus. "Good start eh?"

"Not bad for a young un," agreed Theseus. "Got 'em in the palm of his hand he has. Let's hope he can follow it up."

Paris glowed with internal fire and enthusiasm, he was on a roll and he knew it. "The time has come for a full team meeting to sort out the rumours from the facts. I would like everyone who is not a team member to leave the amphitheatre and I would appreciate it if the team would assist in the evacuation and secure the entrances," declared Paris, knocking another high powered shaft on to his bowstring, just to impress upon all the seriousness of his intentions.

Within five minutes the only presence in the amphitheatre was that of the team. Paris, still standing on the column, levelled his bow at a large statue of Jupiter and let fly. The statue for its part, exploded into smithereens. The team stood motionless, a few remembered to close their mouths. Paris threw a double back full-twisting pike somersault and landed lightly on the ground behind the team and strode forward to the place where the attention was fixed and the statue used to be.

"I did that!" he announced, "not the gods, not any will or whim of the gods, me, I decided. I took aim and I blew it to bits. It was not the will of the gods that this should happen because they would have intervened had it been otherwise, it was the will of Paris that this should happen."

Hercules was impressed, the boy was good, he'd got the attention and he was keeping it.

"Now," said Paris, "we've all had our differences in the past and that's where we have to leave them. We have all fought wars against strangers, against foreigners, against each other. Sometimes pure chance placed us, individually or collectively, on the winning side. However, right there, we are faced with a very strange concept - winning. What exactly did we win? We lost our lands and were unhappy in those we conquered, we lost wives, husbands, lovers, families. We slaughtered whole generations, lost vast fortunes, lost the respect of others, even lost our self-respect - and that was when we won! So we declared a holiday, had a feast and praised the gods who had been so good to us! The same gods in whose name we went out and slaughtered our own kind because their gods were different. So what exactly, you have to ask yourself, did any of these gods actually do for you? They didn't fight the enemy, you did. You made the decisions. You executed the plans. You charted your own destiny. You formed the gods to fit your own ethics and even gave them human traits and characteristics, and why not? After all, you created them.

The ethics of war are the work of men in the name of a god they invented, the only tangible component of the whole setup is men and their kind."

The silence was complete, the information had sunk in. He continued. "Well, I think it's about time that humankind took stock. Stood up and owned up to the fact that nothing happens unless they make it happen and that when it fucks up, it fucks up because they fuck it up. It is not the Gods' fault that things go well or badly and praising them, or failing to do so, will make absolutely no difference to the outcome. If there is a god, it's everyone's and it's free. What we do here on earth, we do. It's about time we faced up to it and rowed our own boat on our own sea.

The gods have got to go and the people have to get in control, mankind needs to declare independence and live up to their own mistakes and fears."

Silence to the point of reverence reigned over the amphitheatre. Theseus leaned over to Hercules and said in hushed tones. "Doesn't seem to be following it up too badly I'd say."

Menelaus, overhearing the remark joined in. "If I'd known he had that kind of spirit, I'd have told him about Helen, I was only too glad to get shot of her. Poor chap," he added sympathetically.

Theseus grabbed Menelaus by the collar. "You fought a ten-year war for the bitch!"

"I know," he replied, "well, it was the lads down the pub taking the piss, wouldn't let a woman treat me like that, you gonna let that Trojan prat get away with that? What's up? Got no balls? All that sort of stuff has an effect when you're pissed up."

"So you had a ten-year war?"

"I just wanted to give him a boot up the arse, you know? Make a point, save face a bit but it got out of hand and we ended up having a decade of a kick-up over an ideal that never existed. The longer it went on the harder it was to pull out. By the end of it no one could really remember what it was all about even. Having a war became the reason for having a war and Achilles' little stint was the final straw. He threw a right wobbly over a slave girl my brother had taken from him and took it all out on the Trojans. Fuckin' hypocrites the pair of 'em, bloody married men both of 'em, screwing around on the side with the same bird. I mean, Achilles wasn't even one of ours, he was just the hired hippie hitman at the open-air rock concert, so to speak. Then I find out that it's all bullshit anyway, Helen wasn't even there she was in Egypt most of the time and, got such a bad name, due to the media coverage, for doing nothing. She met the guy she was supposed to be committing adultery with by accident. I mean, she was pushed into it really. It was all so dishonourable."

Menelaus by this stage was almost in tears. "We had a full-scale ten-year war, with all the associated atrocities, over bugger all. I'm with Paris, the guy's well cool. The gods stink and the whole war deal is a complete bag of shit! He's right all the way. War has no winners."

Theseus was visibly moved and released his grip on Menelaus' collar. Menelaus coughed and turned towards Paris. "Well spoken Paris of Troy Land. I stand beside you all the way. There have been too many atrocities in the names of gods, they have got to go!"

There was much cheering and hooraying about the amphitheatre, hats were thrown into the air, as were javelins, hatchets, pikes and the occasional dustbin, which was followed by a rapid expansion of the team formation to the outer reaches of the amphitheatre, as they all came back down again.

Paris held his hands up. "Friends, tonight we party, which may be the last one for a while, because tomorrow, at say eleven o'clock to allow for hangovers, we get serious."

XXX

WASHING IN A STYGIAN WONDERLAND

Odysseus trudged across the sun fried terrain with the relentless sunshine aggravating his epidermally depleted pate and encouraging the rising aroma of drying shit, both his own and that of some accursed cow. Why the hell was that thing invented to be so hot just when you needed it least, being one among two of his tortured thoughts. The other being, what the fuck was the team's fascination with throwing shit at him, what had he ever done to them? Collectively as a team he had been a good director of proceedings where they were concerned. It was those old school wankers, they were the problem, harbouring grudges that were pure misunderstandings to the average sociopath. They were all things that should be long forgotten over a pint somewhere. Let's face it, wasn't his fault that the bastards were too tight to buy him a beer and apologise for his shameless use of them as human resource. You can't run an employment agency without a solid HR structure. There were KPI figures that had to be performance managed and pursuant disciplinary measures to be imposed regardless of any defence offered by an employee. The figures didn't lie, the figures never lie. Apart from when the wrong questions are asked in order to obtain the results that the figures were invented to elicit, as a method of sacking the inadequate with a provable disciplinary record based on the figures. They were too stupid to know that, only he, Odysseus, the boss knew that. They were heroes for fuck sake what did they know about running a business, brainless cattle fodder with a life expectancy far shorter than would allow them to ever be engaged in the process. They were supposed to die in service not create workforce control issues. Bloody hell, give them an inch and then what? Holidays, sick leave, paternity leave, equal rights, equality and diversity, differentiation, wages? Where would it end? They'd never be happy, they were there to be herded and they just didn't understand that death in service was in itself its own reward! Sod them, they weren't his problem now, that glamour boy from Troy could deal with them and he would step in at the end and steal the glory and the financial benefits and run the lot of them through the disciplinary procedure and sack them for gross negligence.

Such were the thoughts occupying Odysseus while the sun seared his head further. He reached the river and doused his fiery bonce in the cooling waters. Aaah, blessed relief, pure cooling bliss but it was curtailed by a skeletal hand yanking him up by what little hair he had left. Odysseus screamed in pain, "you twisted sack of bones, haven't you got some dead to bugger off and ferry?"

Charon raised his scythe in a menacing manner and slowly drew the point across Odysseus' burned and weeping scalp. Odysseus let out a high-pitched wail of agony. Charon realising that the message was not getting through adopted a tactic that he was beginning to feel at ease with, he spoke. "Pay up you tight arsed twat." Charon was not a ferryman of many words, in fact in the present circumstances he wasn't even much of a ferryman and he was bored shitless and looked forward to Odysseus' visits.

Odysseus found to his disgust that Charon, due to the wrecking by a large boulder of his newest boat, had recently doubled the sewage and supply charges for his stygian produce.

"Bugger it, buggering bugger it," mumbled Odysseus to himself, "covered in shit again, laughingstock in public, scorched, blistered and now, this over boned-xylophonic-washboard, wants double the clean-up charge. What else can possibly happen to the same guy in the same day?"

Providence, that's what can possibly happen and, the inevitable results of tempting it, as became blatantly obvious to Odysseus when, while trying to examine his scorched craniums reflection in the stygian waters, a large voice boomed, "Oddy me old mate." It was a voice that boomed from the vicinity of twenty feet up.

"Oh balls!" replied Odysseus, "and I thought I was already having a bad day."

The giant downshifted a few spatial gears and came to a halt around two feet taller than Odysseus would be when he stood up. "Sharp hair cut man." started Prometheus.

"Piss off!" responded Odysseus without turning. "Seeing you hasn't improved my day so far. What do you want?"

"Just thought I'd check on the team's progress," said Prometheus.

"The team," growled Odysseus. "The team, the sodding bloody team, that's all anybody wants to talk about these days, team this, team that, team the other. The team is fine, absolutely unequivocally top-notch, ay number one, ready for action, tip-top and splendid. Now go away!"

"And the Jason business, resolved?" inquired the giant.

"Yes dammit, the Jason business is resolved."

"I see, and he is a good coach?"

"I haven't got the bloody foggiest idea," snapped Odysseus, "I sacked him, he's finished, he's out, his behaviour in public was a disgrace, totally unacceptable for such a high-profile position."

"Oh!" said Prometheus, "I really wanted him on the team."

Odysseus sprang round glaring, snorting like a bull. "Now look here you overstuffed bird feeder," he snarled as the sun glinted off his blistering pate, "you put me in charge. I say he's de-selected then he's de-selected, okay? He's out, got it? Now fuck off!"

Prometheus swelled a little and inquired. "So who's training the team?"

"If you're so bloody interested, why don't you get your arse down to the amphitheatre and see for yourself, thank you and goodbye!"

"I think I'll do just that," replied Prometheus, patting Odysseus firmly on the head, a number of times and then wiping the resultant burst blister fluid and secondary layer of skin on Odysseus' shoulder and giving him playful slap on the cheek, "not today though, I'm on my way to meet some old smoking buddies for a bit of a session."

"You bastard," screeched a once again agonised Odysseus, "You evil fucking over-inflated fucking bastard."

Charon appeared to be rattling uncontrollably like a bamboo wind charm in the desert breeze. It was a sound never before heard on the planet, it was the sound of the river Styx's ferryman pissing himself laughing so much that he pissed in his own river – for free!

XXXI

OF GODS AND MEN

As with everything that the semi-divine, as they refer to themselves, do, a bit of a session was a somewhat over the top affair, especially when one has not partaken of a joint in well over a millennium. Stoned would be an wholly inadequate description of the state of mind and body achieved at one of these get-togethers, as would, completely and utterly fucking shit faced to the point of cardiac paralysis, but that would be a little closer in descriptive terms to what Prometheus and his smoking buddies were capable of or, with hindsight, what they were incapable from.

Prometheus emerged, two days later, from a mountain that most mortals were regarding as an inert volcano that had suddenly re-discovered magma activity. Bilging plumes of smoke issued at erratic intervals from a number of flank vents and parasitic cones as exhalations of smoke rings were created during joint toking games. Minor tremors occurred due to stoned titans with the munchies tripping over a variety of beer cans, bongs and broken coffee tables on the quest for anything that might still be contained in the fridge or kitchen cupboards. Whether fungally challenged or not it was edible, the attachment of fungus could only add to the enjoyment. Clouds of steam rose from other vents following tremor producing stumbles in search of a place to have a pee because the energy required to actually get to the toilet, lift the lid and pull the chain was just too much hassle man! Having a piss in the magma chamber, it was considered, would attract too much attention at the crater top and might lead to a drug squad raid! Besides, the rest of the place felt cold after you'd been there and that ruined the well-deserved effects of the endeavour.

Reality and a few other states had merged into total symbiosis after a session that would have taken care of the complete gross national product of certain regions of Colombia for a decade, even at the grossly overestimated proportions put forward by many a metropolitan police force with regard to quantity and street value.

Prometheus' left eye had moved so far in cross-eyed that he could see from his right ear hole and his right eye was still frantically searching for anywhere to look out of. His voice seemed to emanate from somewhere in his lower colon which, in the opinion of many of his acquaintance, should be regarded as the point from which he usually spoke and therefore probably no discernible difference would be evident to the average listener, if they could be bothered to listen.

He looked back into the volcano and addressed his similarly conditioned - but wiser and not making any attempt at mobility save for origami with cigarette papers - buddies. "Shit's gone to hell these days, I remember when you could get a good buzz off a few joints of Colombian. Now it's cut with anything that looks like a plant. In fact, the nearest some of that stuff ever got to a plant was being the price tag on the plastic bag at the garden centre. Quality control's gone to hell, you got to smoke so much just to get a hit these days."

"Yeah man, cosmic!" came the reply from a hole in the side of the volcano.

"Gotta split anyhow, gotta check out the team, see if they're managing okay without me," he said, tripping over a badly scorched oak tree that his right ear hadn't spotted and totally destroying fifty acres of vineyard in the ensuing stumble.

"Yah ya dumb fuckin' shithead!" came the voice from the volcano, "see ya in a couple a thousand years."

The vineyard proprietor looked on in dismay and toddled off to instigate a talk with his insurance company about acts of gods. He had a funny feeling that he was in for a year of small print and general dodging of the issue under any pretence to the point where, due to lack of funds, he would probably decide to cut his losses and declare bankruptcy.

He knew that one could not insure against every eventuality just as well as he knew that there would be a paragraph that indemnified against all risks except where an act of god could be invoked as a reasonable defence and that the scenario of a shit-faced giant of divine descent walking on your grapes, more than likely featured in the act of god parameters.

He knew that a flood was not a shortcoming on the part of local authority to invest in flood defences, it was an act of God that was an uninsurable risk. He knew that a plague of locusts was not a shortcoming of the genetic manipulation corporation, the same corporation that introduced terminator genes to ensure future profits, it was an act of god that was an uninsurable risk. He knew that a drought was not the fault of passive town planning that ensured water flow in the town and bugger the farmers that fed the town, it was an act of god that was an uninsurable risk. Along with infestation, tornadoes, whirlwinds, tidal surge, lightning-induced fire, hailstones and Armageddon, all of this he knew. Yet even in the face of all he knew, all that he had paid his insurance premium for, he was still prepared, or pre-programmed, to give more money to the 'phone company, the mail company, the solicitors, the lawyers, the barristers and eventually the church, in the vain and futile hope that he might not actually know what he knew.

He was an independent man who rowed his own boat and, like so many before him, due partly to poor physical design, spent most of his time rowing in one direction while looking in the opposite one. The result of this gave an excellent hindsight view while giving absolutely no vision ahead. This was by design. Those who were in the ahead territory did not want the common man, or the farmer on whom all relied for food, seeing what they were putting round the corner for them loosely disguised as an act of god. This was a state of mind that was to be gracefully passed down the generations from father to son, from mother to daughter and from politician to politician. The best way to proceed was to look the other way while fully believing that you were looking forward!

Prometheus, proceeding in much the same manner but looking sideways, headed for the amphitheatre.

XXXII

COMET CAPERS

The scene in the amphitheatre had undergone a severe metamorphosis. Order had somehow been dragged kicking and screaming from the previous chaos. Javelins stood in racks six abreast, swords stood hilt up in slotted stone blocks, axes, cleavers and machetes dangled from overhead rigging, braziers stood at regular intervals and horses and chariots were ranged along the edge of the spectator stands.

Javelins cut through the air four abreast almost in unison and cut through targets with a single thud. Throwing axes, knives and hammers removed moving targets from mid-air with deadly accuracy and were intercepted by other team members before hitting the ground.

Paris was impressed with his team. He had done nothing and the whole thing had just come together perfectly.

So far as martial prowess was concerned his team was hot, it could fight its way in, or out, of anywhere, Olympus included. It was time to have another pep talk.

He strode towards the centre of the amphitheatre and all training stopped as the team came to attention.

"You people," said Paris, "are ready for any eventuality and it is now time to brief you on the object of your mission. The mission is to take out Mount Olympus and demonstrate the fallibility of the gods. Battle plans and strategies are something you are all expert in. What we don't know is what we will find on Olympus. If our theories are correct, we will find bugger all. If not, we will find gods and you will be tested to the limits of human endurance. To combat this eventuality, we have Hercules and Thor whose reputations for battling with gods precedes them and Sisyphus whose reputation for deceiving the gods precedes him. In the eventuality of an existent gods scenario, these three will formulate all strategies. Any questions?"

"What about the horse shagger?" asked Menelaus.

"Odysseus," replied Paris, "has been observing in what he thinks is secret, from a distance over the last two days. I have fed him the appropriate bullshit about discipline, power structures and strategy and left him believing himself to be fully informed. Odysseus does not figure in our plans and will be dealt with at the conclusion of our activities."

This was met with large amounts of cheering and roars of approval which subsided swiftly at the sound of some equally large crashing noises outside the amphitheatre. Everyone armed themselves and ran for the upper perimeter wall in the direction of the destructive sounds.

They watched in amusement as the figure of Prometheus stumbled through a fifty-acre vineyard and more or less decimated it just prior to arriving on the banks of the Styx.

He stopped, remembering his kerb drill and looked right, because that was about all he could do, before proceeding. The first size twenty-five Doc Marten splashed down sending tidal waves, the likes of which Moses would have been proud to pass between, in both directions. The second was not quite so well placed and snagged on a large rock that appeared to have the remnants of a boat trapped beneath it.

Sisyphus sniggered. Prometheus didn't, he instead, fell headlong over the obstructing rock, craning his neck round frantically so that his right ear could see. All it saw was the ground coming up rapidly and the entrance portal of the amphitheatre as it interacted, due to gravitational forces, with the upper right side of his head and bestowed upon him unconsciousness.

Sisyphus slid down the inside of the wall like a total basket case in fits of laughter.

"Nice one Sis," said Hercules, "I'd recognise that rock anywhere."

"Me too," agreed Theseus, "but that twat didn't."

"You'd think the dumb prat would stick to a smaller body when he's shit-faced," smiled Hercules, looking into the vacant eye sockets that had come to rest two feet from him on the upper rim of the amphitheatre.

"Guess he'll be sleeping there for a bit then!" concluded Paris with more than just a hint of disgust. "Tosspot!"

Zizzsspit!

Perseus looked round, he'd sort of half heard, half felt, the sound.

Zizzsspit!

He looked at Oedipus. "Did you se - ah, hear that?" he asked.

"What?" said Oedipus.

"That, 'Zizzsspit!' noise."

Zizzsspit!

"What, that, 'Zizzsspit!' noise?"

"Yes," said Perseus.

"Yes," said Oedipus.

"What do you reckon it is?"

"Haven't got a clue," replied Oedipus.

"Sounds ominous to me." interrupted Thor.

Zizzsphut!

Which was followed by a puff of acrid smoke from the amphitheatre floor. Oedipus sniffed and turning to Perseus said. "D'you drop that you smelly bastard?"

"Looks ominous to me," said Thor.

"What?" questioned Oedipus, "a fart so thick you can see it?"

Zizzsspit! Zizzsspit! Zizzsphut!

The team ran for the centre of the amphitheatre holding shields above their heads. Craterlettes puffed smoke around their feet as mini meteorites impacted with the ground. Paris grabbed a stout pole and began to play baseball with the incoming cosmic rubble which was now large enough to be seen.

Thor, deciding that this was most definitely ominous, followed suit.

Oedipus bumped into a fallen column and deduced that the best place for him was under it.

As the meteors increased in size they also increased in frequency, calling for the use of much stouter poles for the deflection operation.

Ajax and Neoptolemus whirled large, hardened tungsten, rapid sweep maces about their heads and, more by accident that judgement, succeeded in smiting many a medium-sized meteor into smithereens and showering each other with red hot fallout.

Camilla was a windmill of double-headed, twist grip, pump-action axes, shattering anything, whether meteor or not, that came into her airspace.

Thor stood on the stump of a pillar and, with the aid of his fully reversible, thirty-pound, rotary vibrating, recoilless, titanium, cross-faced hammer, vaporised all passing interstellar debris.

Turnus and Perseus crouched at the top rim of the amphitheatre, opposite the still unconscious Prometheus, transferring direction and inclination to Sisyphus, Menelaus and Paris, who were loading and firing twin one hundred-millimetre, armour piercing catapult slugs at the larger meteorites.

The atmosphere was a blaze of pyrotechnics as meteors of every shape and velocity were split, re-split and shattered into harmless, though rather hot, pebbles. The intensity of the shower lessened to be replaced by an eerie calm. Everyone was on full adrenaline charge, with the possible exception of Oedipus, as the silence fell across the amphitheatre. It was all over, but it didn't feel right.

Turnus and Perseus watched as the horizon became a red glow reminiscent of the rising sun, which they both considered unlikely as they were looking at the horizon behind which the sun had set scarcely two hours previous. The glow glowed more and something that appeared a damn sight larger than the sun came into view with a low, grating, rumble.

"Judas H fucking Jupiter!" pronounced Turnus, as a comet, which had recently had an interaction with a stray celestial mop bucket, bore down upon them. Perseus turned towards the assembled team, "this one's a real bastard, we're fucked!"

Hercules strode forward brandishing a club the likes of which would have left the above-average Cyclopes embarrassed and desperately searching for toilet paper.

Charon watched in amusement from a collapsed giant's length away and a smile crossed his fleshless jaws as he filled a bucket with grade one Stygian effluent and marched in a clickity-clackity way towards the head of the floored titan. Completely unnoticed, Charon ascended the outer staircase to felled giant's ear elevation and lifted his bucket.

Hercules stood on the parapet wall of the amphitheatre and hefted his club in a couple of practice swings. All the angles were correct, the only variant was the incoming velocity, which Hercules judged to be very bloody fast.

The comet now filled his field of vision and with a Herculean effort, for this was something he was particularly good at, he swung the club twice around his head and on the third sweep brought it upward with irresistible force. The impact jarred the whole amphitheatre, cornices crumbled, pillars pitched back and forth and the whole team collectively closed and squeezed hard on their exit sphincters. Charon wobbled on the staircase and dropped his bucket straight into the slumbering giant's ear.

Hercules pushed upwards on the end of his club, which rapidly became fused to the underside of the comet and carried him, from his position on the parapet, across the amphitheatre. He let go and landed lightly on a collapsed column which swiftly gave way - to the sound of, "Ooofyaclumsyfuckingit! Somebody's going to knock the stars out of you one day," - and crumbled down on top of the hiding Oedipus.

Prometheus jerked his head up at the shock of having two gallons of double the price, ice-cold, Stygian filth deposited in his sightless ear and collided with the passing comet, giving it a five-degree elevation of deviation from its recently club deviated elevation and securing for himself an Odysseus style haircut in the process, along with a rapid return to unconsciousness.

The comet, for its part, with club intact, adopted a new vector. It headed upward, which was good, and north east, which wasn't. Well, that is, not from the point of view of a certain mountain, reputed to be the home of the gods, which lay two miles northeast of the amphitheatre at an elevation of five degrees.

The team, having released what was in most cases a successful collective sphincter contraction, now held a collective breath as they watched the comet depart.

The grating rumble diminished and the air became still and calm. The collective carbon dioxide laden breath was ready to return to the atmosphere when it was abruptly blocked by a collective sharp intake of breath as, very suddenly the view exploded into a shower of sparks and jagged pyrotechnics interspersed with flying rock and debris, the like of which Krakatoa would struggle to emulate.

The double collective breath returned to the atmosphere which, as the afterglow bore testament to, now contained a fair proportion of the upper third of Mount Olympus.

"Oops!" said Hercules.

"Yeah well," said Paris, "it's not an exact science! Fancy a beer?"

"Don't mind if I do," replied Hercules. "We'll check out the damage in daylight."

Cassandra, in a preminitionary kind of way, had twelve brimming flagons already pulled and on top of her residents' bar.

XXXIII

DEUS EX MACHINA

The grove of Druids in Stonehenge had called in reinforcements. This was to be a momentous occasion and no expense had been spared in hiring a minibus to assemble head Druids from Scunthorpe to Cornwall in the hallowed Druid cathedral.

They were dressed ceremonially but not ostentatiously. The leaf or acolyte wore grey robes symbolising their formlessness but readiness to learn. The branch, who knew a bit more about which way to face when having a piss in windy outdoor conditions, were in green. The trunks, who knew everything that the previous two knew, plus how to bend natures gifts toward their own fulfilment, dressed in white and due to a lack of faith in washing powder products were barely discernable from their grey-clad subordinate but equal comrades. The roots, whose accumulated knowledge spanned the panoply of all previous levels with the addition of a vast treasure trove on local disabled parking by-lore, wore brown. The Archdruid, who knew everything that all the rest knew and had the upper edge on the metaphysical transposition of matter in post-modern travel agency, was resplendent, though not in any way overstated, in gold!

Stonehenge was an amazingly complex piece of machinery on the grandiose scale. It had no moving parts and operated on the combined power of earth lore concentrated through the psychic collective of the grove awareness by the impresario that was the Archdruid. Its purpose was to move celestial beings between dimensions. It was the interstellar tube train of the gods.

Deep in the lower than lower bowels of Stonehenge on a Sunday evening a bunch of druids farted about with a collection of vibrations and frequencies, while endeavouring to modulate an omnipotence carrier wave.

"Okay," said Barney the gold-clad, the head Archdruid, to his assembled acolytes, "this one's important, so let's get it right."

"Yeah yeah," mumbled an acolyte leaf called Kewistopher, "they're all bloody important."

"I heard that," pointed out Barney the gold. "This one's real important okay?"

"Why?"

There was heard a fizzling sound followed by a medium pop and the time-space reference point, which had contained the questioner, became vacant as a collection of free-falling atoms, which represented the acolyte Kwiestopher, dispersed into the aether. In keeping with the tenets of Druidism the sacrifice was totally painless, though did leave a bit to be desired on the willingness issue. Presumably, had he not been willing he would not have been so stupid as to question the received wisdom of the gold at such an auspicious event.

Barney the gold turned to the remaining acolytes. "I need not explain but I shall. We are conducting an omnipotence transit exercise. The clients are Jupiter and his missus, who really don't need the service but she paid for the full five-star supernova treatment and we are going to ensure that they get value for money. Need I remind you what happened last time?"

"Mumble Lott, mumble wife, mutter salt." came the less than enthusiastic response.

"Yes," said Barney the gold, "that's right, the Sodom and Gomorrah incident, of which we don't want a repeat. So let's get these folks from Alpha Centauri to Olympus without incident. Any questions?"

Having sniffed the air and noted the peculiar aroma created by the mixture of incinerated hair and vaporised skin and bone and, having glanced sideways once or twice to a place that used to be occupied by one of their number, nobody had any questions. Acolyte Woderwick said lightheartedly. "You mean we best not fuck up?" This, as it happened, turned out to be a question which, in the light of current circumstances, was an unwise move, as the ensuing fizzle and pop went some way towards, painlessly and yet again by way of stupidity, willingly, pointing out.

"Incidental bilateral flutter on low-frequency conduit, now stabilising," announced branch in green Woddeny.

"Assume your positions," ordered Barney.

"All systems nominal," asserted Woddeny.

"Temporal inter-dimensional transit helix established." said trunk, in off white-could-have-been-grey, Hawold.

"Angular momentum time shift conservation confirmed," intoned root in brown Percy, whose parents did not suffer from the speech impediment that afflicted other members of the grove's parents.

Barney stood at full attention. "Elevate the ring of the third parallax integer of the root and initiate retro by-pass to vernal equinox - now!"

The ensuing silence was absolute and petrified as the assembly of potential free-falling atoms awaited the outcome of their efforts.

"Well done gentlemen, a complete success," announced Barney.

Acolyte Archibald, with the same similarly un-afflicted parentage as Percy, seeing that the tension was now relieved, decided that now would be the correct time to ask questions and raised a tentative hand.

"Yes Archibald," said Barney the gold.

"Why do we retro to the vernal equinox?"

"Well," said Barney, "you know what it's like up there on midsummers night, wall to wall arseholes, pissed up hippies and bikers, stoned pseudo druids, police squads, weirdos and psychologically disturbed individuals. Also yes, I know that the dividing line between the last three is somewhat of a grey area. Nevertheless, too much interference. That's what happened on the Sodom and Gomorrah transit. We ended up with two shit-faced hippies caught in an inverted temporal vortex between dimensional flux fields and one very pissed off deity blowing fire and brimstone at all and sundry. So we use the midsummer angular vector because it's the most powerful and retro by-pass to the previous vernal equinox because there's never anybody about topside then."

"Oh," said Archibald, who had lost the thread somewhere between mid-summer and psychologically disturbed. However, being a bright lad, living with the ever-present possibility of becoming a fizzling pop, he concluded that he knew as much as he needed to know of the accumulated knowledge of the Druid grove at his present level and that there was nothing to be gained by pushing one's luck.

XXXIV

STRATEGIC WITHDRAWAL

"Well," said Juno. "That was really rather fun, we must do it again some time." Jupiter stood there and said nothing, he just looked while Juno faffed about with the luggage. He couldn't believe his omnipotent all-seeing eyes. Juno picked up two suitcases and turned round.

"Oh!" she gasped, dropping the cases.

"Ow," he groaned, extracting his flip-flopped right foot from under one of them.

"Alright," hissed Jupiter, "so where's the bloody house gone?"

"I'm sure I don't know dear, I thought I left it here," replied Juno, "look, there's the loo!"

"Oh, oh well that's a start," grunted Jupiter, "at least we can still have a crap then!"

"Now now, calm down dear, there'll be a perfectly ordinary explanation."

"Explanation! Explanation! Bloody hell woman, half the shagging mountain's missing. What exactly did you tell the builders to do?"

"It wasn't much, just knock out a wall and a window, the rest was all cosmetic. Don't worry dear I'll sort it all out, you go and do a bit of fishing and relax a while. I'll attend to this lot."

Jupiter did as his wife suggested, after all, he was still in holiday mode, no point getting wound up - yet!

Juno picked up the cases and headed towards the great hall and upon entering it decided that, great ha…, would be a better description, seeing as it only appeared to be half present. The left-hand side, which lay along the east west axis looked good right up to the point where the gothic arches on the second row of pillars intersected with the roof ridge. At this point the great hall stopped being a hall and became the great outdoors. The whole right-hand north elevation was gone, the arches just stopped overhead in an overhanging, fused, stub that resembled the side of a cow after a visit to the butchers, but larger.

At the far end two figures were frantically chipping away at a large spherical rock and a chain of labourers from the underworld were removing the pieces in wheelbarrows.

For the second time that hour, Juno dropped the cases, though with the 'chink' of fracturing duty-frees this time and stomped to the far end of the hall.

She glared at the two builders, who swiftly realised that their best was probably behind them, or not to be at all.

"Fuck me Rameses," she stormed, "I just wanted the cross wall out, a window in and a few arches, look at the fucking state of this place! I can't leave you alone for a minute, can I?"

Cheops stayed in the background feigning invisibility and let Rameses absorb the full impact of the less than amused queen of the gods. "You're just a pair of bloody cowboys, pyramid builders my arse, you two wouldn't be safe on the beach with a bucket and spade, if you're responsible for the pyramids I'm surprised the apex didn't miss itself by a good forty feet. Now get this shithole cleared up and bugger off and expect to receive the full range of contract penalty clauses regarding completion dates."

"Aaha," said Rameses, "if I may interject, we er, did complete on time and then this here sodding comet breezed in and it er, well as you can see," he indicated the truncated arches with a sweep of his right arm, "took out the sidewall, er, and the columns, er, ahem, and the, er, roof and you will, er, perhaps recall that the damages waiver, er, on the Rameses and Cheops Limited, Builders to the Gods, contract does, ah, specifically exonerate us from any damages or liabilities relating to er, acts of gods and er, or natural phenomena."

"Oh, I see," glared Juno, "and what does it say about acts of goddesses? Especially very pissed off ones who are standing in their devastated houses looking for a cocky cowboy builder to blame?"

"Aaah, it er, it doesn't exactly cover that particular eventuality now that you come to mention it," replied Rameses, moving to a position rearward of Cheops and pushing him forward.

"Look Ju," said Cheops, "it's all a big mistake, it could happen to anyone. Just let us get this out and a few acrow-props in, couple of R.S.J.'s, a few picture windows and a lick of magnolia, it'll look great! The conservatory of the future, we can even do it in U.P.V.C., no maintenance, if you want, it'll be great for the tomatoes and herbs."

Juno - arms folded, foot tapping and a facial appearance that could hammer nails into granite - glared.

"Oh, great, that's just fucking great, that's just what I fucking need, a north facing fucking sun house!"

"Aaw, c'mon Ju," chided the builder, "you're just upset, go freshen up after your trip and give us a couple of hours here, things'll look much better then, you'll see."

Juno subsided and turned toward the loo. She stomped off, head held high and a handful of steps later she halted in mid-stomp to wipe stringy sticky stuff off her face. She couldn't see it but she could feel it and as quick as she wiped it off, more of it clung to her. She waved her hands ahead of herself, but the invisible sticky string work still attached itself to her face. Spotting one of the kids she called out, "Diana?"

"Hi Juney," replied Diana, "Good holiday?"

"Excellent, though the homecoming leaves a little to be desired."

"Meaning what?" sighed Diana, getting her facial gears lined up for the blank look induced by the - you never tidy your room, or wash up, or iron, or think - sermon that she suspected was just about to be preached.

"Well, the hall's wrecked, the builders are twats and your old man's going to go ape-shit when he sees it, which will probably result in his flattening the rest of it and there's all this invisible stringy stuff everywhere."

"Ah," said Diana, aborting the facial gear alignment. "The sticky stuff I know about."

"I suppose you and your brother Pol have been down Virgil's joke shop again?"

"No no, Apollo's out having a beer with some woman, Niobe I think. It ain't half winding the old lady up," replied Diana.

"Latona and Niobe go way back," said Juno, "feud being brewing there for a bit really. Anyhow, what about this sticky stuff Di?"

"Spider webs," replied Diana.

"What?"

"Spider webs!"

"What's a spider web, in fact what's a spider?"

"Well," said Diana, "webs are what spiders spin and spiders are eight-legged bugs with spinning tackle in the rear end."

"I don't recall feeling this stuff before," responded Juno.

"No, you wouldn't, they're new and not much use for anything so far as I can see."

"So where'd they come from Di?"

"It's all your fault," replied Diana, "them two fishwives you hired to fix the drapes and tapestries, argued from day one they did, one wanted this scene, one wanted that scene and they ended up having a weaving and spinning competition. Arachne very skilfully, and accurately I thought, depicted the gods as a bunch of pisshead womanisers. Minerva threw a wobbly, stuffed the spinning wheel up Arachne's arse and turned her into a spider and now she's spinning webs all over the shop."

"I'll sort this out," snapped Juno and walked on calling, "Minnie? Minnie you little shit, where are you?"

"Amma oger 'ear," came the very muffled reply from the only dark corner that was left.

Juno looked at what appeared to be a white fluffy sheep propped up on end in the corner. As she got closer, she could discern the face of Minerva behind millions upon plenty of fine silvery threads.

"Et mne ovaf ear."

"You dumb bitch," snorted Juno, a tad derisively, "how many times have I told you, if you can't control it get well out of its way before you invent it." Then picking up a large stick removed the cobwebs from Minerva's face.

"Okay, now change Arachne back please."

"Can't."

"What do you mean can't?"

"The bloody thing proliferated so quick, within a couple of hours there were hundreds of them. I don't know which one's her anymore and every time I tried to change the wrong one back it just multiplied."

"You stupid cow," said Juno.

"No, that's Io!" replied Minerva.

"So I suppose we're stuck with the sodding things now then?"

"Er, looks that way," responded Minerva, sheepishly.

"They'll be in all the corners, under the furniture, up the candelabras, spinning bloody webs everywhere, as if we women don't have enough to do without having to clean up sodding spider webs as well. I wonder about you sometimes Minerva, like, just who's side are you on? Go on, clear off before Jupiter gets back." Minerva remained stuck to the wall.

"Er, how?"

Juno looked intently at the swaddled mass in the corner which burst into flames, allowing a singed and smoking Minerva to do as requested. Juno continued along her chosen path and opened the loo door. "Aaw bloody Norah!" she exclaimed. "Angelo? Oy Mick you toe rag, what the fuck kind of white-wash do you call this?"

The head of Michelangelo appeared from down behind the toilet bowl.

"Issa good yes? You likea ma work?"

"White I said," exploded Juno, "bloody boring, ordinary, seven colours of the rainbow mixed, white. Can't anybody follow simple instructions around here? This is not bloody white, is it Mick?"

"Aah, no, issa no white, issa godda soma da white see, here anna here, issa godda bit adda artistic licence."

"Bollocks," said Juno.

"Si, si," said Michelangelo. "Issa godda da bollocks dare anna dare," he said, pointing strategically.

"No," stared Juno, "Bollocks - complete and utter but, just out of interest, what is it?"

"Issa God an he maka da man an he giva da man life, si?"

"Bloody hell Mick, Jupiter ain't going to like this, he'll blow his stack after all the Prometheus stuff, save it for the Christians you prat. Now get it painted out bloody pronto, si?"

Michelangelo stared "Si? - No, no si, amma worka ma bollocks off, amma maka for you bellissimo muriel all over da walls, amma even gedda da door 'andle so issa right onna da knob, jusa fora da laugh, an now you say, issa no good Mick, painta da dam thing out Mick, well amma say issa stay!"

Juno pointed a vicious forefinger and elevated the hapless decorator into the top corner of the lean-to ceiling and very determinedly said. "An amma say, if Jupiter sees this you won't have any balls left for working off, or anything else come to that, kapisch? Now get it bloody white-washed!"

The power of elevation was withdrawn. *Schthunk!*

Michelangelo was left, a ten-foot drop later, rubbing a rather bruised posterior and babbling in deference to a goddess. "Si, si, issa okay, amma godda da whitewash brush right here, amma get right on it."

Just then, from the doorway, an omnipotent voice boomed. "Juno, what the fuck is going on here?"

"Nothing I can't handle dear," replied his queen, not quite as calmly as she thought. "Everything's under control, don't you worry about a thing."

"Under control?" thundered the thunderer. "The bloody place is a shambles, half the hall's missing, presumed vaporised, the bog's covered in pissin' porno paintings and everything's shrouded in sodding cobwebs."

"Well," said Juno, "you always get a few cobwebs when you've been away for a bit."

Jupiter hauled her out by the hair from the loo. "Look!" he snarled, "look at the not so great bloody hall, it's going to take more time and energy to fix it than it would take to make a new one and as for spiders, them little bastards aren't in the programme for another thousand years or so. That's it, that is it, fuck 'em, fuck 'em all, we're pulling out, bollocks to earth. I want the gods out by dinner time. Let the pissing mortals have it for a couple of thousand years, they'll wipe each other out and solve the problem for us!"

"Oh dear," replied Juno tentatively, "I won't bother unpacking then dear?"

Jupiter stormed off to the far end of the remaining hall and abruptly tripped over. "What the fu…" his booming voice trailed off as he looked at what had tripped him up. Juno sniggered. "Mind that club that seems to be sticking out of that comet dear."

"Hercules you little bastard," thundered Jupiter.

This is going to be good, thought Juno, that'll teach him to go putting it about, having troublesome kids right, left and centre. "Is that one of young Herky's clubs dear?"

"Bugger off," said Jupiter, "And you two, bloody pyramid pushers, piss off!"

Rameses and Cheops, not requiring a second dismissal, dropped their chisels and ran, scattering spectral wheelbarrows and their shady shovers in all directions, while creating in their haste, indelible skid marks in the very rock of the substructure.

Jupiter rose to a height of one and a half Prometheus's and, sweeping his giant hands over the mountain top, removed everything that dared to rise above seven feet. "Right," he said, "let's go," and, noticing a bucket of unused lightning bolts discarded in a corner, he picked them up by the sharp end and indiscriminately showered them all over the unexpectant mortals.

"What?" questioned Juno. "Just like that, let's go?"

"Yeah, what other way is there to go?"

"Well, I thought there'd be a sort of transition period, like a skeleton gods staff in a purely hands-off capacity or something like that."

"What's the point," said Jupiter, "Sod 'em."

"What about Hercules?"

"What about him?"

"Well, you're not going to let him get away with this are you?"

"Let's get out of here and set up somewhere new," replied Jupiter, "and I'll come back and sort him and close up the operation, okay?"

"Yes dear," said Juno, placated by the fact that the spawn of her husband's adultery was about to get his bottom well and truly slapped. Just to be sure she slipped away for a few minutes on an errand of a personal nature.

In a cupboard under where the stairs used to be, she scrabbled about and withdrew from the rubble a magnificent robe. It was delicately handcrafted and covered with a multitude of jewels, stones and precious metal threads. It was also fully impregnated with Centaur blood from a half-man, half-horse guy called Nissus.

With five minutes to spare Juno dropped in on an old adversary in the sexual Olympics stakes. "Dee baby," she said to a woman who was casually sitting in front of a roaring fire in her own front room.

Deianira looked up and, even through the disguise, instantly recognised Jupiter's jealous missus. "Who let you in?" replied Deianira.

"The door was open, there's no need to be defensive," said Juno, "I've come to make amends. All that stuff with Hercules and the lady Iole was just a silly joke on my part, so by way of reparation I would like to give you this splendid robe, over which Venus has personally laboured to ensure the return of your husband."

"Oh yeah?"

"Yes indeed," returned Juno, "you must give it to Hercules and he will never look at another woman again. It's the least I can do. There's just one rule. You must let no other handle it apart from Hercules."

"Okay," said Deianira, "I'll take it under advisement. Now get out!"

"No problem," said Juno, with a smile of unknown intent, to Deianira at any rate.

By eleven forty-five am the earth was totally devoid of godly presence.

XXXV

THE SACK OF OLYMPUS

By eleven forty-six am, after substantial hangovers and much Paracetamol later, the team was assembled in the amphitheatre, fully kitted out and ready for the final push on Olympus.

"Well," announced Sisyphus, "after last night I'd say these bleeders have got it coming!"

"What?" asked Oedipus, trying very hard to develop a questioning look in his sightless eyes.

"All that celestial crashing and banging about, there I was trying in vain to have a hangover in peace and what do I get? Lightning bolts, that's what, thunder and bloody lightning half the night."

"Oh," said Oedipus, "The storm, didn't see it myself as it goes but I heard a few pops and bangs and rumbles, definite case of unnecessary noise pollution I thought."

The two-mile hike took the rest of the day and night was falling as they reached the new lower altitude summit of Olympus.

What they saw was somewhat surprising and not a little disquieting. Walls rose before them to a height of seven feet, just high enough not to be able to see over.

Hercules stood with his back to the wall and Paris climbed onto his shoulders.

"See owt?" questioned Sisyphus.

"Not a lot," replied Paris. "It's a bit dark to make it out. There are loads of walls about seven feet high with some gaps and interconnecting passages, it's a bit of a maze really, you can't tell where they start or stop and there's rubble everywhere. It's a regular bloody labyrinth."

Theseus came forward. "Leave this to me, I know a bit about these things. Turnus, get that ball of string out of your backpack!" Theseus caught the ball of string and wound off about fifteen feet and tied it to his belt. "Here Oedipus, hold this," he said, throwing the ball to him. "Butterfingers! It's on the ground, no not there, six inches to the left!

"Yeah, okay got it. What is it?" Theseus rolled his eyes skywards, mainly because he could. "It's a ball of bloody string, now hold on to it. You can manage that can't you?"

"Now look here Theseus," began Oedipus, "you are looking, aren't you?" There was no reply, just a tug on the string which, Oedipus realised, meant that Theseus had gone and he had to hold the string, which he did.

The rest spread out and examined the outer walls and kept watch, just in case there was anything to keep watch for.

Two hours later Theseus decided that the labyrinth was, apart from his, devoid of life, which did nothing to alleviate the strange feeling that something was following him. He turned about face and began to rewind the string and retrace his steps. He heard a noise, a scrabbling scratching sound, very close, right round the corner where the string led. He inched round the corner in the gloom and could just make out a, blacker than the surrounding blackness, blob, about two feet high moving from side to side and bobbing up and down. It was making low guttural noises. Theseus froze, if there was one thing he knew about better than anyone else, it was Minotaurs and this, most irrefutably, certainly, positively, definitely, wasn't one.

It came closer and was apparently unaware of Theseus as it scritch-scratched and snorted. "'Sitgone 'stard, f'king fing, 'sit naw 'ollocks - 'asit gotcher." The blob rose to six feet tall and Theseus charged at it with drawn sword. It jumped to awareness, it's right limb appeared pushing the sword hilt aside with a side-step, it turned clockwise and followed with a sharp blow of its left limb to the now passing skull of a most surprised Theseus, who hit the debris strewn ground, rolled, jumped, span with the alacrity of a scalded cat and deftly tripped over an indiscriminately placed pile of rubble.

The enlarged blob said, "Aah Theseus, there you are."

"Oedipus, you dumb shit, you're supposed to pay the string out, not hold on to it and follow me!"

"I know, it had a knot in it and I dropped it, it's taken me the best part of two hours to find it but it's okay now, I've got it." said a triumphant Oedipus. "The hearing becomes so much more acute when the sight's gone you know!"

"I see!" snarled Theseus on purpose and emphasising the second part, "and just how do you propose we get out of here now, you brainless excuse for a bat?"

"Ah," said Oedipus, followed swiftly by, "Ouch!" as Theseus introduced his blind bonce to the sword's hilt.

"Hi ya, boys," called Hercules, who was happily trotting about on top of the walls, "thought I'd best find out if you were lost or anything. The door's over there, three lefts, a right and a 'U' turn."

Theseus scowled, viciously shoved Oedipus out of the way and took the next right.

Three rights and a left later Paris gave him new directions. "Oh, fuck it!" responded Theseus. Aware that his reputation as a maze master was now in some doubt, he admitted defeat and climbed up on top of the wall with the aid of the not very cooperative Oedipus' right ear which formed the second tread of a human staircase shortly after his solar-plexus had bumped into Theseus' air bound knee in the gloom. "That's not what I'd call a labyrinth anyway," he grunted.

"No," agreed Paris, "but it is what you might call half a house and just over there we have what you might call half a hall," he said, pointing to the remainder of the great hall. "Strange that, it appears to be halved at ninety degrees to the house though."

Theseus followed Paris' indicating finger. "Must have been a hell of a divorce!" he grinned.

"Perhaps they've had the builders in," stated Camilla, noticing a hammer and cold chisel that looked recently and hastily deserted.

"Guess they didn't get paid," commented Thor, noticing the skid marks presumably left by recently departed tool utilisers.

"Here that's mine," noted Hercules, shortly after tripping over the remnant of his club, which was still attached to the remnants of a comet. "Guess I did this then," he said, indicating the atmosphere where the missing half of the hall no longer stood.

"Naw," said Perseus, "It was Prometheus, he stuck the nut on it!"

"Looks like he achieved his aim by default," sniggered Hercules. "Well, let's do what we came to do, eh?"

"Good idea," agreed Ajax who, though possessing an inordinate amount of neurons, generally found that, from a synaptic point of view, they did not talk, or for that matter in any other way, interact with each other for most of his conscious hours. "So what was that then?"

"What?" questioned Neoptolemus.

"That," replied Ajax

"That what?" inquired Menelaus, who was also having a bit of a forty-watt awareness capacity at the time.

"That what that we came to do," struggled Ajax, managing against all the odds to get a synapse to fire.

"Oh, that what," said Menelaus, visibly struggling with the ramifications of logical thought and turning to Paris and Hercules for enlightenment. "Tell the sheep shagger why we're here boys," which got the heat off him, not being exactly sure of the why bit himself.

Hercules whispered to Paris, "Well, we did pick them for their muscle tone I suppose!"

"And splendid choices they were too," replied Paris.

"We are here," announced Hercules, "to give the gods a boot up the arse and dispel a few myths."

"My old man used to do that," said Oedipus.

"What?" enquired Perseus.

"Distil Meths," replied Oedipus, totally dispelling the myth that impaired senses in one department were necessarily an indication of increased acuity in another.

Hercules and Paris exchanged a look that was laden with increased acuity and required no verbal assistance.

"Excuse me?" said Sisyphus, "not wanting to piss on anybody's fireworks or anything like that but, there doesn't appear to be any deific presence of a godly nature hereabouts," which, if nothing else, proved that he had learned at least one lesson during the rock and roll years.

"Okay," Hercules clapped his hands, "job done, myths dispelled, gods ousted and fully arse kicked. Well done everybody, now we, the mortals, are in charge, let's see what we can do with the place."

"Hold it right there! Not so fast you don't." The voice belonged to Odysseus who, in a remarkable parody of the Holy Ghost, seemed to have just appeared. The only drawback to the illusion, seeing as the Holy Ghost was reputed to travel in ones or threes, was the fact that there were two of them and, even in low gear, Prometheus stood out by being a good head and a half taller.

Camilla turned to see. "Just when I thought I was having a good day," she muttered, unslinging a medium weight, ball pein, throwing hammer from a set that Thor had given to her for her last birthday.

Hercules moved in and rested a restraining hand on hers, "Hang on a bit, I think a little finesse is required here."

"Oh," said Camilla, "I've never tried one of those, can I waste him with it?"

"Let's hear what he's got to say first," replied Hercules. "He may be bearing gifts."

Odysseus and Prometheus walked to the comet location, looking very much like newly promoted monastic abbots.

"Oddy baby!" Paris hailed the pair heartily, "Nice haircuts boys!"

Odysseus ignored the remark and elbowed Oedipus firmly in the solar plexus in passing. Oedipus folded neatly in the middle and followed up by venerating a Promethean Doc Marten with his chin, in descending.

"Sodding horse shagger," said Menelaus to Turnus. "Two of them on to one blind man, no class, and no style - no gifts either!"

"Right!" exclaimed Odysseus severely. "We'll take it from here."

"Why?" said Neoptolemus.

"Because matey," replied Odysseus, "we are the brains behind this operation."

"I'm with Ginger," said Turnus, indicating Menelaus. "The only thing you ever got behind was a horse."

"Your comments have been noted and will be very useful in determining the ranks to which you may be allowed to aspire to in the new world order."

"Bugger off you pair of dip-shits," called Sisyphus. "Mohicans are the other way round, you keep the middle bit you dumb bastards!"

A sound resembling, *zischunk*, rent the air and Sisyphus disappeared into the ground below the weight of the comet that Prometheus had just picked up by its club handle and transferred in a swooping arc to the place that was occupied by Sisyphus.

Some miles distant, back in the residents' bar, Cassandra sniggered to herself, "Told him so, gobby twat!"

"No Prometheus," screamed Odysseus, "you dumb, oversized excuse for a second-generation junkie," but it was too late. The ground cracked into two north-south, zigzag lines and the mountain was rent in twain.

Prometheus - still holding the comet crowned club and wearing the gormless expression generally reserved for the post-shit-faced, which planet am I on condition - suddenly followed the comet in a downward direction. He grabbed Odysseus frantically who, equally frantically – in the, my life is passing before me and there's not much to look at mode - grabbed the nearest thing to him which just happened to be Theseus and the three rapidly vanished into the ever-widening ravine.

"Oh dear," said Thor, looking over the edge. "That's a bit unfortunate."

"Indeed," agreed Camilla. "Sisyphus and the other pair belong down there but not Theseus, I liked him."

"You wait here," announced Hercules to the remainder of the team. "I'm going in. I have to rescue him, he could be going through hell down there!"

"Hercules?" cautioned Paris.

"Yeah?"

"Best take the dog eh?"

With that, one man and his, three dogs in one, canine began their descent into the new underworld entrance.

XXXVI

IT'S HELL DOWN THERE

Hercules worked his way down the ravine cautiously. Generally, and especially since he had stolen the dog, the entrances to the underworld were unguarded but why take chances? There was the odd Cybele still around and now and then a token harpy would take a look out. It was really a rather pointless exercise guarding the entrances to such a hideous realm because nobody wanted to get in anyway and the place didn't have exits, unless you happened to be a semi-mortal superhero of course.

This one, however, was different, Pluto and his underworld hordes had just developed a new back door that wasn't of their making and, sooner or later somebody, or more likely something, was bound to notice it.

When Hercules reached the bottom, he could see that the ravine had become a funnel with a large round rock at the base. The two and a half bodies on top of it were vaguely identifiable, two by the prematurely induced baldness and the half by the fact that it was wearing Sisyphus' loincloth but missing most of the rest of him. There was no sign of Theseus, not even parts that might have belonged to him.

Hercules looked up and around and spotted a ledge twenty feet higher with a few boards across a crack in the rock. "They work fast round here," he grumbled to himself, "couldn't get a window boarded up that fast back home."

They climbed back to the ledge and Cerberus, scenting the aroma of untreated timber, promptly cocked his leg against the boards, which promptly disintegrated.

"Oy you!" shouted a female voice. "I've only just finished that, now look at it!"

"I'm sorry," apologised Hercules into the darkness. "It's the dog you know, he's only a puppy, he gets a bit excitable."

"I'll give him excitable," said the voice coming nearer. "What do you want?"

"I'm looking for a friend of mine, might well have come this way recently," replied Hercules.

"I know that voice," said the voice. "Herky isn't it?" Well, how the hell are you, haven't seen you round here since the dog incident."

"Persephone, you little doll, is that you?" inquired Hercules.

"Betcha life it is!" she replied.

Whadumph!

"*Sulersch, sulersch, sulersch!*"

Persephone was flat on her back with three canine heads licking her face in a frenzy of delight. Hercules hauled the dog off her and she sat up wiping her face.

"Cerby baby, I've missed you so much, it's been real boring without you around."

"Waruff!" issued all three heads in synchronicity.

"He's looking good, I knew he'd like it topside. It was disgraceful keeping him chained to the wall in that damp old cave like that. You know the only exercise he ever got was frightening the odd errant shade back down the cave, poor pooch, and even that bit of fun was taken from him when Pluto had the re-fit and put the nine levels in with them gigantic chain link fences and all. Made him right vicious it did, put him off his food altogether, didn't it Cerby?"

"Waruff!"

"So, how's Pluto these days?" inquired Hercules, "still a grumpy old git?"

"It's a funny thing," she replied, "but he doesn't seem to be about anywhere, in fact, there doesn't appear to be any gods anyplace. You remember he did that deal with the old lady over me and they set up that timeshare arrangement? Well, I've just come to do the six months down under tour and this is what I've found. The place is a complete shambles. The levels are all mixing together willy-nilly. Old Con's mixing with new ones, no segregation, drugs everywhere and a sodding great hole in the roof with a boulder with a club stuck to it in it. On top of that, there are three newcomers, two of them with inside out Mohawk haircuts, frantically belting around the corridors, right rough-looking bunch they are. Anyway, come on in, have a cup of tea and a chat."

Hercules followed her along vaguely familiar passageways he had never intended to re-visit, after first propping a few newish planks across the hole.

"You'll have to excuse the mess," said Persephone, "but that's men for you. I mean, I leave him alone for a couple of months and I come back to a right pigsty."

"Aw c'mon Seph, Pluto's a busy guy, you can't expect him to do the domestics as well," said Hercules.

"I don't," she replied, "he is only a male after all, but he could pick up a few things as he goes along. Like, there's a pile of unused man traps by the front door going all rusty. The rack's pulled out at forty degrees half blocking the passage. His trouser pockets are full of thumb screws, never takes them out before throwing them where he stands instead of in the linen basket. I mean, you walk down any corridor and you won't get ten feet before you trip over a dismembered leg or skid on an ear regardlessly tossed over his shoulder. Bloody iron maidens under the stairs, a few 'save 'em for laters' stuffed in the freezer, eyeballs marinating in the pressure cooker, lost souls in the coal cellar, it's just bloody ridiculous he's such a messy bleeder."

Persephone rattled about in the kitchen and locating the kettle filled it with water, after first removing a collection of, this'll make your eyes water, trophies from its interior.

"Oh balls!" asserted Hercules.

"I know," replied Persephone, "he keeps things in the strangest places."

"What?"

"Pluto, I said he keeps things in the strangest places."

"No, I didn't mean that," replied Hercules, "the dog's wandered off was what I meant."

"Oh don't worry about him," she said absently, "he knows his way round and it'll clean up the corridors a bit if he's hungry."

Persephone put the kettle on top of a magnificent range style cooker, opened an access door and poked Ixion and his wheel to get some back draught and a bit of air conditioning going.

A few minutes later she brought the tea into the lounge and, stepping over a discarded guillotine blade after ducking under the new club ceiling fixture, seated herself in a splendid dragon's head rocking throne.

"So, why are you here Herky?"

"Well, the short version," replied Hercules, "we've had a bit of a revolution topside and got shot of the gods in the process and, along the way I've lost Theseus down here somewhere, so I thought I'd best come and get him back."

"I see," said Persephone, stirring her tea. "So it's your fault Pluto's missing?"

"Well," replied Hercules, "by default perhaps, we couldn't make exceptions for some gods now could we?"

"No, I see your point you either have gods or you don't, a new order does require the displacement of the old one but it doesn't really help me out very much does it?"

"Look Seph, I'm really sorry…"

"You will be mate if we can't contain this lot down here!"

"… you've become one of the unconsidered victims of change."

"Too right pal and it's all entirely your fault."

"Well not exactly, the instigator in all of this is Prometheus. I, er, inadvertently set him free you see," said Hercules shamefully, "but he's down here now, one of the inside-out Mohawks."

"How interesting," mused Persephone, "and who are his two companions?"

"Sisyphus and Odysseus."

"Oh, how lovely," replied Persephone. "Okay, I'll make a deal with you. I know Sisyphus and, to be honest, he's done his time and deserves a break. So you round them up and put him in charge and get them to run this hell hole and I'll give you Theseus back."

"Sounds like a good deal to me," responded Hercules. "Done!"

From beyond the living quarters a sound reached their ears. Not the usual background noise - of moaning and wailing and gnashing of, in many a case gold, teeth and an even greater gnashing of teeth - but something more refined, more refreshing, the sound of sheer unadulterated panic. The kind of sound one might expect to hear from three newly created shades, which had only just crossed over and come to the realisation of their status, while standing in a dead-end corridor of Hades with a three-headed hound slavering at the other end. Which was exactly what the sound was.

"Sounds like," interjected Hercules, "as well as sheer panic that is, that the dog's found something."

"Indeed," replied Persephone. "Finish your tea first and we'll go and check it out."

He did and then they did.

As expected, the dead-end stub of an unfinished excavation contained three of the most panic-stricken shades in the history of history.

Odysseus was trying to hide behind Sisyphus, who was trying to hide behind Prometheus who just happened to be hiding behind Odysseus, who was - as well as trying to hide behind Sisyphus - cowering very close to six eyes, three snouts and an awful lot of sharp foam-flecked teeth, which were in constant motion and backed up by a high intensity, fully synchronised snarl, of the rabid lip curling category. And, as if that wasn't enough, the whole thing was on the front end of fifteen stones of perfectly conditioned muscle, sinew and fur that had suddenly developed a lust for blood sports.

"Hmmm...?" mused Hercules. "Guess the puppy's come of age then. Oh well, three down, one to go!"

Much to the dog's disappointment, they contained the panic-stricken shades where they stood, or cowered as the case actually was and set off to locate Theseus. He was nowhere to be seen but he had left a trail.

Ixion's wheel now sported a natty pedal arrangement with a trough of diverted Stygian water to push it round.

Tantalus, who had for so long been unable to reach the water around him, or the fruit above him, now held a cup in one hand and the branch of an overhanging tree in the other and was smiling.

"This will not do you know." Persephone pointed out. "They have been bad lads and they're here for punishment."

"That's Theseus for you, so kind-hearted, he'll help anyone if he can," replied Hercules.

"Yeah well, there's help and there's cocking up the whole system and Theseus is tending towards the cocking up scenario," snapped Persephone. "It's a delicate balancing act down here you know. We need Ixion on the wheel to keep the air circulating and Tantalus is blocking a hole between two dimensions down there. Change may be good but let's have it a bit more structured eh?"

"Fair point," conceded Hercules. "There's a rock in the roof that can do Tantalus' job and I know just the guy to roll it down there too," he said, considering that Sisyphus wouldn't have much else to do now, "and Ixion can be put in charge of a water wheel for a change. Prom and Oddy can oversee the contract in a 'hands-on' capacity, which they will readily accept when the alternative is playing with Cerberus. So all we have to do is find Theseus before he does the whole thing single-handedly."

Suddenly, off to the left, a gigantic roar, that far excelled the moans and roars from elsewhere, rent the stuff that passed for air. Hercules turned swiftly. "What's down there?"

Persephone gave him a knowing smirk and a look loaded with information. "The Minotaur pit."

"Oh shit!" exclaimed Hercules. "He really hates those guys."

Dimensional physics, being what it is, made interaction between mortals and shades in the underworld conditions virtually impossible. Of course, where superheroes are concerned, the impossible, when approached with a deep-seated, long-standing sense of hatred, rapidly becomes the improbable which, after two minutes of wholehearted piss-taking, becomes the unlikely. The unlikely, being what it is, happens all the time.

They stood and watched as Theseus circled the pit making motions like somebody reading - well, looking at and fantasising over - a porno' mag might well perform. This was followed by a single fingered salutation involving extensive use of the middle finger in an upward direction which flowed into a burlesque hop, skip and pirouette, culminating in the descent of his trousers and the waggling of a large hairy arse in a general pit-ward direction.

Theseus looked over his shoulder in mid-waggle, turned rapidly, while pulling up and fastening his trousers, shrugged with a smirk at Persephone and Hercules and then overbalanced.

"Oh fuck!" he managed to say, before performing a half twisting back somersault and landing in the pit with sword drawn. A moment of intense calm and silence followed while a collection of Minotaurs swapped glances and the merest parody of a grin that their bovine facial features would allow.

A deafening roar, which was suppressed by Theseus' war cry, hit the atmosphere and Theseus vanished in a cloud of airborne dust punctuated by a blur of glinting, flashing steel with much grunting. His blade whirled in a smear of motion as hoofs, horns, tails and other general Minotaur paraphernalia took to the air without having anything vaguely resembling a Minotaur attached to them.

Three minutes later the pit contained a red figure holding a sword firmly in two down stretched arms that resembled tree trunks and wearing a look laden with determination without the 'de' prefix and, one cowering anally unretentive Minotaur.

"Oy you!" bellowed Persephone. "Stop that! Stop it right this minute, do you hear me? That's a protected bloody species, now back off mister and get out of there this instant!"

Theseus smirked. "Not very well protected if you ask me," he replied, walking over to the cowering Minotaur and giving it a right good kick in the balls before using it as a step ladder.

"What'd you do that for?" screeched Persephone.

"Just making sure it don't breed," said Theseus casually.

"With what?" groaned an exasperated Persephone, looking around a pit that was awash with Minotaur spare parts and fluids.

"Well, you can't be too careful with these sneaky bastards you know," grunted Theseus. "Done you a real favour here I have. I can still finish it off if you want?"

"No! No thank you."

"Aww go on."

"No!"

"Please, just one more that's all."

"Sod off."

"Well can I just beat it up a bit more?"

"Bugger off will you?"

"Well, there's gratitude for you. This is my last offer."

"Fuck off!"

"Okay."

"Hercules?" said a quietly determined Persephone. "Take this twat and get out of here and don't bring him back. Oh yeah, and leave the dog on your way out."

"Can't do that Seph," answered Hercules, "I may still need him topside."

"I said, leave the dog!" quaked Persephone.

Hercules looked at Theseus, who re-drew his sword and turned back towards the pit.

"All right! All right!" growled Persephone. "Take the sodding dog and piss off - now!"

XXXVII

TERRAFORMER

The inhabitants of the Crab Nebula were rather new to the concept of life. So new in fact that if there hadn't been something around that understood the concept to tell them, they would probably never have known and probably been a lot happier for a lot longer. They didn't realise what hit them when the gods arrived, they didn't even know that they had been hit, in fact, they didn't know anything. They were unicellular and existed simply because they could, they didn't need a brain and in any case, didn't have the room for one - yet!

Jupiter stood on the shore of a primeval swamp. He took a long inhalation of the new air and sneezed, then he coughed, then he hawked up mightily and gobbed upon the water. "It's breathable. It'll do," he announced, turning, belching and letting rip with an almighty (well, what else?) fart.

Enzymes, proteins, nucleotides, atoms, diatoms and a few other minuscule particles suddenly came together around a god gob in a swamp and went.

"*Burdleurdleurdlelurp.*"

And thus it was that the God performed every basic function short of having a shit upon the waters, and saw that it was good.

And thus it was that a basically content unicellular organism, began it's ascent to awareness, guilt, regret and the never-ending search for what had hit it in the first place.

"Right," said Jupiter, "Get set up and settled. I'll be back in a bit."

"And what are you going to be doing?" inquired Juno.

"Minding my own business," he replied, "you ought to try it sometime."

"Oh yeah, that's right, we'll do all the work while you swan off idling about. This needs lots of planning you know," snorted Juno.

"Bloody hell woman," he bellowed, "It's easy. Raise a few mountains over there, a couple of plains down there, the odd volcano there and there," he pointed indiscriminately, "and get this water flowing, surely you can handle that?"

"Yeah, so where will you be?"

"If you must know, I'm going to close up the earth operation, okay?"

"Oh," said Juno. "Turn the sun off, put the cat out, that sort of thing?"

"Something like that dear, yes."

"And, er, take care of Hercules?"

"Yes dammit!"

"And one other thing dear?"

"What now?" groused the exasperated king of the gods.

"Well, sweetie, I was thinking, a couple of giants would come in handy my love. Perhaps Typhoeus, you know, the guy you dropped Mount Etna on top of and, er, maybe Prometheus?"

"Not a fucking flying chance. If Prometheus is lucky I'll drop him down there with the rest of his junkie buddies.

Now get on with it!" he growled and turned promptly and headed for earth.

XXXVIII

THE SECOND GOING

The team had set up a camp while Hercules was down below and spent the rest of their time fabricating ropes out of anything that came to hand. By the time Hercules and Theseus were halfway back up, they found the ends of the ropes and were dutifully hauled up by the well-practised team, a ride which Cerberus found totally undignified but it was easier than climbing.

"Good holiday?" inquired Paris.

"Spiffing," replied Hercules, "but don't eat the food!"

"Too right," added Theseus, "It hasn't done Seph any good at all. She's a totally different gal down there, bitchy, uptight, miserable, a right pain in the arse."

Menelaus looked at him while remembering his sister-in-law Clytemnestra and Helen and Jocasta and Medea and a good many others and said quite innocently.

"And this is unusual in a female?"

Kadumph!

The flat face of a meteor pocked battle-axe was brought into very close proximity, at considerable velocity, with the back of his head by Camilla.

"See," spluttered Menelaus, from his new position face down on the ground. "Strange creatures, unpredictable," followed after a nano-second pause by, "Oompfsh!" as the battle-axe owner found the side of his rib cage in much the same manner but with a steel-shod foot on this occasion.

"Was it something I said?" asked a confused and aching Menelaus.

Hercules waited a good five minutes for the raucous and hysterical laughter to subside and said. "Well, it looks like you've been busy in my absence and I think some down time is called for. I suggest we camp here for the night and have a few games and more than a few flagons!" A suggestion that was loudly endorsed by the team members as they set fire to anything that looked like good campfire fodder and broke out their hidden supplies of 'for medicinal purposes only' medication. Hercules continued, "In the morning we'll have to something about closing up this new back entrance to the hell zone but for tonight let's have a little fun and keep an eye out for anything that thinks this entrance is an exit." Everyone cheered and the business of getting pissed and playing with weapons commenced with great exuberance.

Meanwhile, in the underworld, Persephone was doing a tour of facilities with her new right-hand man Sisyphus. They had viewed various aspects of general site maintenance and had compiled enough remedial work to keep Odysseus and Prometheus gainfully employed for the foreseeable eternity.

They now sat in the, not as spacious as it used to be due to a large rock in the ceiling, kitchen. Persephone produced a bottle of ten-year-old single malt and two glasses and filled both. "Cheers," she said, downing it in one. Not wanting to appear ungracious Sisyphus followed suit and Persephone refuelled both glasses. "This though," she said, indicating the club extended comet, "has got to go, it's getting right on my tits! I can't cook with this in the kitchen it's totally fucking up the Feng Shui. This was the only tidy, harmonious place in this hell hole and now it's as big a shit hole as the rest of the place. Herky thought it would do a good job of filling up the dimensional gap that we've been using Tantalus to plug for the past few hundred aeons."

Sisyphus grinned broadly and said. "Leave to me, I have just the right men for the job. You get a good night's sleep and it'll be out of here and the ceiling shored up, replaced and decorated by tomorrow morning. I think we should begin as we mean to go on. In my opinion, a night shift followed by a day shift for the foreseeable future will be good for those slack arseholes Oddy and Prom. Plus, if you're agreeable, I'll have Tantalus as a contracts manager from tomorrow."

Persephone thought for a moment while throwing another glass of spiritual fuel back. "Yeah, sounds fair to me," she smiled. "Tantalus has done a reasonable community service stint down there. Under The Rehabilitation of Offenders Act, he deserves a phased return to society with responsibilities to live up to."

Sisyphus looked surprised. "You operate under a Rehabilitation of Offenders Act, down here?"

"Well, it looks like I'm wearing the in-charge hat now, so I can do whatever I want. I've just invented the concept, to justify employing my first reformed offender in the realm – you!" She winked at Sisyphus.

"You are setting a dangerous precedent here you know? What if the twats up top adopt it? They'll be setting all sorts of criminal shit sacks free to re-offend, there'll be some real bad lads on the loose up there." frowned Sisyphus.

"They are already on the loose up there and that's Herky's problem. He'll have them locked up doing hard labour but he has compassion, he'll go this way eventually. What harm can it do? It might even work!"

Sisyphus was not convinced. "What if it doesn't?"

Persephone smirked. "They got rid of the gods up there and with them they also got rid of the heaven concept. This place is not so mythical, Hades on earth is still a viable concept. There may be no heaven but, there is a hell. If it doesn't work up there, we get them, and down here there is no rest for the wicked!

"Cool," said Sisyphus, washing down another glass of ten-year vintage, "employment continuity contingency ensured."

"It sure is," grinned Persephone, "and I still get six months holiday topside to spread the paranoia and frighten the shit out of the morons." Persephone, sniggered, then she tittered and within seconds both employer and reformed employee were laughing like they were having a hell of a time.

Morning dawned and the team dawned much later. "Right," said Hercules, "let's get this hole closed… er… filled up," he corrected as he looked down to where a comet had vanished and a solid granite composite floor now lay. Good old Sisyphus, he thought, make the bastards labour from day one "Thor, would you like to direct this operation?"

"No problem," replied Thor, suddenly producing a hammer that easily equalled the club that had instigated the hole.

"Stand back!"

His muscles rippled as he hefted the titanic hammer with mountain splitting force and brought it down to a sickening dull, *Schurrglursch!* instead of the expected resounding crack that resembled a lot of nitroglycerin under vast pressure. This was followed by, "Aaarrgh, aaarrgh, aaarrgh, damn, shit, bollocks, you fuck-arsed little bastard you," Which was followed by the sight of the king of the gods, who had just touched down, leaping about wildly on one foot while clutching the big toe of the other one between both hands in a dance of throbbing agony.

"Ooops!" said Thor.

"Oh shit," said most of the rest of the team while scattering in any direction available.

"Bloody hell Dad," said Hercules. "We've got everything under control. We don't need you coming round and putting your foot in it, now sod off will you?"

Most of what was now the top of Mount Olympus fractured and split under the pressure of the hopping deity and cascaded down into the hole before the agonised Jupiter subsided nursing his pulsating, oversized - even for him - bigtoe.

"Where did I go wrong, son?" asked Jupiter. "I just wanted to create a good world for my kids to live in, safe and secure, free from fear and guilt and look what I get, chaos and a scruffy ungrateful little urchin who keeps outsmarting me."

"It's 'cos it changes of its own accord pop," said Hercules. "Your perfect is your perfect and it fits you and your world, but it's not your world anymore, it's the mortals' world now. They have a conscience and a will and you have to give them a shot at it. Now please, sod off, and leave them in peace."

"Or else what?" inquired the bright red-shifting-to-purple toed one.

"Well," replied Hercules observing Thor's wicked, twisted, grin, "you still have nine more toes!"

"Er, okay, have it, what the fuck, you'll only screw it up, who cares!" he responded nonchalantly rising and turning on his heel because the other end was too painful.

Squelch!

Cerberus sniggered briefly, the brevity induced by the application of an almighty, omnipresent, deital (same as before) foot to his triplicate rectals as he descended rapidly back to the underworld. "Sorry son but that mutt needs discipline and a strong master, or in this case, mistress, besides Seph needs him more than you to stop them new reprobates developing notions above their station!"

And Jupiter was gone.

One by one the team surfaced from a variety of cleverly concealed hiding places, all except Ajax who had decided that, no matter what the prize was, he'd had enough, even before the mountain had split. He had made a run for it with the appearance of Jupiter and had reached the plains below Olympus before being jumped by an evil band of Trojans who surrounded him and began making fun of him.

"Baaah – baah," they kept repeating cruelly, he could take no more.

XXXIX

A NEW CONSTELLATION

Deianira sat in front of the same fireplace now roaring with a different fire, staring into space when her son Hyllus burst into the room. "Mum, Mum," he said breathlessly, "The old man's shown up!"

"Hercules? Where?" she gasped.

"He's up on Olympus, well, what's left of it."

"I might have known, when a mountain suddenly blows up, that he'd be involved," she replied. "I must go to him."

"Well, let's not be too hasty eh, Mum. I mean, he did walk out on you to shack up with that tart Iole."

"No, he didn't. I got that all wrong. He never touched her but all the scandal left him thinking I'd be better off without him and all the embarrassment."

"Oh, I see," grunted Hyllus, "so where'd you get that one from?

"The queen of the goddesses visited me last week in disguise but I'd recognise that malicious bitch Juno whatever she dressed up in. Anyhow, she told me it was all a wind-up head game of hers and she gave me a magical robe to give to him that would ensure his return but I couldn't find him to give it to him.

Hyllus looked at his Mum, not fully convinced, seeing as Hercules had more or less returned in any case, robe or not, but humouring her anyway.

"Hyllus you must take it to him and you can return together."

"Aw Mum, it's bloody miles away, do I have to?"

"Yes, please do it for me."

"Yeah all right then, where is it?"

"It's here in this bag, make sure nobody but Hercules touches it, I want him to be the first to see it, okay?"

"Yeah sure," replied Hyllus and set off for Olympus.

After an uneventful day of trudging along with his parcel, muttering to himself all the way, he decided to rest under a large overhanging rock on the plains for the night. The sounds of animals and creatures drifted around him. The cooing of birds, the grunting of hedgehogs who were having real trouble finding any hedges to be hogs under, the odd distressed squeak of small furry wildlife as it became the evening meal of larger furry wildlife and the gentle bleating of a nearby flock of sheep. "Baaah - baah. B - *schunk!* Ba - ba - ba! *Schunk, schliss, kerchink!*"

Hyllus stood up and peered into the twilight. "Oy, you, what are you doing to those sheep?"

"What sheep?" Questioned a large dim figure as it continued its wholesale flock slaughter.

"The ones that you appear to be carving up there."

The figure bounded toward him, horribly bowel loosening-ly spattered in sheep blood with tufts of wool attached to it, giving the overall appearance of a severely mentally deranged, psychotic, Santa Claus. The breath flared in his nostrils, his eyes wild and staring as he slashed at Hyllus, who dodged well and dropped his parcel which, in his own opinion, was preferable to being disembowelled just prior to shitting himself.

"Ah, and what have we here?" Snarled the madman, ripping into the parcel.

"It's yours, take it," cringed Hyllus, "It's your size and definitely your colour, go on, try it on," he pleaded desperately, as the sheep slasher did that very thing. "Oh yes, yes, it's definitely you, you have a nice day now, I have to be going."

"Not so fast," said the maniac, "Aarrgh! It's too tight," he gasped, pulling frantically at the place where the buttonholes used to be but that had now magically vanished.

"Aurgh, can't get it off, aah, aargh, aaarrgh!"

Hyllus watched in horror as the mad sheepicidal nutcase struggled with the rapidly contracting robe. Veins rose on his arms and temples, his eyes bulged, his whole head swelled.

Pookurgh! - Exploded the man, viewed by Hyllus in an over the shoulder fashion as he ran like hell through what remained of a severely dismembered flock of sheep.

An hour later he was still running and halfway up the remainder of Mount Olympus when he came to an abrupt stop which removed what little air his lungs still contained. A large hand had caught him, right out of the blue, in the solar plexus. He looked up from his new profession of sitting on the floor in winded agony and followed from the large hand along the equally large arm to the face and gasped, "Hi Daddy!"

"Hyllus? What brings you up here?" Quizzed Hercules.

"Well, you," spluttered Hyllus, "the old lady's missing you; she wants you to come home. She sent me with this new robe for you."

"What new robe?

"Aah, that's a tricky one, I er, sort of got mugged on the way here and it, er, sort of got stolen by this guy who was slaughtering sheep by the flock load, but believe me, you didn't want it - really!"

"I didn't?"

"No, no definitely not, I mean, I watched the guy put it on and he just went berserk, well, more berserk than he was already going. He was raving and screaming that he couldn't get it off and it was getting tighter and tighter by the second. He stood there fighting against it, muscles bulging, veins standing out everywhere, eyes popping and all that, looked like he was under a lot of pressure he did and then – boom baby, he just exploded."

"I see!" mused Hercules, "and what did he do then?"

"Eh?"

"After he exploded, what did he do then?"

"Er, well, nothing. There was nothing left to do anything, just, Kaboom Daddio! He was splashed all over the stars, sort of up there," Hyllus pointed towards a constellation that bore more than a striking resemblance to a man with a club.

"Hmmm… I see, well I guess they won't be looking for me anymore then!" replied Hercules. "So what about the Iole business?"

"Aw that's okay now, Mum knows all about that. It was just a big mix up stirred up by that half a horse's arse centaur Nissus. He wanted to get you back for that business with the old lady when he tried to steal her away and you shot him. Well, that's what I reckon."

"So where did the robe come from?" inquired Hercules.

"That's a bit confused in its origins," replied Hyllus, "but it looks like Juno gave it to the old lady."

"Aaah! That explains all," said Hercules.

"It does?"

"Oh yeah, she was pissed off with Jupiter over the incident with my old lady, your grandmother, Alcemena, 'cos she claimed, quite rightly I might add, that I was Jupiter's kid. You see, all the labours and that were all Juno's work, trying to get rid of me. Looks like she had a final stab at it and presumably thinks she's succeeded. Okay." he said and under his breath added, "Sorry about this Ajax old mate but from now on that constellation will be known as Hercules. I'm retiring from public life." Then to Hyllus he said, "I've just got one or two little details to sort out, tell your Mum I'll be home for tea."

"What?" said Hyllus. "So now I've got to go back and then it'll be, tidy up your room, clean up the house, stick the fatted calf and get your Dad's slippers out 'an all that crap?"

A moments silence was broken by, "Ouch!" emitted by Hyllus as he performed a ten-foot length of cartwheels at the impetus of Hercules' backhand.

"That's right, and the sooner you get back the quicker you can get it all done!"

"You ain't changed much," sneered Hyllus, scrambling further out of range. "Suppose you'll be wanting to go clubbing afterwards too?"

"Oy you, watch your gob. That wasn't my fault, that was Juno, okay?" growled Hercules.

"If you say so, looked like you to me. Blame the gods why don't you, everyone else does," replied Hyllus, practising his duck, cover and run routine.

XL

BAR STOOL BUSINESS PHILOSOPHY

The team seemed suddenly to have found something else to talk about to each other and made a particularly good show of showing that they had not heard a word of everything that they had just heard, when Hercules turned back to them and said, "Anyone fancy a beer or six?"

"Well if you're offering," said Theseus, "The six bit sounds good to me."

"All courtesy of Oddy," smiled Hercules, "He may be gone but he's not bankrupt - not yet at any rate!"

"Back to Cassandra's?" Inquired Paris.

"Well, it's a start," said Thor, "as the instigators of a new world order it seems pertinent that the first order of the new order can only be properly proffered with the assistance of an innkeeper and the aid of a bar between the two."

Cassandra, in a prophetic sort of way, had ten flagons ready and waiting and a new slate running especially to inaugurate the new order.

Halfway down the first one Thor stood up and announced, "Camilla and I would like to thank you all for making this a splendid holiday, we haven't had so much fun for years. God bashing has been a favourite sport of mine for as long as I can remember and now we have a new sport to take home that's even better, God annihilation, don't just bash them, get rid of them totally. I'd never considered that before and it has the added bonus of being damn good fun. So we are going to go home and sort out a few Nordic chappie God types, anyone who wants to assist will be more than welcome."

Neoptolemus, being young and still full of beans, raised a flagon to Thor. "Yeah, I'll have some of that," he quaffed.

"And me," shouted Turnus.

"Okay boys," said Thor, "how'd you like to be my independents?"

They looked at each other, then at the ale and Turnus asked, "Do we get an expenses account?"

"Expenses?" thundered Thor, "Expenses, gentlemen we get the world!"

"Suppose that'll do." conceded Neoptolemus.

"Good," said Thor, "now let's get pissed."

This was received with resounding agreement.

"Pub crawl," shouted Menelaus, to a good smack in the gob from Cassandra, who hadn't quite foreseen that all the night's profits were not to be hers. Menelaus looked at her startled and said, "I love a woman with spirit. Close up and come with us. You can advise me on the holiday resort possibilities of a castle I've recently inherited. We could be good together."

Cassandra consulted her pocket crystal ball and said, "Hmmm… What's it like and what's the castle called?"

"It's a lovely place. It's got hardwood floors throughout and an independent energy and heating supply. It's all on one floor level, sort of bungalow style with a two-acre footprint plus extensive landscaped gardens. The roofing is all oak, hammer-beam trusses, kingpost trusses, seeing as I am one and queen post trusses too, just in case! The whole thing is exposed in the interior, every roof plane and intersecting roof planes. It is a sheer masterpiece of geometrical carpentry and joinery. I call it, Trussed House," replied Menelaus proudly.

"I see," pondered Cassandra, because in an oracular type of way she certainly did, "and where is it?"

"About forty miles away, on the other side of Olympus. We could have signs between the two and corner the market." said an inspired Menelaus.

"Hmmm…" hmmmed Cassandra, "come with me I'd like to show something."

She led Menelaus outside to where she had recently had a new hand-painted sign-written board fitted. The board was covered and Cassandra removed the cover to reveal a work of art that bore the legend:

TRUSSED HOUSE
40. →

"You have a weird sense of the prescient Cassandra that never ceases to awe and amaze," replied Menelaus. "We could have an expressway between the two and a sign the other end."

CASSANDRA CROSS Inc.
←

"Yes, it has possibilities, the names need some adjustment though but the expressway, I like that, that'll do nicely," she said, pulling the bar shutters down.

Perseus was the first to leave Cassandra's and therefore the first to trip over the rope, which had been stretched tight at shin height across the threshold. "Ooh fucoof!" he uttered as the rest of the team followed suit.

"Bloody typical," pronounced the clerk, "follow like sheep you do. So where's Oddy then?"

"Aah!" spoke the head of Theseus, emerging from between Cassandra's legs and a tangle of limbs formerly known as the team. "Oddy won't be joining us on account of his being dead at present."

"Dead?" repeated the clerk questioningly.

"'S right," said Turnus past the pointy bit of Thor's battle axe which had just insured that he would not be picking his nose for a bit. "Completely brown bread at the moment."

"No shit!" replied the clerk, "and you're not expecting his condition to improve or anything like that?"

"Not particularly," mumbled Perseus from a place where none of him was visible. "It's generally the way with death that when you're dead it lasts for a long time,"

"That's right," agreed Oedipus, whose head appeared to match his feet but was a hundred and forty degrees out according to his shoulders. "That means that you have become the proud owner of a job shop and dating agency okay? Now would you mind awfully if we continued with our pub crawl?"

"Yes, of course, gentlemen and ladies, sorry to detain you, in fact, the first round's on me," said the clerk.

"Wrong," stated Paris, "this is the second round and they're all on you! With the inheritance of a business comes the inheritance of its debts, including any current expenses accounts set up by the previous proprietor."

The team were now upright again and forming a menacing martial circle about the clerk, who, for some strange reason, suddenly felt incredibly small and increasingly vulnerable.

"Yeah, okay no problem, business is business."

Menelaus clapped him on the back with the proportional efficiency of a mousetrap upon its unsuspecting victim. "That's the spirit, come and have a few with us."

Andromache's Bar and Bistro was fairly quiet as they approached it - due mainly to the fact that most people didn't get paid 'til Thursday - but this condition was about to come to an abrupt end as Oedipus, who was leading the way by accident, suddenly became the victim of one and misjudged the transition from kerb to bar floor, entering arse first and tripping the whole team up for the second time in the same pub crawl.

Andromache eyed the rowdy fallen heroes suspiciously "Somebody's birthday? Christenin'? Weddin'? Leavin' do? Or are we just extendin' the weekend?"

"Leaving do," grunted Perseus from some place amid the tangle of team.

"That's nice," responded Andromache in a 'humour them' tone, "Oooz leavin'?"

"Left," stated Turnus.

"Okay," said Andromache patiently, "Oooz left?"

"Well, we are," said Menelaus, "Sis and Prom and Oddy didn't make it they…"

"Menelaus," cut in Paris.

"Yes Chief."

"Shut up!" Snapped Paris. "Don't think, drink."

"Well that's very kind of you," said Menelaus, "but I thought all the drinks were on Oddy's boy and his new found business."

Theseus looked at Hercules and felt compelled to add voice to the look. "What d'you reckon he smokes at night?"

Andromache grabbed the nearest collar to the top of the pile, which by some strange quirk of fate, happened to belong to Oedipus. "Okay mister," she demanded. "Oooz left?"

"Don't know, can't see who's still here," answered the sight-impaired convincingly.

This just wasn't fair, she was the landlady, the centre of the hub and the vessel through which all information, be it scandalous or otherwise, passed. Somebody had left and nobody was missing and nobody was saying who wasn't there anymore. She now had Paris in a neck lock threatening him with the dreaded extending swivel action, night rolling pin. "Who, has, left?" asked a falsely calm Andromache, recalling her private education and, for once, the product of her extravagantly costly elocution lessons.

Paris, having had firsthand evidence of the power of the instrument in question, whilst in the control of his beloved Helen, answered promptly. "Oh, just Jupiter."

"What? The king of the gods is gone. You mean there's no one in charge anymore?"

"Well," rasped Paris, through the landlady's cast-iron grip, "there's nothing left to be in charge of any more 'cos all the rest of the blighters have gone with him."

"You mean we're all on our own down 'ere?" she responded.

"Andro, baby," said Paris, "we always were. All that's changed is that now we know for sure. It's ours to run and shape and live in."

"Bloody 'ell," gasped Andromache, "you mean all the things that 'appen don't 'appen because the gods make 'em 'appen?"

"Yes," croaked Paris, as Andromache released the neck lock.

"First one's on the 'ouse," announced Andromache. An announcement that only the clerk paid any real attention to, as he could set off some of the night's extensive bar tab against it.

In the process of so doing, a light twinkled and brightened to full luminosity in the convoluted synaptic pit that was the mind of the clerk. He had a job centre where people, often on benefits, spent many a jobless day but no money. Now if there were some catering services, money would come in more often, if only in the form of passing trade from those mistaking it for a coffee shop. That, in turn, would lead to a transfer of skills from further afield as some would stay and that would create jobs further afield, in new occupations, and create a mobility of labour set up, all running through his place.

The clerk pulled Andromache to one side for a quiet chat. "How do you fancy running the catering franchise for my job centre?"

"Wot's in it fer me?" replied a slightly suspicious pint proprietor, with an air of, 'I've heard them all before', about her.

"Well, you get paid and there would be more people in town overnight drinking ale in between contracts."

"And wot about the dating agency side?" asked the less suspicious pint purveyor.

"Scrap it," he replied.

"Oh no, no don't do that," she responded, "expand it, blind dates at Andromache's Bar and Bistro, good food, friendly atmosphere, congenial surroundins, live music an' probably get laid as well at the end of it. Everybody's idea of a good night out an', in the process, they spend lots!"

"I like your way of thinking," mused the clerk.

"Okay," said Andromache, "'ere's the deal. I keep the bar and bistro, we go fifty-fifty in the date a mate set up, you keep the job shop and we split the catering franchise profits seventy-thirty in my favour."

"Fifty-fifty," said the clerk.

"Sixty-forty," said Andromache.

"Done," said the clerk.

"Probably," said Neoptolemus who had caught the bartering end of the conversation.

"Hey, Cassy?" called Andromache.

Cassandra looked over the verbose crowd and shouted,

"Yeah, okay, I'll go along with it."

"How does she do that?" snorted the clerk.

"Ah, that's Cassandra for you, probably looked the deal over last month sometime," said Andromache.

"What deal?" inquired the clerk.

"The one where we go inta business togevver and Cassy puts up the overnight stayers."

"But, we've only just discussed that, how could she know?"

"Oh, it's just a God thing, I'll explain it one day - if I ever work it out myself," smiled Andromache.

Cassandra was decoratively draped across a bar stool chatting to Hercules. "So, what now Herc?"

"I'm retiring properly this time, I'm going back to Deianira and Hyllus for some family fun."

"No you're not but then again you are," replied Cassandra.

"Look Cass, there's no gods, we got shot of them."

"So?"

"So," replied Hercules, "you can prophesy but Apollo messed it up and confused the interpretation. Well, seeing as there's no Apollo anymore, the confusion should be no more, so either you can prophesy or you can't."

"I know," replied the prophetess, "but it's much more fun saying I told you so, after an enigmatic prophecy."

"Like Sisyphus and the rock you mean?" asked Hercules.

"Aw that was just a bit of fun, his time was up anyway, death was looking for him, it was just a question of method of death really."

"So you always saw clearly but couldn't make the description coherent to anybody?"

"That's about it Herc, lucky escape you had with that robe by the way, that's not the way I saw it you know. I saw the constellation of Hercules and the first of the victorious to leave Olympus wearing a robe dipped in the blood of Nissus, which was poisoned by the arrow you shot him with. Who could have foreseen Ajax cracking up like that and doing a runner?" replied Cassandra.

"Oedipus had a vague idea," said Hercules, remembering his threatening comments from beneath a crumbling amphitheatre pillar.

"Really? I must talk to him, he could be useful. Anyway just for you, 'cos you're a mate of old, you don't retire but you and the family bit works out and you and Paris have to get some organisation up and running 'round here."

"We do?"

"Of course, the folks are a bit stateless at the moment, got no gods, no future, no reason for doing things."

"But that's exactly the reason, because they can do things, for themselves, for their future, for the greater good of everyone," replied Hercules.

Paris, who was standing close and accidentally on purpose overhearing, said. "I know that and you know that, but them, the great unwashed, unenlightened, partially religious, general public don't."

"Guess we'd better show them then!" responded Hercules.

"Yeah," agreed Paris, "but after eleven tomorrow though."

Oedipus, regardless of his disability, was having no difficulty at all in locating and using the bar. The fact that he was on a stool at one extreme end with a wall to the right, another one behind and the bar to the left allowing just enough room for elbows and a white cane, might have been instrumental in alleviating any location problems. As for supply, seeing as it was free, everyone who came to the bar got one in for Oedipus too.

"Watcha mate," said Oedipus recognising the familiar clicking sound at the bar beside him. "You must be Oddy's boy?"

"Please," groaned the clerk, "I was just a business associate, I worked for him that's all."

"Everybody worked for Oddy," replied the blind man. "Oddy never worked for anybody but Oddy, ah, ha ha, even Oddy worked for Oddy!"

"How did you know who I was?" ventured the clerk.

"That clicky thing, Oddy always had one. Every time we landed, there he'd be - click - click, click - click, clicketty - clicketty - click, "oh damn it," click - click clicketty etcetera. An electric slate he called it, adds, subtracts, divides, multiplies and generally enrages and aggravates."

"You got that right," replied the clerk, "So you went on voyages with Oddy?"

"Yeah sure did. Set a lot of 'em up I did. It's often a case of who you know not what you know."

"And, er, you know a few people then?" enquired the clerk.

"It's a funny thing being blind," said Oedipus, "but there seems to be a certain amount of pathos for my unfortunate circumstances. I mean I know I'm probably not the first - to be born in opposition to the gods will, pierced through the heels with a pointy stick, strung up in a tree, rescued by a shepherd, attacked by thieves, one of which was my old man and I killed him, only to return to his kingdom and marry his wife, only to find out that she's my mother and that my sons are also my brothers - but never the less, royals do seem to be biased towards my predicament, kindred spirits I guess, and they do make useful contacts."

"I see," mused the clerk. "Would you like another drink?"

"What - you buying?"

"Well, yes actually I am. The tab's Oddy's, I seem to have inherited it," replied the clerk.

"Nothing new there then!" said Oedipus. "Never saw that tight arsed bastard buy a beer when he was alive, guess there's no chance now."

The clerk who, though doing the buying but not doing the drinking, was sharp and alert. "You mean you can see?"

"Eh?"

"You said you'd never seen Oddy buy a beer."

"Okay, okay," rasped Oedipus. "Keep your voice down. It's a recent thing. I reckon that, seeing as the gods drove me to blind myself to the apparent horrors of my actions whilst under their guidance, now that they've gone my sight has returned."

"Would you like a job?" inquired the clerk.

"As what?"

"Technical consultant for a little business venture I have just entered into with Andromache," replied the clerk.

"You want to match-make with the rich and famous?" asked Oedipus.

"Something like that," said the clerk, clickety-clacking at his electric slate.

"Okay, but don't tell anyone I can see, it could be a good advantage to a new venture."

"It could also be the start," the clerk pointed out, "of a more peaceful association between neighbouring nations, if we match them up well. If not it will make good plot lines for reality stage shows."

"Yeah well," said Oedipus, getting off his stool and fumbling towards the loo, "it'll keep 'till tomorrow!"

"Snerrfph!" said Theseus, as Oedipus bumped into him for effect and assisted him in drinking his ale by the snorting method.

"Oedipus you bumbling shi..." blustered Theseus, raising a mighty arm terminating in a mighty hand with the intention of smoting incredibly verily the blind man. "...thead." A hand, which was arrested in mid-smote by Perseus, who for an old guy had a cast-iron grip, the result no doubt of being a pensioner often taxed with the daunting task of holding onto that fifty Drac piece for the gas meter.

"You don't want to do that These. He's just a blind guy, it's not his fault."

"Aw c'mon grandpaw, he does it on purpose and it really gets on my tits!" responded Theseus.

"Violence never solved anything Theseus," replied the wise old man.

"It bloody well showed a Minotaur a thing or two and it seems to have sorted a few gods recently - it works for me!" snapped Theseus shortly.

"Extreme situations demand extreme measures, but a blind piss-head in the pub is hardly extreme, now is it?"

"You wouldn't say that if it was your beer you had just snorted so far up your nose it made your ears leak," grunted Theseus.

This was a theory on which Perseus was just about to receive a new perspective as Oedipus, an ablution later, bumbled back through the bar and bumped into him creating the second, "Snerrfph!" of the evening, it was a "Snerrfph!" which was rapidly followed up with, *Tischwack!* As Perseus backhanded the blind man back to his corner seat in a manner that left him sliding down the wall facing completely the wrong direction round for the purposes of sitting.

Theseus raised a quizzical eyebrow along with an unspoken question.

"Yeah well, extreme situations demand extreme measures!"

"Indeed they do Perseus," cut in Cassandra, "and this is where you get yours - or at least get to know about it. You will meet a woman of unholy nature whose hair will have a life of its own. Homicidal towards men will be her aspect, a devious mind to parallel that of a serpent will be hers and a stare the like of which will sour milk in the udder and vitrify stone."

"Jesus!" said Menelaus, not realising his own prophetic powers. "However will you know which one it is?"

"Yeah," added Theseus, "why do you have to be so obscure, couldn't you narrow it down a bit?"

"Well that's where you're wrong," announced Perseus, "'cos I've already done that Gorgon Medusa stuff."

"This I know," returned the smug Cassandra. "On your way home you will meet your future mother-in-law."

"Aw no," cringed Perseus, "you mean I've got to get married again?"

"Just my little joke," said Cassandra. "Now go and help Oedipus off the wall and back onto his stool, before I tell you what really happens."

"You mean I don't have to get married again?" inquired a visibly relieved Perseus.

"No you don't have to," replied the obfuscating oracle with a sly wink at Theseus.

"Oedipus me old mate," called Perseus, "a little misunderstanding, let me give you a hand there, can I get you a beer?"

"Sho you can," replied the blind sleight-of-hand expert, as he expertly palmed a few fungal growths of an hallucinogenic nature into the gorgon slayer's ale.

"Is he really going to marry again?" asked Theseus.

"If he's thick enough it could well happen. Considering you're only honorary relatives," replied Cassandra, "you have much in common really!"

"We do?"

"Sure, neither of you were built for marriage but you keep on trying to make it fit."

"Well excuse me," answered Theseus, "but you and Menelaus there appear to be getting things together in a rather marital way."

"And that's where the similarity ceases," smiled Cassandra, "I've just invented living together, all the advantages of marriage and none of the sweaty sock, blowing your nose in the shower, wiping bogeys under the bed, skid stained underpants and general empty beer can in the loo modus operandi that seems to accompany most marriages."

"How?" asked Theseus, thinking it an improvement in real terms on the more usually proffered, why? Though, 'why?' would probably have been more appropriate.

"Separate houses forty miles apart with a business in each, easy see?

"Ehm, I don't suppose you could give the wife a job in the further away of the two, could you?" inquired a hopelessly hopeful reluctant husband.

"Hippolyte? Yes, she'll need something to keep her occupied while you and Hercules are adventuring about organising the world!"

"Eh?" said Theseus, involuntarily snorting his beer of his own volition on this occasion. "Adventuring about? You mean more monsters and shit?"

"Not exactly. Corporate monsters and Tyrants sort of thing from now on, a few despots perhaps, nothing too taxing," smirked Cassandra. "Paris can't do it all on his own can he?"

"Can't do what?" inquired Paris in passing, with his hands fully occupied by four large flagons.

"Run the world," replied Cassandra.

"Oh, is that all," shrugged Paris, "no problem, tomorrow after eleven okay?"

"Three separate and individual persons with differing but equal powers all working as one towards a unified peaceful world?" interrupted Oedipus while bumbling past on another toiletry mission. "Sounds like a crock of shit to me and, may I add, a dangerous precedent to set!" With that said he bumbled ever onward leaving Cassandra and Theseus to stare after his departing rear.

"He may have a point there," declared the prophetess.

"Aww don't start Cass," replied Theseus.

By degrees measured in quarts, the ale level in the cellar fell and the internal capacity of the local heroes was approached. Paris and Theseus moulded themselves into a men-at-work-relaxing, art piece with the assistance of a stool, an ashtray, a sticky bar top and the remainder of lots and lots of ale.

"Wassat?" Theseus attempted.

"Wasswat?" replied Paris.

"Schh, lissen," instructed Theseus.

From the corner, earlier on occupied by Oedipus, grunts and snores issued, interspersed with, "No, snumpfh, Jesus no, not you," and, "Aaagh! Spawn of the devil, evil bitch."

They leaned out precariously past the corner of the bar to peer, at ninety degrees from where they sat, at the twitching troubled figure of a subconscious Perseus who, thanks to the fungal intervention of Oedipus, was presently traversing the fetid slime holes of his old adversary but things were not going in his favour at present.

Perseus was tripping his face off in gorgon gallery, where he was about to walk up the aisle with a bunch of blushing serpents decoratively permed around the delicate head of a sabre-toothed cobra. Lizards - artfully snatching flies from the rancid air, to keep them off the bride - lined the walls. Cockroaches carpeted the floor and large gilt-framed mirrors reflected, not only himself and his suppurating bride, but also the hysterically laughing figures of all his ex-wives and lovers in various positions of copulation with Minotaurs, Centaurs and a variety of other crossbred farmyard creatures bearing the faces of many a past arch-enemy.

This was the fungally controlled wasteland that was the mind of Perseus enduring the best of the worst of a troubled past. His greatest fear he was later to recall was the horrifying prospect, in the postnuptial consummation, of any type of blow-job scenario.

The whole mystical, hallucinogenic journey was to leave him, forever after wondering, if the whole mythology thing was some product of a civilisation based on the abuse, by the forefathers, of many a class A leisure pursuit.

Eeeerrreekrunch! rent the air as Andromache's two remaining bar stools gave way simultaneously and deposited two super-heroic piss-heads on to a lightly saw dusted floor.

"C'mon boys," called Andromache, "sod off 'ome an' take 'im wiv yer."

"D'we haff to?" questioned Paris.

"Move it!" replied the barkeeper.

"It's late, I'm tired, Astyanax is on a school trip tomorra, an' I've got sandwiches to make yet, now piss off!"

"No," said the plastered Paris, "I meant d'we haff t'take him?"

Andromache walked over and deposited a jug of water on Theseus' head. Then she picked it up again and emptied the contents over him instead. "'Vad a few myself," she said and as Theseus spluttered into life, "'e's your grandad these days, now pick 'im up an' clear off."

Bemused and dampened Theseus replied, "You only 'ad to ask."

"I just did," declared Andromache.

Theseus struggled to his feet. "Oy, Percy, wake up you ole fart, gorra go 'ome."

"Murrmph," said the pile of Perseus from the corner, "Fuckin' cow, slithery slippery bitch…"

"Er, sorry about this Andro, 'e dint mean it really."

"'E's out of 'is 'ead on mushrooms," replied Andromache "'ave seen it before, twat! 'E's barred, I don't want no drugs in 'ere."

Perseus suddenly became totally lucid and announced. "A fact, madam, which is plainly illustrated by the alcoholic content of the ale you serve at this establishment!" He then lapsed even more suddenly back into his fungal foraging, as Andromache punched his nose out level with his ears and followed up with a knee jerk reaction that, probably brought the mushroom trip into the oral sex domain, along with bringing tears to Theseus' eyes and definitely creating in Theseus a sense of relief that his own testicles were at least two feet away from his surrogate grandfather's.

"Aaww, nice one Andro," said Paris, "Like it would have been easier to get him out of here if there were some semblance of consciousness in there."

"G'night boys," she called as the members of a garish three-legged race team stumbled out into the night.

With an arm over each shoulder Perseus was conducted by Paris and Theseus to his mobile chariot vanette and dumped, without ritual, in a position where his head, quite by accident, wedged itself between the wall of the van and the 'Emergency Use Only' toilet, which was displaying definite signs of having serviced an inordinate amount of emergencies of late. It was not quite brimming over but the stench was airborne and they saw Perseus' nostrils twitch as his internal mushroom voyage moved to a setting more in accordance with the external stimuli, which got rid of the gorgon set up and mirrored surprisingly the transmutation of many a marriage. As if in a dream, it started bad, it got worse, and both parties ended up in the shit in the back of a camper van. The only redeeming factor that Paris and Theseus could see was that, for Perseus at least, it wasn't real. He would wake up in the morning, smelling of shit granted, but not knee-deep, in a matrimonial sense at any rate, in it.

This produced somewhat of a sobering effect on the two heroes as they parted company and went home to their wives.

"See you tomorrow?" inquired Paris.

"Yeah, and we can put the world to rights," replied Theseus.

"Wot again!" exclaimed Paris.

"Bloody hell," said Theseus, "never thought of it that way. Now we got nothing left to talk about in the pub."

"I have an idea about that one," answered Paris, "It's called sport, politics and religion and it can all be neatly abbreviated to one thing - sex!"

"Not bad," said Theseus, "for the married men anyway, if you aren't getting any you can at least brag about all you don't get by telling everyone you get so much that you had to come out for a beer just to get a rest from it. Then men can develop the power of their own neurosis and psychosis and remove the sexist element involved with regard to women holding all the cards in the psychological defects' department."

"Goodnight These," replied Paris, wishing that Darwin would hurry up and come into existence while the last example of the missing link was still available, and then rapidly deciding that this was Helen's lucky night!

XLI

SHE'S A BIG SOFTIE AFTER ALL

Theseus stumbled along the garden wall and eventually located the gate and, snagging his arm on a couple of strategically positioned four-inch nails, booted the offending article in. It gave way with surprising ease and speed and, when he was halfway through it, came back with a similar amount of ease and speed and stopped when the Suffolk latch jammed into his right ear and the lock hasp jabbed him in the groin.

Theseus stumbled, more so, and fell frantically clutching at an acrow-prop which slid across the house wall and fell on a thirteen-foot builder's plank, which was lying across a roll of roofing felt with an ugly garden gnome on the end of it. The gnome for its part experienced an overcoming of inertia followed by acceleration and responded with the sounds *Tischinkle!* and *Scphutt!* immediately following its passage through the descent half of a parabolic curve that intersected the greenhouse roof en-route to the one remaining prize tomato.

"Aaww fook!" Theseus managed to utter disgustedly before strange noises broke upon him.

Gurdat! Disching! Zirdink! Dizing! Duzunk! rent the night air as Hippolyte, roused from her slumbers by the passage of her newly acquired garden gnome, set about the back of Theseus' head with a recoilless, spring action baking tray.

"Oh!" she stopped surprised, "It's you. I thought it was that thieving rag and bone man, sheep fiddler, Ajax."

Schtwak!

"Ow."

"So where…"

Duschunk!

"… the hell…"

Kradink!

"… have you been for the last god knows…"

Kadonk!

"… how long. Leaving a poor defenceless woman all alone."

Schurkrink!

"To fuckin' hell an' back," replied Theseus truthfully, grabbing the baking tray and balling it up like used tin foil at a picnic. "An' I'm in no mood for this shit. Now get inside, get upstairs and get undressed. Now!"

"Ooooh, oooh Theseus, I never knew you could be so masterful."

"Masterful is it? Look, the last few days I've had death's doll 'Sephone, soddin' Minotaurs, bloody giants, fuckin' comets, bleedin' gods and filthy sodden super-heroes up to my tits. I'm pissed up, pissed off and pissed about and right now I need a damn good shag!"

"Ooooh These, These baby, I love it when you talk dirty. Take me, take me now."

XLII

IT'LL ALL BE OK IN THE MORNING

Helen, on the other hand, ran down the path kicking over the empty milk bottles and next door's cat at the sight of her returning husband. "Busy day at the office dear?" she quipped, grabbing hold of Paris and treating him to the full French, tongue to tonsil massage. "I was so worried, all that gossip about martial training in the amphitheatre, Mmmwah mmmwah, and the top sheared off Olympus, bits of meteors everywhere, Mmmwah, I'm so glad you're safe, Mmmwah. I love you Paris, let me take care of you."

Paris came up for air, "Stone the fucking crows, if I'd known women could be this good when left to their own devices I'd have gone off and got shot of the gods a long time ago!"

"Shut up Paris and get inside, I want you, I want to strip you in private, slowly. I want to share with you the passionate love that is the whole reason for our lives for the rest of our lives," said the most stunningly beautiful woman in the whole world ever, pressing her thigh against his rising spirit.

Paris gave next door's cat, who had been stupid enough to hang around, a quick boot up the arse just for good measure - and to impress upon it the wish that it should go and crap in its own yard - and caressed his wife the rest of the way to the house. Then, in the spirit of mutual unity, groped her just about all over the rest of it as they tore at each other's clothes and screwed each other senseless for a very, very long time, ignorant of the world around them and ignorant of the fact that all around the town, for the second time in twenty-four hours, the earth moved for an assorted variety of heroes.

These heroes all intended to make the most of it because tomorrow, they knew, they would awake to a new world. A world where gods were banished and mortals were in control of their own destiny. A world in which mortal mankind would have to be responsible for the consequences of their own actions. It would be a world where the delicate balance between the environment, environmental health, industrialisation, economical growth and human rights, with all of their hideous possibilities, was purely, totally and completely the responsibility of mankind.

"Oh shit!"

Acknowledgements

Everything in this book is historically inaccurate - maybe - but beer was always there!

I would like to thank Virgil, Homer, Ovid, Sophocles, Euripides, Aeschylus and Apollodorus for the cast and supporting chorus. Thanks for the characters - sorry for what I did to them!

Big thanks to Josh, guitarist, vocalist and drummer extraordinaire, for laughing in the right places and making dinner while I was busy and bouncing ideas off him!

Thanks to Simon Derry Photography - for not making the mug shot too incriminating.

Thanks also to Hannah Cross, a proofreader with ideas, for spotting the glaringly obvious and making this possible.

Thank you to all the people at MTP, the few that I have worked with and the many I haven't run into but who all aided and abetted admirably in getting Mythistrone published.

Finally, I extend my gratitude also to the multitude of bar and pub theorists for their rhetoric, sagacity, sarcasm and cynicism - you know who you are, as do some of the local and international constabulary - cheers guys!

About the Author

Eddie Woods was born in Shardlow at a very early age, the first rung on the nuclear family ladder for a serial fisherman and a clever woman who saw more to life than messing about on, or in, the river. He was educated in state schools including the godly indifferent, daily punishment beatings, Paramilitary (religious) division of the Christian Brothers.

Following the demise of the nuclear family unit, due in no small part to an excess of serial fishing, Eddie served a seven-year reality apprenticeship in the woodworking disciplines, which funded many travels to the leftovers of the Greek Empire where he never discovered the ruins of a

5,000-year-old pub. Surely they'd had at least one - seeing as every second doorway of his travels appeared to be one!

After life in the trade, followed by the disseminatory process of 'passing on the secrets' of the ancient masters to subsequent generations of the disinterested hoody clad and the genius inspired interested alike (in the most altruistic manner that college-based bureaucratic red tape would allow) the subject of academic difference of opinion featured largely. Education became transformed, by forces who apparently knew better, into edutainment with little educational value but much more efficient funding options. Having learned from the experts who systematically decimated the educational system, Eddie realised he needed a change because change was the only constant which ensured that difficult questions would not be postulated or asked.

After spending many years in a variety of Greek and Roman locations looking for the right stone, generally in the wrong field from the point of view of some local authorities, Eddie wondered what it would be like if all the ancient myths, heroic figures and creatures co-existed in the same space and time with present-day insecurities and views of societal community structure and he launched, at full throttle, into the task of combining the characteristics of the world's greatest theorist thinkers, chroniclers, action personas and creatures.

The place to start was in the centre of many a community, the hub, the place where counselling is free, the place where business dealings are forged, the font of all irrelevant but useful knowledge, the place where free thinking theorists abound - the pub! Thus Andromache's Bar and Bistro was created in the heart of the Greek Empire from the heart of the rapidly diminishing English Empire.

Could we have a world where bar room theorists, heroes, heroines and creatures ran the world? Apart from funny how bad could it be?

Despite the attractions of the Greek lifestyle and wonderful weather, Eddie still lives in the centre of England with his son and still makes 'stuff' from wood by hand, when he's not playing music or engaged in rewriting world history - from the correct perspective of course!

γεια μας

*Available worldwide from
Amazon and all good bookstores*

———————

www.mtp.agency

www.facebook.com/mtp.agency

@mtp_agency

www.ingramcontent.com/pod-product-compliance
Lightning Source LLC
LaVergne TN
LVHW041623060526
838200LV00040B/1416